Advance Praise for *Seven Heavens Away*

"In *Seven Heavens Away*, Ashraf Zaghal gives us a many-layered portrait of a young man trying to live under, and resist, longstanding occupation. Zaghal offers characters that are forever caught between fear and gumption, between faith and desire, between clarity and indecision. In Zaghal's hands, heroes are rarely immune from hypocrisy, and scoundrels are not devoid of a measure of nobility. The result is a debut novel that is nuanced, searing, and unforgettable."

—SAEED TEEBI, author of *Her First Palestinian* and *You Will Not Kill Our Imagination*

"Ashraf Zaghal's *Seven Heavens Away* embraces the soil of Palestine and its people with fury and tenderness. Here is the fidelity of friendship and family, the hunger for intimacy, the rage against the occupier, the heartbreak of first love, the guilt of escape, and, astonishingly, the dignity of hope. A fierce and beautiful novel."

—DAVID BERGEN, author of *Away from the Dead*

"*Seven Heavens Away* is a beautiful and complex portrait-in-words of boyhood, masculinity, and the growing pains of figuring out who to love, what to believe, and how to show up in a world that is set on ensuring you don't survive it. The tension in Ashraf Zaghal's prose is palpable; it's clear in every line that this coming-of-age story has life and death hanging in the balance. A remarkable debut."

—JESSICA JOHNS, author of *Bad Cree*

"*Seven Heavens Away* is a beautifully written and moving novel about Palestinian life in occupied Jerusalem. In evocative and authentic detail, Ashraf Zaghal tells the story of Aziz, a teenager trying to navigate his sorrows and desires in an unstable and violent world. Aziz is a narrator who will win over many readers. In depicting the harsh realities of the Israeli occupation, the novel also celebrates the richness of Palestinian culture and community and the bond between friends. A powerful debut."

—GHASSAN ZEINEDDINE, author of *Dearborn*

"In *Seven Heavens Away*, Ashraf Zaghal brings the alleys, storefronts, and paradoxes of Palestinian Jerusalem to vibrant, messy life. What elsewhere would be typical rites of passage for a teenaged boy—first love, first job, first rebellion, friendships, pranks, confrontations with the larger world—are here fraught, harrowing, and haunted by death, thanks to the reality of Israeli apartheid, dehumanization, and violence. An engrossing and enraging addition to the growing canon of Palestinian Canadian fiction."

—AARON KREUTER, author of *Lake Burntshore*

SEVEN HEAVENS AWAY

SEVEN HEAVENS AWAY

A NOVEL

ASHRAF ZAGHAL

Published in Canada and the USA in 2026 by House of Anansi Press Inc.
houseofanansi.com

House of Anansi Press is committed to protecting our natural environment. This book is made of material from well-managed FSC®-certified forests, recycled materials, and other controlled sources.

House of Anansi Press is a Global Certified Accessible™ (GCA by Benetech) publisher. The ebook version of this book meets stringent accessibility standards and is available to readers with print disabilities.

30 29 28 27 26   1 2 3 4 5

Library and Archives Canada Cataloguing in Publication

Title: Seven heavens away : a novel / Ashraf Zaghal.
Names: Zaghal, Ashraf, author
Identifiers: Canadiana (print) 20250266229 | Canadiana (ebook) 20250266261 | ISBN 9781487013486 (softcover) | ISBN 9781487013493 (EPUB)
Subjects: LCGFT: Novels.
Classification: LCC PS8649.A34 S48 2026 | DDC C813/.6—dc23

Cover and text design: Alysia Shewchuk
Cover images: iStock.com

House of Anansi Press is grateful for the privilege to work on and create from the Traditional Territory of many Nations, including the Anishinabeg, the Wendat, and the Haudenosaunee, as well as the Treaty Lands of the Mississaugas of the Credit.

Canada Council for the Arts   Conseil des Arts du Canada

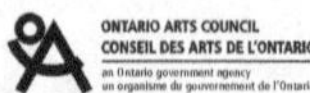

CERTIFIED CANADIAN PUBLISHER

With the participation of the Government of Canada
Avec la participation du gouvernement du Canada | Canada

We acknowledge for their financial support of our publishing program the Canada Council for the Arts, the Ontario Arts Council, and the Government of Canada.

Printed and bound in Canada

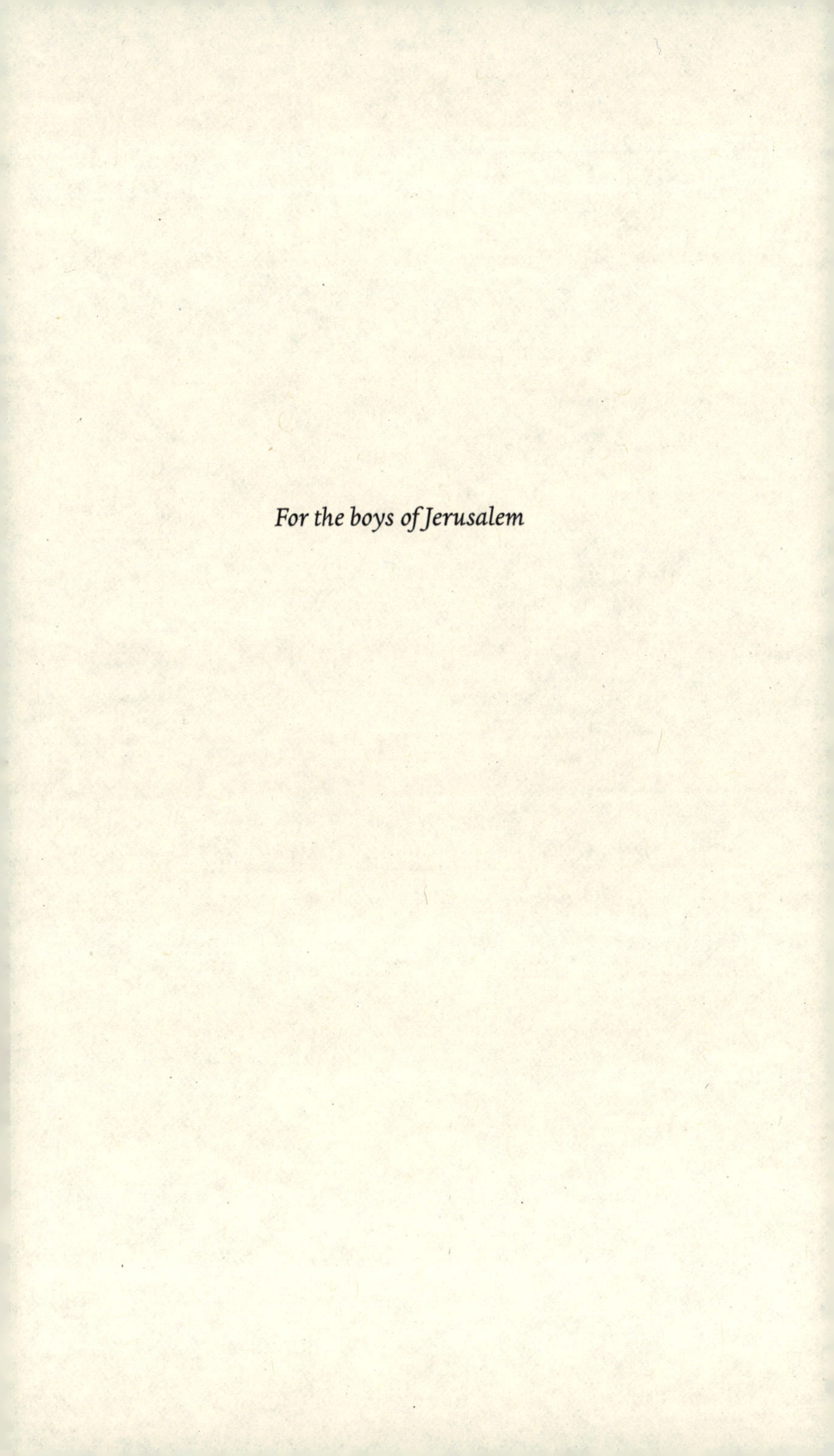

For the boys of Jerusalem

PROLOGUE

My flight has left the ground.
I have a window seat.
From above, everything is small and sullen:
Flat and mute, lines and dots, curves and squares.
I can see the Mediterranean.
Nothing looks like the Mediterranean, not even the Great Lakes.
I see clouds and water. No pigeons. No seagulls.
At this elevation, birds can be as dangerous as rockets.
My chest hurts. I lean forward;
My nose touches the fabric of the seat in front of me.
I smell coffee with cardamom and sweat on prayer rugs.
The flight attendant hovers over me. I fasten my seat belt.
She walks off. From behind a curtain, she announces,
"We welcome you aboard our flight from Tel Aviv to Toronto …"
Tel Aviv is a forty-minute drive from Jerusalem.
I knew some who could make it in twenty minutes
And some who could not make it in twenty days.

People give you a thousand estimates
Depending on where you live in Jerusalem—
East, West, old, new,
Valley, hill, walled, unwalled.
Sometimes people lie;
Sometimes they get confused
Because distance is relative,
Because distance is like beauty;
It's in the eye of the beholder.
Sometimes you walk two steps, and they are only two steps;
Sometimes you walk the same two steps and find yourself
Two alleys away, two gates away,
Two hills away, two seas away,
Two continents away,
    Or seven heavens away.

FALL 2015

1

October 22

We walked toward Jaffa Gate. It was called Jaffa Gate because, long ago, at the end of their journey from the port of Jaffa, pilgrims walked through it. Now, brooding nuns walked through it. Priests with brown cloaks and long hoods walked through it. Bearded imams with long robes and bearded imams without long robes walked through it. Haredi Jews in wool suits walked through it. Settlers with guns and foreign money and searching eyes walked through it, and past us. They had occupied two houses in the Muslim Quarter last year, not in my neighbourhood but close enough to see their guns and flags waving on the roofs.

We went up the twisting alleyways, and they went down, and surveillance cameras, standing like owls in the armpits of balconies, watched everyone. To fail facial recognition, we lowered our eyes like the devout. Since September, Captain Moussa had arrested half the boys of the Old City. If you sneezed without showing your nose to the camera, he would arrest you. He was the Shabak officer responsible for our neighbourhood. He'd been around for a long time, but nobody knew his real name. People whispered stories about him as though talking about cancer.

I pointed to one of the cameras. "Hassan, since you're good with computers, why don't you hack that?"

He opened his backpack and pulled out a screwdriver. "This only hacks wood," he said, and we laughed.

Hassan had been chosen by our physics teacher, Ustaz Salim, to participate in science experiments supervised by professors at the Hebrew University. Genetic engineering took his fancy, but Hassan's father didn't like the idea of messing with God's creation.

Dragging his feet on the cobbled stone, Hassan shoved the screwdriver back into his backpack and said, "I can't be late getting back home."

He lived in Wadi al-Joz, just outside the Old City wall.

Mustafa chuckled. "We have all night."

"I don't have all night," Hassan said.

"I'll get you the biggest shawarma ever made in the history of Jaffa Road," Mustafa said. "And ice cream. We'll get ice cream."

I told Hassan it was Mustafa's wish to celebrate his first paycheque from the car wash he had started working at this summer. "We must go," I said, and he told me something about his parents giving him a hard time about being out after a certain hour.

"Don't worry, we'll walk you home," I said, jokingly.

He wore a large white shirt, and I asked him if it was his father's. He scoffed, his glasses bouncing on his nose. I liked to tease him because he always had a serious face.

My theory was that he sat at his computer for too long. Mustafa's theory was that it was because Hassan had five sisters—he not only had to protect them but also win every argument with them.

The light of the day was fading. Shopkeepers swept the dust off their doorsteps and pulled back inside carousels of postcards, embroidered dresses and cushions, and T-shirts with maps and logos on them. They yelled at some boys who were setting off firecrackers and chasing cats, threatening to tell their fathers and older brothers if they didn't go away.

My shoelaces were loose, and I bent over to tie them. A Haredi Jewish man, walking in the middle of the road, flinched and changed his path. As his arm brushed against the concrete wall, the wool of his suit crackled.

"You scared him!" Mustafa said as the man trotted down the stairs, mumbling something—a prayer, a curse.

Haredi Jews never scared me. They walked fast, but they minded their own business all the way to the Jewish Quarter. I envied them. They read books and prayed, and got paid for reading and praying. In the old days, when Muslims had a great civilization, their smart and pious people also got paid for being smart and pious.

Mustafa and Hassan stood under a dim streetlight. "You scared him!" Mustafa ribbed me again.

WE CROSSED THE ROAD that separated the Old City from West Jerusalem. The road was nameless, or none of us recalled its name. After the Nakba of 1948, a line of rubble and barbed wire had split the city in two portions: East and West. Following the 1967 war, a rope of asphalt had replaced the rubble and barbed wire, meandering through the city like an unwanted river.

It was a short walk to Ben Yehuda Square, but when the streetcar stopped in front of us, we jumped on. We patted our pockets. Hassan paid with his card, and I pretended to look for mine. Then I turned and looked for Mustafa but couldn't find him. The seats were full, and I started to wonder if he'd made it. Then he signalled to me from up front. He had found a seat beside a woman soldier.

"Aziz, come!" he said, and I made the mouth-zipping move. We had an agreement not to speak Arabic on the streetcar. "Do you remember when Abu-Yousef's donkey ran to the municipal park and ate all the grass?" He snickered and pointed to the sidewalk. "They arrested the donkey right there. Abu-Yousef had to pay a big fine!"

The soldier remained still as though the archangel Gabriel was talking to her. Passengers in front and behind us whispered, a few stood up, and some clung to the bars and handles. I was stuck between a pregnant woman who was chewing gum and a man who kept looking at my waist. The sweatshirt I was wearing was loose. It looked like I was hiding something. I was not hiding anything. I clung to a handle and my eyes shot straight toward the road.

The streetcar stopped near Ben Yehuda Street, and we jumped out. We were hungry. Mustafa cut the line at a shawarma place and shook hands with the cashier boy. "Everything?" he called out to me and Hassan, and we nodded from the end of the line. "Everything" meant a hundred toppings on the sizzling meat: tomatoes, cucumber, eggplant, cabbage, tahini sauce, hot sauce, amba sauce, hummus—you name it. Standing by a thin tree with quivering leaves, we wolfed down the sandwiches and volleyed the wrappers onto a crammed garbage bin.

We strolled to the café where Mustafa's brother, Marwan, worked. We called it Marwan's café because he practically ran the place. He spoke Hebrew better than his boss and gave us ice cream for free. The café was packed. We stood in the doorway as waitresses wearing shorts or skirts slit up the thigh leaped across the dining area like ballerinas. Minutes later, Marwan came out of the kitchen, his apron splashed with tomato seeds and parsley. He was in his twenties but had a boyish face.

Marwan let us in, smiling his naughty smile as if he were letting in thieves. Then he disappeared inside the kitchen. Between us and the kitchen pass-through window, which was the size of a small TV screen, stood a bright-red coffee machine and an ice cream refrigerator.

I browsed the buckets of ice cream.

"Shalom," a tall girl with curly hair said from behind the containers of many colours. She smiled as if we knew one another.

I turned and looked at the other boys. They said nothing, and Marwan shouted from behind the kitchen's square window, "Two scoops each, vanilla and chocolate."

"Maybe we want something different this time," Mustafa said, raising his arm.

"Hurry up!" Marwan said. "Trouble outside."

The tall girl arranged her curls behind her ears and handed me three cones with vanilla and chocolate.

"Thank you, todah," I said.

"You're welcome, ahlan," she responded, resting her tongue longer on the *l* and the *n*.

Mustafa grabbed the cones from my hands, and we went outside. Around a corner that faced all the action on Jaffa Road, we arranged ourselves on top of an oak tree stump, ate ice cream, and smoked. Only Mustafa and I smoked. I only smoked in this part of the city and only with Mustafa.

Hassan was annoyed by the smell of cigarettes. He stood up and said we blew too much smoke because we didn't inhale properly.

"Why don't you teach us how to inhale properly?" Mustafa said, laughing, extending a cigarette to him.

At times, Mustafa talked to us as though we were little boys. He was a year older—sixteen. He carried an ID card; we carried our birth certificates. In the eyes of the government, he was a man. In our eyes, he was also a man, and we were catching up with the hair growing on his face, his muscles, and his manly, prickly words.

Hassan was looking at his phone, his face serious.

"What's wrong?" I asked him.

"It's too late to go home," he said. "I'll take a taxi to Beit Hanina and spend the night at my grandparents' place."

Hassan turned away and stood in front of a closed shop. He started talking on his phone, his arms swinging.

Mustafa shook his head. "What a whiner."

Across the street, four Border Police soldiers carrying long rifles threw glances at everything and everybody.

"Maybe he's right," I said. "Maybe we should have gone to Beit Hanina."

"No girls in Beit Hanina," Mustafa said, and pointed at the middle of the square, where music was playing and people clapped and danced. "Staying home for too long has spoiled you."

"Maybe you're right," I said.

I turned and watched the lineup at Marwan's café behind us.

"She's gorgeous," I whispered to him.

"Who?"

"The waitress."

"Dafna?"

Dafna. Nice name.

"How old is she?" I asked him.

"My age, I think," he said.

"I like her name," I said, without thinking. "I wouldn't mind if a girl named Dafna seduced then assassinated me."

"She's taken," he said with a snicker.

"Someone like her has to be taken," I said, looking over my shoulder, imagining a Jewish bodybuilder with swollen arms leaning over her slim body, hugging her from behind, breathing into her neck, telling her smooth things that would make her melt like the ice cream we had swallowed minutes ago.

Mustafa whistled a tune, and I followed him, and we laughed when we didn't sync. A passerby turned around and gave us a strange look.

"I hate it when they give that look," I said.

"What look?"

"Like we're monsters with horns."

"You're too sensitive," he said in a singsong tone. "Just look them in the eye. I learned this from Marwan. They'll only respect you if you look them in the eye. Try it."

He challenged me to bum a cigarette, but I didn't speak Hebrew. Only a few words: *shalom, todah, boker tov*, and *cigaria*. The plan was for me to use one word, one perfectly pronounced word. I practised the word *cigaria*, rolling the *r* to sound like it came from the back of my throat. I swished the letter around my mouth: *Cigarrrrrrrrrrria*. First I asked a woman. She clutched her handbag and crossed the street. Then I asked a man my father's age, and he stopped and raised his eyebrows. He pulled back and asked why I wanted the cigarette. I panicked and said something in Arabic. He cursed at me, and I gave him the finger.

I retreated and told Mustafa I was done for the night. I bent down to tie my shoelaces. They were constantly coming loose. I needed new shoes. Mine were dirty and worn out. I liked Hassan's. I looked up toward his location in front of the closed shop, but I couldn't see him. The sidewalk was more crowded than before, or maybe it had been crowded the entire time. I couldn't tell.

I stood up, and at the corner, I saw the man I had asked for a cigarette was talking to the Border Police soldiers. He pointed in our direction, and they pointed their guns and came howling toward us.

"Run!" Mustafa roared.

I froze, unable to talk, unable to run, unable to move, unable to think, like in a bad dream, except that it wasn't a bad dream. I could see Hassan now. He was standing on the sidewalk, in front of a lotto kiosk. I could not locate Mustafa anymore, but Hassan was in my line of sight.

Behind Hassan, a bald, muscular man yelled something

in Hebrew, and his two arms stretched forward, pointing at Hassan.

Hassan turned around. Then I heard BANG, BANG, BANG.

Hassan collapsed before my eyes.

I turned back to face the soldiers. A trembling grew in my arms and legs, and I shouted, "Don't shoot! For the love of Allah and the prophets, don't shoot!"

2

October 23

A soldier shouted my name. I got up, grabbed my things—phone, wallet, birth certificate—and walked through the metal gate. Outside the police station, Uncle Fahmi was waiting for me. He wrapped my shoulders with a blanket. "I promised your mother I would keep you warm," he said, as we walked down a narrow street. It was dark, and we were alone on the sidewalk. I stretched out my arm and touched the nettle leaves on the low walls. I touched the dew on the leaves, and my stomach ached.

My uncle looked at his phone. I pulled out mine; the screen was broken, the battery dead. When I asked him the time, he said, "Four in the morning."

"Can I use your phone?"

"Let's cross the road first," he said, swinging a small thermos in his hand.

We crossed the wide empty road bordering the city walls. Then we looked over our shoulders as the traffic lights changed colour. In front of a small store that had stacks of crates at the doorstep and a tattered awning, my uncle opened his thermos and poured stale coffee on the ground. He then disappeared inside the store, and I sat outside on a bench. I gazed at my sticky hands, opening and closing all ten fingers to feel the traces of last night. I stretched my eyes open to stay awake for the dawn prayer, when angels clamber down from the seventh heaven to scrub dust and static off Jerusalem's stones and door hinges, when they sweep the believers' floors, heat their water, and clean their bedsheets.

An old man sat beside me. He wore a thin shirt and held a lighter. He coughed. It was windy, and he was shivering. I could give him my silly blanket. I had no use for it. I was shivering no matter what. Wind or no wind, I was shivering.

Then I threw up. A strange liquid, the colour of amba sauce, burst out of me. I threw up on the bench, then on the old man's shoes. He did not get mad at me. He patted me on the back and told me to let it all out.

Then my uncle came, tore off a piece of bagel, and gave it to me. "This will help your stomach," he said, and I took the bagel and bit into it.

On our way home, through the Old City—the souk and the winding alleyways—pigeons brushed against low arches. Some descended onto our path, picking at trampled vegetables and candy wrappers; some stayed on the roofs. Faint lights came from behind gridded windows. Kettles clattered, and the pulse of wary waters seeped through the cracks. Lazy feet scraped the floors behind the windows, and the smell of worn carpets clutched the iron bars.

"Did they hit you at the station?" Uncle Fahmi asked without looking at me.

I shrugged and asked again for his phone.

"Why?"

"To call Mustafa."

"Don't worry about Mustafa," he said. "They let him out early."

The call to prayer descended from the high minarets: "Allahu Akbar. Allahu Akbar... Prayer is better than sleep. Prayer is better than sleep."

I repeated after the adhan as passersby said "Salam alaikum" in loud bursts.

My uncle responded to them one by one, "Ahlan, Hajj," "Ahlan, habibi," "Salam!" He knew them, or maybe he didn't. He greeted them, raising his arm then dropping it heavily on his belly. I repeated after him, with a voice full of vomit and sesame.

I tripped over a jutting stone. I slapped my face to stay awake. Looking down at the cobbled street, I saw my shoelaces were loose and dirty yet again. I did not tie them. At the turn of the road, two cats sprinted in front of us, leaping over trash cans. The trash cans fell. My body shook.

"What happened to Hassan?" I said. "Where did they take him?"

My uncle cleared his throat. "You don't know, do you?"

"Know what?"

"He died."

"Who died?"

"Your friend Hassan. He died on the spot. I thought you knew."

We walked two more steps, and then kept walking, our shoes stepping on spoiled fruit and seeds spread out like a skin disease. My head drifted up to the clouds. A blaze of red and black took over the sky, and water filled my eyes. The cobbled road felt bumpy, and I could not tell if it was the work of my imagination, or of the shovels and earthmovers starting their day in front of Al-Aqsa Mosque, seeking tunnels from the time of Solomon.

My uncle pulled out his keys and opened the main door leading to the lower courtyard. The courtyard and its walls, and the neighbours behind the walls, were sleeping, but the square of sky above our heads was wide awake. The shadows of the lemon tree stretched across the stone floor and the musty smell of the old cistern filled the air. Our shadows mixed with the tree branches. We went up the steep stairs toward the dim lightbulb dangling from the ceiling at the top of the staircase. At the top landing, by the jasmine tree that separated his house from ours, my uncle patted my arm and talked about life and death.

I was not listening. I opened our door and collapsed on my mother's chest. My eyes were between open and closed. The sun was rising behind the back door. Car horns blared, pushcart vendors yelled "Make way! Make way!," and ambulances wailed.

Afternoon

The news arrived slowly on the internet: first social media, then CNN and Al Jazeera. "The terror suspect," said CNN, "had flashed a sharp object." Nobody claimed responsibility for the "attack," which had left no other "damages." None of the Palestinian groups claimed the attack. The bullets that killed Hassan had come from "an armed civilian," Israeli television announced. Hours later, Al Jazeera interviewed Hassan's father, Abu-Hassan, or Sheikh Abu-Hassan, as people who went to his lectures at Al-Aqsa Mosque called him.

"My son is a martyr," he told the journalists. "He died in the service of Allah and Jerusalem. He's not the first, and he won't be the last."

Stars flashed across a map of Jerusalem that filled the television screen. Each asymmetrical red star represented a knife or a bullet. The news ticker below the map showed the date and time of every stabbing and every shooting since September, when the police had erected barriers and started banning people from praying at Al-Aqsa.

I was sitting on the cold floor of the living room when the television went silent. My father had turned it off. He came from behind me, opened the back door, and flicked a cigarette onto the terrace. He slipped one of my books under the heavy back door to keep it open. I watched my book as it carried the load of the door. I watched his cigarette's last breath on the concrete floor—one dot in a heap of grey dots. I watched the wind tickle the satellite dish and the cables and the broken cover of the solar water heater. I watched everything as the neighbour's baby cried behind the wall of our living room as his father divorced his mother for the millionth time.

"What's your problem, boy?" my father suddenly said. "Did I or didn't I tell you not to go to West Jerusalem? Why don't you listen? This time they detained you for a few hours. Next time they'll keep you for six months or a year. Maybe then you'll become a man."

He scratched his arm. The scratching sound was loud. As loud as the sirens coming from the streets. As loud as the call to Maghreb prayer from Al-Aqsa, a stone's throw from our house.

"God forbid, God forbid," my mother said, walking between the two sofas, bringing him his cup of coffee. She made it before he went to work, but also when his mood was rough.

He drove a taxi, working two shifts: mornings and evenings. Until this summer, he had worked between West Jerusalem and Tel Aviv. But now fewer tourists were coming to the city, and Jews did not feel safe riding with him because he had an Arab name, a thick accent when he spoke Hebrew, and an unshaven face. Now he worked in East Jerusalem and behind the separation wall in the West Bank, loading and unloading people between checkpoints.

My mother went back to the kitchen table and started stuffing zucchini. Some of the rice escaped her oily hands, landing on the ceramic tiles to hide between the patterns.

"Broke my heart, the poor child," she suddenly said. "I can't get his face out of my head." She looked at me. "Aziz, habibi, tell me. They say the martyr went to your school. Was he your friend?"

I nodded with a shiver. How is it possible for a friend to become absent and holy and scary in one day, one word, one breath?

I looked up at the square window above her head. The little window, overlooking the alleyway, was closed because of flies and foul smells coming from the waste of the souk. The house had no oxygen. The open back door was not enough to let the house inhale. The branches of the lemon tree, extending from the lower courtyard to our terrace, brought a nice scent to my sofa bed every morning, but it was not enough.

"Have you done your homework?" she asked, her voice barely reaching the back of my head. The thing about my mother's voice—I needed to look at her face to make out the words.

I nodded again and went to the bathroom. The corroded water heater hummed and groaned, and I hit it to make it stop. *Good-for-nothing piece of shit*, I hummed back, and splashed my face with cold water. I squeezed a pimple the size of a meatball and changed into a clean shirt. When I opened the front door and peered outside, the wind was striking pyjamas and underwear on the sagging clotheslines on the neighbours' roof. My mother followed my gaze. She stared at me with her wide green eyes. I stared back.

"I'll be in the neighbourhood," I said.

"Don't go," she said.

"Why?"

"My heart tells me so," she said, looking up at the square window, "and it's getting dark."

"I won't be late," I told her, and she sighed.

My father said something about her spoiling me. She responded with something about the war outside. It bothered me when she called what was happening outside "war."

It wasn't war, yet.

Evening

I met Mustafa near his house in Bab Hutta, at a corner with no streetlights or surveillance cameras. We sat on a patch of gravel as dirty water ran down the neighbour's stairway and trickled past our shoes. Mustafa carried a bag of chips and ate them in threes and fives, the skin of his fingers wrinkled from soaking in soapy water at the car wash.

"I saw Hassan's father on the news," I said.

"He hired a lawyer."

"Why?"

"To release the body," he said.

I closed my eyes and saw *the body* lying on a metal table with squeaky wheels.

"My fault," I said. "Hassan is dead because I told him to come with us. Curse the minute we decided to go to Jaffa Road! Curse the shawarma! Curse the ice cream!"

Mustafa raised his arm. "Khalas! Enough! He's with God now."

"With God? He's not with God! He's in a morgue! A freezer!"

He put his hand on my forearm. "You're saying things you should not say."

"'Pardon us and forgive us and have mercy on us,'" I mumbled, looking up at the bitten moon.

Mustafa pulled out his pack of cigarettes and we smoked. He inhaled half his cigarette at once, and I puffed slowly, blowing through the sounds and faces from the night before. He glanced up at the end of the alley. Then he said, "Did Hassan ever mention any plans to you?"

"About what?"

"You know," he whispered.

"No," I said, rolling gravel in my clammy hands. "He told me nothing." Then I thought of something. "Didn't he have a screwdriver in his backpack?"

Mustafa nodded. "Why was he carrying it, anyway?"

"For his experiments with Ustaz Salim," I said. "They dismantled old computers and learned about their hardware."

"Was it in his hand when you last saw him? When the soldiers came running was he holding the screwdriver?"

"I don't remember."

"A screwdriver can be deadly," he said, swinging his thick arm. "Especially if you direct it to the neck or the chest."

"I don't think anybody would have shot him because of a screwdriver."

"You never know," Mustafa said. "Soldiers shoot at plastic bags nowadays."

"It was not a soldier who shot him."

"How do you know?"

"On the news, they said it was an Israeli civilian."

There was a silence, then I said, "Maybe Hassan got scared."

"Of what?"

"Maybe somebody asked for his ID card. Maybe he couldn't say that he wasn't sixteen yet. That although he was the height of a palm tree, he still carried his stupid birth certificate. You know how nervous he could get. Also, he didn't speak Hebrew. They must have thought he was from the West Bank or something."

"Who asked him for his ID? The Border Police? Some guards? I thought he was alone the entire time. I thought he was in front of some shop or kiosk or whatever."

"When the soldiers ran toward us, I started searching for both of you. I saw him. He was alone. Then there was a bald man standing behind him. But maybe he wasn't."

"Stop rambling, for Allah's sake," he said, pulling out another cigarette.

"I'm trying to think!"

We brooded as people started closing their doors and windows, and tourists walked out of the Old City toward Mamilla to stroll on proper sidewalks and sleep on proper beds. When the image of hotel beds and feather pillows came to my head, my chin sank to my chest.

Mustafa nudged me. "Yousef will know something we don't."

We got up and walked to Abu-Yousef's bakery. As we entered, heat rushed to our faces, and the sound of drums and nasheed drifted from the flour-coated CD player on the counter: *"Our martyr's blood is debt around our necks until the end of days."*

We sat on the wicker chairs by the wall as Abu-Yousef's son, Yousef, swung his stick into the oven and clawed back bread and bagels and pies. He threw some on a wooden tray in front of us. "Eat," he said.

I was not hungry. Mustafa ate, and then helped Yousef carry barrels of pickles out of the storage room.

Yousef's biceps ballooned as he carried the last barrel of pickles. "New, shiny machines," he said, grinning and looking over his shoulder at the boxes of equipment for the gym he was building in the back area. "I'll show you the manuals. All in English. You know me, I'm a donkey in English. I need your help!"

He was stretching his words at the same time as his muscles, and he winked. Joking or serious, he always winked, and I hated that about him. He and Hassan were cousins, but they did not look alike. Only their ears looked the same—small and pointy.

Why all this stupid talk about his stupid machines? Why wasn't he talking about his cousin?

Mustafa and I stood between the oven and the refrigerator like idiots, waiting for Yousef to tell us something useful. If their family had heard anything from the police. If Hassan's body would be released this week or the week after. The heat from the oven was making me sweat and I was feeling nauseous. Spilled sesame seeds covered the tiles under Yousef's feet, and I was about to pull out the hosepipe by the door and wash down every particle.

I was about to say something when Yousef looked down at the lines of sesame seeds and said, "May Allah have mercy on Hassan. My head is about to explode. I can't believe it. You know how much I love him. He's not only my cousin, he's my little brother. Only two years separate us. When I saw him two days ago, he was flying with excitement. He helped me carry most of the boxes. He wanted to grow his muscles. He wanted to translate the stupid manuals for me."

We stopped talking as people came in to buy bread and bagels. Yousef waved to his helpers to finish kneading the dough and stack the baked loaves on wooden trays against the soot-covered wall. On the counter, the flour-coated CD player vibrated, the sound of drums drifted, and the nasheed blared, cutting through the hot air and the clatter of baking trays.

Stepping outside the bakery, Mustafa and I recited the seven verses of Al-Fatiha.

"Amen," I said in a low voice. I wanted to say it louder for the surveillance cameras and the satellites in the seven heavens, to share it with the universe. But Hassan would have said it in a low voice, so that's what I did.

3

October 24

At school, the gym teacher went up the staircase and did the Vitruvian Man: legs apart, arms apart, but belly sagging. His voice echoed across the schoolyard: "One, two, three, four. One, two, three, four."

We followed suit, elbows shoving and ramming in the centre of the yard. Then the lines moved, and I trotted through chlorinated corridors. Sitting in the back of the classroom, under a ceiling with exposed wires, I pulled out a notebook and drove my pen through the pages. The windows were half-open, and I wanted them flung wide to peddlers, hawkers, beggars, cars, and trucks backing up, beeping loudly. I wanted all of them to rush inside and drown the noise in my chest.

Two hours later, Ustaz Salim arrived. Hassan was his favourite of all the grade ten students. Hassan's hand always reached high to answer a question, no matter how complicated. Ustaz Salim would nod and grin. Now he glanced at the vacant seat by the window and said nothing.

Say something, you spineless coward.

He leaned against the yellow wall. "Today, I will explain the physics concept of work," he said. "I will give you an example: If I pushed this wall from now until tomorrow, would it move?"

There was a long silence, then a student in the back stood up and said, "Maybe, Ustaz. God forbid, if they keep digging under our feet to build their temple, all the walls will move. All of them, Ustaz! Do you think they'll find what they're looking for under Al-Aqsa Mosque? They've found nothing. My father drives a big truck for one of those excavation companies that dig near the city walls. He sees them—the engineers, foremen, labourers, and what-have-you. Sometimes he takes pictures. In secret, Ustaz, in secret! If they found out, they would impale him!"

The class laughed loudly. Ustaz Salim did not laugh. He stared directly at the boy and said, "Very funny. Now sit down and listen."

The boy sat down but continued. "They search through all buried things: tiles, mangled pipes, ceramics, bricks, sand, gravel. What do you think, Ustaz? Will they?"

"Will they what?"

"Will they find what they're looking for?"

Ustaz Salim pounded heavily on the textbook in front of him. "I don't care! Not my job. Not yours, either. You should read this book. Only ask questions and give me answers from there. I teach you science. If you want to learn something else—religion and history and the rest—ask somebody else. They'll tell you the *One Thousand and One Nights* stories. They will make you happy!"

Religion and history made him scowl—he was an atheist.

Students in the back, including the one who had answered the question, started to mimic his flailing arms.

He noticed them and said, "You know what your problem is? Mental decay. That's your problem."

Ustaz Salim liked to say difficult words. He had a doctorate in physics. Some called him "Doctor" and praised him for coming back from abroad with a Russian wife, who was also a doctor. She had converted to Islam and wore a hijab, and he didn't like it. His blond kids went to the mosque with his father, Abu-Salim, and he stayed at home with the women of the house.

Minutes later, noise erupted from the surrounding corridors and classrooms: stomping, knocking, cracking, whistling, singing, and screaming. Four or five senior students pushed open the door and told us to pack our things and leave.

"*You* leave and let me teach," Ustaz Salim told them.

"There is a martyr in the city!" they growled at him.

Everyone left the school except for the teachers and the headmaster.

The clashes had started on Sultan Suleiman Street—the entire street, from Damascus Gate to the Rockefeller Museum. Students from my school and others carried rocks in the hems of their shirts. I hid behind a parked car and covered my ears as flying rocks and bottles made a bang and rubber bullets whistled and made another bang. I located a small rock by the car's front tire and threw it at a passing military jeep. I missed. The jeep was not far away, but I missed by plenty. I looked for another rock—none in sight.

The army rushed through the side roads, filling them

with tear gas and skunk water. I pulled my shirt up to cover my face. Dampness was building in my armpits and behind my knees. I snuck inside a barbershop.

The barber brandished his blades. "Curse your father! Get out of here!"

I rushed out and turned left, then right, then left again. At the entrance to the public library, policemen riding heavy horses waved their sticks in the air. I took a parallel road and stopped at a small mosque squeezed between houses. I went up the stairs and then into the toilets. I gulped water from the faucet and did my ablutions.

Like a frightened lizard, I darted into the sanctuary. Sitting by the mihrab, in the deepest recess, facing the qibla, where believers' voices were received, I shrank myself and shaped my hands like a bowl. I knelt, asking God to give me strength and answers. I asked God for refuge.

I said, "I am your slave, Aziz, the son of your slaves, Khawla and Omar, and I am asking for refuge."

With my right hand, I reached for my heart. I recited His names: "The All-Compassionate, the All-Merciful, the Absolute Ruler, the Pure One, the Source of Peace, the Inspirer of Faith, the Guardian, the Victorious, the Compeller, the Creator, the Maker of Order, the Shaper of Beauty, the Forgiving, the Subduer, the Giver of All, the Sustainer, the Opener, the Knower of All, the Constrictor, the Reliever..."

Afternoon

Peddlers pushed their carts down the alleyways as I lowered my head and counted my steps. Every two or three steps, I turned to check if I had been followed. I walked slowly. The power I had gained from my prayers was receding. Fear and weakness shook me from the knees upward.

The smell of zaatar and cinnamon hovered throughout the Khan El-Zeit Market. The air was so heavy, I could not tell spice from dust from skunk water. The sight of buckets of pickles and chickens spinning and kebabs grilling made me want to eat, or think about eating, but I convinced myself not to be hungry. I chewed gum and with it I chewed the heavy air.

Peasant women held straw baskets and leaned against one another. One of them noticed my famished glances and reached for a persimmon on top of her straw basket. She offered it to me, and I hesitated. I disliked the unripe, stinging fruit. But then I grabbed it and moved to the side of the road. Brushing the dusty persimmon with my fingertips, I watched men shoving one another, haggling over the prices of vegetables and herbs that had been cut the night before from the slopes of Bethlehem. The peasant women entered the city without a permit, sneaking through holes in the separation wall or hitchhiking a ride with do-gooders from Jerusalem. They hid their faces with their veils, afraid that the police would blast through the market and kick them back to the slopes of Bethlehem.

There was a sudden surge of people, and I surged with them. A commotion up the road. I hid in a corner and craned my neck as people stood and took pictures. They were pointing and gasping, then pointing again.

Is it one of those flag marches? I pricked up my ears. I didn't hear chants of "Am Israel Chai" or "Death to

Arabs." I hadn't seen anything in the news. "Jerusalem is relatively calm," they had reported, "and so is the weather."

The settlers would not march through Khan El-Zeit. Too crowded, and not as protected as the parallel road, Al Wad, on which Ariel Sharon, long ago, had bought a house overlooking half of the Old City. Now Sharon was dead, after a very long coma, but his house, the size of five houses combined, had become a school for the loudest settlers.

"There they are," someone said, startling me.

I craned my neck once more. I couldn't see anything, and then I saw two masked men, jumping between even and uneven steps, full and trimmed arches, keystones and stone benches. They carried black flags and a banner with a large face—Hassan's face!

On the banner, Hassan's round glasses were resting above the Dome of the Rock, and the Dome rested above chains and barbed wire. There was a little wind, and the banner fluttered and made a strange noise. My heart raced, as if Hassan's face were real, as if he was about to talk to me from the afterlife.

Seconds later, Abu-Hassan slipped through the crowd. He wore a white dishdasha, and he held his head stiff as marble. A surveillance camera was perched on top of the shop behind him, and he glared at it. Fire grew in his eyes, and he continued to glare at the camera as if condemning Captain Moussa, the Ministry of National Security, the army, the Knesset, and the prime minister all at once.

"They killed my son," he said. "They won't let me bury him. They won't let me kiss his forehead and say a prayer.

But they won't escape the wrath of Allah! They won't escape the wrath of Allah!"

At the foot of the banner stood a masked man carrying a megaphone. He started speaking about Jerusalem and how the martyr had taught us to raise our heads high. The masked man's words were like poetry, but also not so much like poetry because they weighed heavier on the heart than regular rhyme and rhythm.

The crowd was growing. Nobody had other business. Nobody was leaving. Nobody was afraid. Women with babies strolled on the margins, plastic bags caught on the soles of their shoes. Schoolgirls, with uniforms and without, with headscarves and without, huddled on stoops and doorsteps. They took pictures and gasped, then they wept. They looked so beautiful, wiping their tears with the backs of their hands.

Then everybody started chanting: "Hassan is a martyr, with the pious and martyrs in Paradise! Hassan is a martyr, with the pious and martyrs in Paradise!" The chanting sprang from a thousand hearts, and shouts of "Allahu Akbar" grew like a vine behind closed doors.

Abu-Hassan's lips moved soundlessly. He smiled. I saw it. It was a tired smile, but he smiled. He went down the stairs toward Al-Aqsa, the masked men flanking him like a guard of honour. They floated like secret angels as the sun mingled with the rocks and tombs on the Mount of Olives. The sun mingled with the footsteps of prophets and soldiers descending the mountain. The sun mingled with the echo of earthmovers pouring through the Kidron Valley, south of the city gates. The sun mingled with everything, and there was smoke.

4

October 24
Late Afternoon

When I got home my aunts were visiting. I came in, and they threw themselves on my chest, kissing me four times on the cheek. They asked how I was, and I said, "Alhamdulillah for everything."

My mother was frying eggplant in a deep pan. I stood beside her, glancing at a strip of salted fried eggplant laid on a ceramic plate. I shoved it into my mouth. It burned my tongue.

"He's taller than you now," my older aunt told my mother. Then she started telling stories about her youngest son, who had beaten a gang of thugs on his own a week before. "They threatened him with swords," she said, eyes wide. "They wanted to take his parking spot by our door, but he stood up to them. Now he has two parking spots instead of one."

My other aunt, whose hair was dyed with henna, said, "Mashallah, the whole town talks about your son's courage."

I realized I had not greeted my grandparents, who sat near the back door and said nothing. I kissed their hands, and my grandfather seated me beside him. "I swear to Allah, I miss you," he said. "Why didn't you come to the olive harvest?"

"School," I said, and he nodded. He always nodded when I gave short answers.

"I like it when you are there," he said, looking in my aunts' direction. "Your cousins are harsh on the trees."

It was a good year for olives, he told me. When he was my age, his father would take him to the oil press in Silwan, south of the Old City, hold a slice of taboon bread to the millstone at the crack where the oil oozed out, and make him taste the fruit of the harvest.

"Life was easy then," he continued. "The food was plentiful. Springs ran along the Bustan. Every house had its own garden, not like now. We had figs and olives and watercress. Your grandmother used to make the best pies."

"She still does!" my older aunt interrupted him. "May Allah keep these golden fingers!"

"We ate and gave to the neighbours," he said, looking away. "When we went to Al-Aqsa, we walked all the way from the bottom of the valley. We did not worry about getting thirsty. Inside the walls, fountains from the time of the Mamluks stood at every corner. Good people gave away bagels with dates. Now you have to buy a measly bottle of water. It costs a fortune and never moistens your throat."

He glanced over at the kitchen table at his daughters, all of them present except Aunt Sarah. We called her "the Canadian" because she had been living in Canada for many years. Now my mother decided to video-call her. When

Aunt Sarah answered and displayed the view from her window, the red and yellow leaves on the trees made my aunts exclaim in wonder. My grandmother, who sat on the floor, away from the phone, did not look at the forest outside my aunt's window. Instead, she asked God for her youngest daughter to return and find a good husband.

My grandfather rolled his prayer beads. "Only the pure of heart can make it in this city," he said with a sigh, and my grandmother frowned at him and looked the other way.

Aunt Sarah asked to talk to me. "How are you, habibi?" she said, and I waved to her from the space between the two sofas. "Come visit me. I'll take care of you. You like nature. I'll take you to see nature."

Years back, when she still lived here, Aunt Sarah would take me to hike across the mountains of Jerusalem and in Wadi Qelt near Jericho. She had studied ecology at Birzeit University. She knew lots about nature, what grew in this soil and that soil. She knew every kind of wildflower, every kind of snake and porcupine and hyena. If there was a flower she could not name, she would take a picture of it or snip a small piece of it and take it back to my grandmother, who was an expert in all things old and wild. Now she was doing her postgraduate education in Toronto, studying other forms of nature, ones that grew or lived in lands with plenty of water and trees.

My mother's voice interrupted my thoughts. "Take him! Take him!" she cried.

When the video call ended, I went to stand by the television to try to find a good channel for my grandfather. He wanted to watch the news, but my grandmother wanted the sound off so she could talk quietly to her daughters.

My older aunt told me to keep the volume down. Then she asked me how school was going.

"Good," I said.

She raised one eyebrow and waited for me to say more. "We hired five tutors for my son," she said, addressing my mother, shreds of dough dangling between her fingers. "His school, the Frères, is the best in the city. You know that, Khawla! It has the best teachers, best classrooms, best textbooks, best everything."

My mother remained silent for a moment. Then she said, "Why would your son need five tutors if his school has the best teachers?"

"The more the merrier! You have to do what is best for your kids. Right, Khawla?" She pronounced the *la* at the end of my mother's name as if it were a torn flag flying in the wind.

My mother stared at the dough between my aunt's fingers, then reached for the faucet. She turned it on full force. "My son is smart," she said. "He doesn't need tutors."

The family chatter was making my head spin. I went to the bathroom, splashed water across my face, and walked through the back door to the terrace. Climbing the rusty iron ladder to the roof, I could still hear my mother's voice. "He studies up there sometimes," she said.

True. I studied on the roof. It was also my watchtower, my outpost. Now I looked down at the alley. The shops were about to close, and people from across the city carrying groceries and treats hurried toward Damascus Gate to catch their buses toward Silwan, Sawahera, Shuafat.

Up the road, a long line had formed in front of

Abu-Yousef's bakery. He sat on the doorstep in his wicker chair, greeting customers and friends. Everybody called Abu-Yousef "Hajj" because he had just come back from Mecca. He was very proud of his pilgrimage, and he cursed the gods and prophets of anyone who didn't address him as "Hajj." He was the elder of the alley and knew the origins of every family—the ones who had lived in the Old City for hundreds of years and those who had moved here from nearby villages and spoke with a village accent, like my family.

The sun was setting on the city, and the Dome of the Rock outshone all the other domes. From the wooden crate that held my keepsakes, I pulled out a book about a boy who had been left to fend for himself on an island. A pigeon perched on the broken antenna behind me and scanned the Muslim Quarter. I wondered if I could figure out the world by watching it like a pigeon, or like a boy left alone on a secluded island.

I checked social media on my phone to see if there were videos of the masked parade. I found some, but they were bad quality. In my head, the parade was still going on. I had been there. My guts started churning and a feeling of uselessness took over. The corner where I had lurked to watch the parade was closing in on me—the walls and its garbage and the smell of piss on the singed stone, all of it. Yes, I had been there. But doing what? Craning my neck like an idiot? Tapping my foot on the ground in time with the chanting? I was disappointed with myself. I was angry. I pounded the crate with my stiff arm; the books inside jostled each other, and the lonely pigeon flew away.

My mother called from the terrace, "Aziz, why don't you answer me?"

She threw wet sheets on the clothesline, and water trickled beside her feet. It was breezy, and she pushed her prayer dress down to cover her legs. She was talking to Nuha, our neighbour who lived at the end of the lower courtyard. Nuha lived on her own since her mother had died two years earlier. They had always lived by themselves. Their roof was across from our terrace, and I could easily jump to it from our house or get to their front door by climbing down the lemon tree.

Nuha's laugh rang up to the clouds. She was always happy. She wore a housedress and sucked on a lemon. The wind teased her hair, and she did not mind it. The wind teased her dress, and she did not mind it.

My mother went back inside, and Nuha stayed out with me, taking her dry laundry off the line. She stroked her laundry one piece at a time. Her purple nightgown was the last piece, and she slipped it off the clothesline and dropped it in the basket. What a basket it was—Paradise of threads and hidden cords! Paradise of shades!

Descending her roof ladder, Nuha went back into her house, and I remained with my fantasies.

"'Pardon us, forgive us, and have mercy on us,'" I mumbled to myself.

The prayer was not calming me down. It was not working, and I snatched a tattered blanket from the crate. One rusty nail stood in the way, and I pulled harder, covering my lower parts with the freed fabric. Lying in the shade of a floating cloud, I closed my eyes. Now Nuha was taking off her clothes. All of them. She was moaning, her lips calling my name, stretching, and straining the *i* in *Aziz*, then landing tenderly on the *z*. Now I was caressing her legs and biting her nipples. Now I was raising my hand to the cloud and masturbating to the wind.

5

October 30

I went to see Mustafa. He whistled from his roof, and I climbed the stairs. Face covered with cement dust, he carried a bucket and zigzagged between jack posts. He gave me the bucket to sit on.

"Look at our new house, Aziz. By the life of your mother, look!" He pointed to the scaffolding spread across the roof.

I could not tell the bedroom from the kitchen, but I said, "Mashallah!"

"For Marwan and his future wife." He laughed, looking down. "Or for me. First come, first served."

We both knew his brother would not get married in a million years, but his father's only wish was to see his eldest son with a wife and kids. Since the death of their mother years back, nothing seemed to please their father, and Mustafa wanted to please him. Using both hands, he counted the cement bags and steel bars he had purchased out of his own pocket. He had consulted with an engineer—a relative of his—who had said the columns were good enough to withstand a Japanese earthquake.

I asked if he had gotten a construction permit from the municipality.

"Fuck those sons of whores," he scoffed. "They're busy licensing for the settlers."

"But, God forbid, they could give you a fine or demolish—"

He patted me on the back, and we went downstairs. I sat on a couch with burn holes in the upholstery and kept busy scratching the embroidered saddle of a horse figurine on the coffee table.

"Leave my horse alone," Mustafa said playfully, and then went to make tea.

Shortly after, his father came in, carrying his decorated nargileh and a charcoal holder. He placed them at the foot of his bed, situated in the far corner of the living room.

He asked if I had seen the roof. "You know, we have no sunshine," he said, pointing to the door at the end of the long living room, which had no windows. They would leave the door open to let in some air and light. It didn't help much, though; neither did the high ceiling.

"How's your father?" he asked me.

"Good."

"Abu-Aziz and I," he said, spreading the charcoal pieces evenly on the nargileh's head, "go back years and years. We met after he finished his studies in Jordan. He knew the history of Jerusalem like the back of his hand. He drove a small Fiat, and I did the guiding. Tourists came to see camels and goats. They expected them to be in front of the city gates. Your father and I talked to Bedouins in the south, rented one camel and two goats, hauled them around, and made sure the tourists were happy. They paid well!"

He spoke slowly and smiled wearily at the end of every sentence, staring at the cracks in the wall in front of him. He was a quiet man, unlike my father, who had a short fuse. I wondered how they had gotten along when they were friends.

Stroking his white beard, he continued, "You and Mustafa remind me of that time. Sadly, I don't see your father anymore. He doesn't come to Al-Aqsa. You should bring him with you."

I imagined holding my father's hand, leading him to the mosque, showing him how to bow and kneel, looking from the corner of my eye to check if he was following my movements. I smiled at the thought, and then looked at the opposite wall, which displayed a framed verse of the Quran that said: "'And your Lord is going to give you, and you will be satisfied.'" Underneath it were pictures of Mustafa's family—his parents' wedding, family of four on the beach, the father as a young man, wearing shorts and holding trophies from his time as a boxer.

Mustafa came back with a teakettle and three glasses. He poured the tea and added a ton of sugar. His father's hand shook as he took his glass, grabbing it from the narrow base and blowing air at the steaming liquid.

"Did I ever tell you he was a champion?" Mustafa asked me, as we sipped the sweet tea on the couch. "He competed in Amman, Cairo, and many other places. He was international!"

"Long time ago," his father said, exhaling smoke, then coughing loudly.

Mustafa handed him a glass of water. "See the years on the trophies?" He pointed to the edge of the shelf where three trophies and five wooden shields stood. "They stopped here."

"Why?"

"He went to jail."

"For what?" I asked, trying to understand the full story.

"He beat a collaborator, sent him to the hospital with broken ribs and a collapsed lung."

His father shook his head. "It was wrong. We didn't know better."

His eyes travelled across the room, and he started to play with the strand of prayer beads around his thin neck. He was a Sufi now, gathering often with friends at corners across the city and in Hebron and Nablus, where he sometimes spent two or three nights in a row.

"You should be proud you beat that asshole collaborator!" Mustafa said. "Every Palestinian should have done what you did. Had your generation cleaned up your shit, we would have had a free country, not the fake authority in Ramallah. We are pathetic, and the world knows it. The Israeli army fucks Jerusalem daily and Gaza nightly. The settlers build villas with swimming pools in the West Bank, buy and steal houses in Jerusalem, live in our neighbourhoods, against our will, with their guns, in our bedrooms, inside our underwear..."

Patting his pockets, Mustafa prepared to smoke but then remembered he could not out of respect to his father, who was looking down at the floor, his legs shuffling, searching for his slippers. When he found them, he got up and rested his hand on his son's head.

"This city has seen the good and the wicked," he said. "Don't push the wicked, he'll fall on his own."

Evening

Mustafa's room fit two small beds and a night table with drawers. He lay down on his bed, mouth pursed shut like Vin Diesel, whose picture from *The Fast and the Furious* hugged the inside of the door.

I sat across from him, on Marwan's bed. "We have to do something for Hassan," I said.

"Like what?"

"Like what? Don't you find it shameful that strangers from God-knows-where parade and call for revenge while we, his friends, hide?"

"Like what?" he said again.

"At least visit his father and console him."

He sprang up and started rummaging through his packed drawers. His fingers poked inside the top drawer, then the one below. Cards with pink and golden hearts fell to the ground—gifts from his girlfriends. One card said, "'Mustafa, you are my destiny.'"

"Not now!" I said, and he turned.

"Here," he said, pulling out a piece of cloth. "This is what I do for Hassan."

"I don't understand."

Spreading the cloth across his face, he mumbled behind the mask, "How do I look?" He ran to the door, opened it, ensured nobody was listening, locked it, and then flew back to sit beside me. "I was there."

I glanced at the mask, then at Mustafa, imagining him with and without it. "You?"

"Yes!"

Then I found myself saying, "Was it you on the megaphone?"

Only now did I realize the voice of the masked man on the roof had sounded familiar.

He slapped me on the back. "Did you watch the parade? Did you recognize me?"

"I saw it on the internet," I lied.

I could not handle the memory of that day, of standing idle in the market, idle like a stranger, like a passerby, like a nobody. I could not deal with the thought of not having stood alongside Mustafa and the other masked men.

"That was me!" he said. "I had the strangest feeling down in my stomach. Strange but delicious, like I was eating my own words! I don't know how to describe it. I marched in front of twenty men. Imagine that, Aziz! I led them, Aziz. I led them! Twenty men in uniform! We marched like a military—like a military unit would march into a liberated city. People pointed at us and cheered. They said: 'May Allah give you victory and power.'"

I grabbed the mask from his hands. It was light and soft. He told me to try it, and I laid it on my lap, flattened it, and traced the eye holes with my fingers. They were cut in perfect circles, the holes. Only for the eyes; the nose and the mouth were covered.

"Did it take long, the parade?" I asked him.

"One hour maybe." He looked up at the ceiling. "Minutes maybe. It didn't matter. It felt like eternity. Happy eternity!"

He made me swear not to tell a soul. I agreed, but I felt betrayed. I asked how he and the twenty people had organized the whole thing while avoiding the army, cameras, and all. He could not tell me because he had sworn an oath.

"An oath?"

"Yes, an oath," he said, pacing the room. "Written by Abu-Hassan. The martyr's father himself wrote our oath!"

"What was in the oath?"

"I swore to secrecy," he said. "But forget about the oath. Did you hear my poem?"

"I don't remember."

Pulling out his phone, he started reading:

The martyr taught us to hold our heads up high, for
you, Jerusalem,
the blood in our veins is yours, Jerusalem,
our flesh, complete, torn, or burned, is yours,
Jerusalem,
our houses, big and small, brick and stone, complete
or ruined, are yours, Jerusalem—our mother,
Jerusalem—

I interrupted him, "So, about the oath?"

He confessed it was all Yousef's idea—the parade, the poster, the oath.

"You could have told me," I said. "I could have joined you. You know how much Hassan meant to me. He was my friend, more than any of you in the parade."

"I suggested your name."

"And?"

"Yousef said no."

"Why?"

"I don't know."

"I don't believe you."

"You were at school that day."

"That's no excuse!"

He rubbed his nose. "Maybe you're not the type. I mean, you're into studying and science. Yousef and I dropped out last year. We couldn't catch up to you and Hassan." He paused. "And Yousef said your father wouldn't allow you—"

"I don't need permission," I said loudly.

I knew what he was thinking. He was reminding me of the time when I had asked my father if I could throw rocks at the army—a stupid question. Mustafa was fourteen, already with a deep voice and a moustache. I was thirteen, trying to be strong, mature, and worthy of my father's respect. But not only did I not get his respect, he grounded me for a week.

I threw the mask on the floor, raising my tone to cover my cracking voice. "Yousef only cares about himself. He wanted the whole show for himself. 'Look at me! I can jump between roofs! I can climb walls!' Hassan didn't even like him. He only went to the bakery to meet up with me there. Yousef is a liar, a selfish bastard."

"You don't know Yousef," Mustafa said, folding his arms.

"And you don't know me!" I said, heading out the door and onto the street.

6

November 9

Rumours had spread that Hassan's body might be released. His family drove to Abu Kabir morgue in Tel Aviv. They waited there for hours, and then at the police station in Jerusalem. They waited on the streets, in the cold, the entire day.

Late at night, Mustafa called. He said he was angry.

I said, "Me too."

He said, "Let's do something."

We met in front of our school. He carried two spray cans and two masks. We put on the masks and jumped over the school wall. Under the ledge of our classroom window, where he used to sit, we wrote: *Hassan was here.*

From street to street—Al-Zahra, Salaheddin, Sultan Suleiman, then the Musrara Market—we sprayed Hassan's name in red and black on every bench and every wall. When a police car blinked its lights and pulled over and the police came out and started chasing after us, we hid and waited until they were gone, and then we wrote his name, again and again.

Now drivers on the wide road cutting through the Musrara could see Hassan's name. Pedestrians and police officers and truckers and streetcar drivers could see his name. And the Haredim, walking quickly with their books, or slowly with their strollers, could also see his name.

November 12

Hassan's body was finally released. The police had warned that only immediate family could attend the funeral, but his family refused to obey the orders. Boys from his neighbourhood, mine, and Mustafa's also refused to obey the orders. Captain Moussa, who was Jewish but used his fake Arab name and his Arab informants to scare and bully people, could do nothing about Hassan's funeral. And it went as planned.

We helped carry Hassan to his headstone. Mustafa and I competed for who would carry him the longest, and his coffin glided on our shoulders, through Bab-al-Rahma Cemetery, along the Eastern Wall of Al-Aqsa, past dry trees and stubborn thorns and dust.

The gravediggers pushed aside loose rocks and dry palm leaves and sank Hassan into the ground. They removed the flag covering his chest and laid it beside the shovels. A large crowd had gathered around the grave, and I pushed through until I could see Hassan—not all of him, only his upper body, his face, which was pale, very pale. White tissues sealed his ears, and his mouth was neither closed nor open, as if, at that moment, he was watching the angels, unsure whether he should tell us about them or remain silent.

I wanted to talk to him. I wanted to squat near the headstone and whisper a story or an old secret. But the gravediggers obstructed my view of him as they filled the grave with earth.

"God have mercy on his soul," a tall man beside me said. "He's lucky he's so close to Al-Aqsa, the place he loved."

Slim rays of light descended from a dark cloud above the Mount of Olives. The rays touched the twisted trunks of olive trees in the Garden of Gethsemane, and then travelled down into the Kidron Valley, which lay deep under everything, under the asphalt roads, the stone walls, under all the graves of Jerusalem and above all the graves of Jerusalem.

Abu-Hassan stood by the new headstone and said that our friend's grave was a piece of Paradise. "My son will promenade here," he said, "blessed with the glory of Allah. He is praying for all Muslims to join him. He is a groom today. Jerusalem is a beautiful bride, and my son is a groom."

What an honourable thing to say!

Most people would have said, "We are dust and to dust we shall return," but Abu-Hassan knew that martyrs do not turn into nothing. They keep their shape and form, their smell and smile. Hassan was not only alive. He was a groom, walking across heavenly gardens, where there is no sickness or old age, no flies, no predators, no evil, and where humans live like angels, and animals do not attack or bite or sting.

It was a martyr's wedding, and we marched to the nearest gate to celebrate. We marched with the breezy winds of heaven. We carried the martyr's father and chanted all the way to Lions' Gate. Carved lions stood above the archway, saluting one another by joining paws. We lifted Abu-Hassan up to join paws with the carved lions, but as soon as we walked through the gate toward Al-Aqsa, soldiers with helmets and heavy jackets jumped us. They fired rubber bullets and beat us with metal sticks.

And they arrested the martyr's father.

Evening

Going home, I came nose to nose with the army. When they saw me, the soldiers pushed me into a corner and told me to lift my shirt and take a spin. They asked if I was carrying a knife.

I said, "No," but they frisked me again.

I gave them my birth certificate. They said, "ID card."

I said, "Fifteen, katan."

They laughed at the word *katan*, meaning "small" in Hebrew. Or maybe it was the way I said it. They glared at my lanky legs, then kicked them apart, wide apart. They slapped me two or three times, turning my ears into tuning forks. Then they threw me back into the alleyway.

By the time I got home, I was a sight, with dirt on my shoes and enough sweat on my back to fill a bucket or two. I walked through the front door, and my mother shrieked.

She asked if I had been in the clashes.

I said, "No," and she scanned my head.

I told her "I'm tired," walked two more steps to the sofa bed, and fell flat on my face.

An hour later, our kitchen faucet was dripping, and

the neighbour's baby was crying again. I was still awake, scratching the red skin on my leg, using the roughness of the sofa to subdue the pain from one or two rubber bullets. I went to the bathroom and pulled down my pants. A bullet had left a purple whiplash mark on my upper thigh. I probed the burning spot, and electricity rushed through my arm. I covered it with toothpaste in the hope it would cool down.

When I went back to lie on the sofa, my mother was pacing the living room, worried my father was stuck somewhere dangerous.

Another hour passed, and his keys jiggled in the door. He coughed and tossed his key chain on the table. She asked him if something was wrong outside, and he said, "Everything!"

He asked why the lights were off in the stairwell. "You knew I was coming!" he said.

"I forgot," she mumbled, and he nibbled on something at the table.

"Why's the food still out?" he asked her. "It will go bad."

"I saved it for Aziz," she said. "He did not eat."

The next morning, crumbs from my father's breakfast covered the table, and I sucked them up like an anteater. The coffee on the stove was foaming, and I rushed to move the kettle. I was too late. The stove was flooded, a brown lake. The gas ring was a choking monster. I stirred the remainder of the coffee round and round until my mother came and took the spoon. She leaned closer and sniffed me. Her nose wrinkled. I needed to wash, she said. And then she told me I was not allowed to leave the house, except for school. "Your father forbids you," she said.

"He should mind his own business," I told her.

She got on the phone with Aunt Sarah. She complained about my manners, then handed me the phone.

"Why are you doing this to your mother?" my aunt said. "If something happened to her—God forbid, if anything happened to my sister, I'd come and kick your ass, and your father's."

"Why not?" I said with a grin on my face. "You should come."

"I'm not joking!" she said. "I watch breaking news after breaking news. I watch maps with dots for stabbings and shootings, and every time, I think of you, every single time. Your mother is worried. I'm worried. It's dangerous out there, habibi. Be careful."

November 15

I woke up to cries, heavy things being moved, the sound of metal, and more cries. Settlers from the next alley had attacked Abu-Salim's family and occupied the two-storey building, the balconies, and the yard with pomegranate and mulberry trees. The neighbours gathered and started yelling at the settlers, who started throwing down the furniture and kitchenware. The army intervened and beat up the neighbours. The settlers had pushed Abu-Salim aside and gone in. Like a sheep, he fell on his side and died in the doorway. The women of the house beat their chests and pulled their hair. His son, Ustaz Salim, was kicked out in his pyjamas with his wife and kids. He poured gasoline on his head. His wife kissed his feet and begged him to stop. He stopped, but he was not himself afterward.

November 17

Ustaz Salim arrived late to school. He walked into the classroom in a stained shirt. Whenever students asked questions he did not like, he bumped his head against the wall and cursed. During recess, the other teachers had planned a game of volleyball to cheer him up, but he shouted at them, at the ball, and at the broom in the janitor's hand. Then, as the game was wrapping up and his team was losing, he cursed God and the prophets. The headmaster, watching from the sidelines, was about to kick him out of school, but the teachers talked him out of it. His misery broke my heart.

I called Mustafa. "Let's do something," I said.

November 18

We met at dawn, fifty metres down the road from Abu-Salim's stolen house. With his slingshot, Mustafa broke the streetlights in the area. Wearing our masks, we brushed against the walls. I zipped my coat to my chin and threw my hood over my head. We scanned the new residence—floodlights and fences with daggerlike wires had turned Abu-Salim's house into a military compound. Sadness filled me.

"What's wrong?" Mustafa whispered. "Give me the cans."

With the black spray can, I outlined the Palestinian flag. Alongside the flag, Mustafa started writing *Death to settlers. Death to traitors*, but he stopped when a long shadow appeared. He stepped back to check but saw nothing up or down the road, nothing on the balconies.

I tiptoed to the wall, scanning the would-be flag as it flashed in the dark, waiting to come to life. It had to be big. It had to caress the earth, hug the fences, grab the stars from their holes in the sky.

Then the shadow reappeared, this time larger than before—two shadows in one. *Click-clack*, and we shouted together: "Run!"

My heart was about to stop, but I ran. We darted through the winding alleys, one ascent of stairs taking us to the next, one sharp turn to the next. At one turn, I tripped and scraped my knee. I got up quickly, looking up and forward. Looking back can kill you—the first rule in escaping a hunter's bullet, the first rule mother gazelles teach their babies: *Don't look back!*

The stone under my feet felt like the arms of Azrael, the angel of death. Lungs gasping for air, I expected to feel a sting in the back, the leg, the neck. The sting of martyrdom—it feels like the sting of a bee, they say.

We crumpled on the ground, breaking out in cold sweat. I took off my mask, wiped my nose with it, and placed it on my trembling knees. Morning people passed before our eyes, carrying lunch bags and prayer beads. The sound of walkie-talkies came from the four corners of the city. We did not move. Traces of light came from the nearby houses. Every time more lights shone into our eyes, we blinked and prayed. My fingertips glowed with the flag's colours. I brought the mask closer to my face. I let the fabric touch the pimples on my damp cheeks. The pores of my skin grew wider as I looked at the mask, and as it looked back at me.

7

November 23

It did not take long for Captain Moussa to visit the neighbourhood. At four in the morning, I awoke to banging on the neighbours' doors. There must have been a hundred soldiers and policemen storming through the alley. I trembled, and my hands crept between my legs for steadiness. I buried my head under the stiff pillow and prayed for the noise to go away. It did not go away. I went to the bathroom and drank water from the faucet. I opened the small bathroom window and saw circles of lights and heard things rolling down the alleyway.

I was still awake when the call to dawn prayer sounded from the minarets. The water was cold when I did my ablutions, but I felt warm immediately after I dried myself and went out to the terrace. The air was crisp, the birds were chirping, and there was talking and coughing through the alleyways. The army must have left, though I could not take my chances and walk over to Al-Aqsa. The soldiers, roaming through the alleys, or the police, standing by the archways and the low doors to the sanctuary, might stop me. Last week, only people over fifty had been allowed in. This week, orders were left to the mood of the police at the low doors.

Safer to pray at home. I laid my prayer rug near the edge of the terrace, by the top branches of the lemon tree, where the sun would touch first. Reciting Quran verses pacified my heart. I took my time between the kneeling and the bowing, and I imagined myself inside the sanctuary, surrounded by the breath of other believers.

I had done my prostrations and was rubbing my eyes when I heard Nuha's voice from the lower courtyard. "May God accept your prayers," she said, her voice sleepy but loud.

"Mine and yours," I said, looking down at my prayer rug.

"You have a beautiful voice," she said. "I swear, much better than some who call themselves muezzin!"

I turned around, shifting to the edge of the terrace to be able to see her.

"How are you, habibi?" she said.

I blushed. I did not like it when she called me habibi. I was not a little boy anymore.

She stood in her doorway, well dressed and ready to go to work at the Ministry of Local Government in Ramallah. She was the office manager for some big shot at the Palestinian Authority. Her hair fell straight to her shoulders and her lips were bright red. Her smell was strong—stronger than the smell from the lemon tree, stronger than the bakery up the road and the butcher down the road. She arranged her clothes and tightened the strap of her handbag. Her eyes widened. "Did you hear the noise last night?"

"I did."

"I heard their boots and walkie-talkies. They were very close. I thought they were in the lower courtyard. I thought they would barge inside my house any minute. I was so scared."

She lived alone—no parents, no husband, no children. She had a Persian cat, Lolo, whom she allowed to roam outside whenever she left the house.

Nuha took one slurp of coffee after another from her thermos, making soft *shhh* sounds as the warm liquid flowed smoothly.

"Were you scared?" she suddenly said.

"Why would I be scared?"

She giggled. "Just joking!"

I nodded, and when she looked at her phone, I asked her, "What time is it?"

"Half past early," she said, laughing. "I have to be in Ramallah by eight. I take the bus to the checkpoint, then a taxi. Life is not easy. How's school?"

"Rolling," I said.

"Do you want anything from Ramallah? Tell me. Don't be shy."

"From Ramallah? No, nothing."

She smiled and walked past the cistern, her high heels clicking. Waves of new and old voices danced in front of me. I remembered the long nights with Nuha and Aunt Sarah, playing board games or cards until dawn. Many times I had stayed at Nuha's place, pretending to be sleepy, dozing on her puffy cushions, waiting for her to ask me to sleep over. "For breakfast," she would say with excitement, "we'll dunk Arshalleh biscotti in hot milk."

The light in our kitchen went on, and I could hear the bubbling of the kettle on the stove. The back door opened. My father came out and walked in my direction, followed by my uncle.

"We'll have our coffee here," he said, calling out to my mother.

"Such a nice day," she said, walking through the back door and placing the silver tray on a clean spot on the floor. She brought a blanket, on which my father and my uncle sat. My father scratched the knotted hair on his chest and talked about a mechanical issue with his car.

"Bring it to my shop," my uncle said. "I'll take a look." He owned a car repair shop in the industrial zone in Wadi al-Joz. His specialty was German cars, but he fixed other cars too, especially for people he cared about.

"I'll stop by this afternoon," my father said. "But don't give it to that donkey-boy, Ramzi. Last time, the car broke down on Route 90, near the Dead Sea."

My uncle chuckled. "You should have taken a swim!"

"*You* take a swim!" He slapped my uncle on the back, and they laughed.

My mother laid mattresses and pillows out in the sun. Nuha's cat, Lolo, sauntered between her feet, and she shooed her away. The cat walked slowly toward my father, who stroked her gently while sipping his coffee. The cat purred softly, rubbing against him as she basked in the sunlight.

My uncle joked about Lolo being in heat, and the brothers snickered like little boys.

My mother shook her head at them and smiled faintly. "Scandalous!"

My father's phone lay on the ground, and he looked at it as a series of messages appeared on the screen. He said he had to leave. Then he looked at me. "Why are you still here?"

"Still early for school," I said.

He left, and my uncle stayed to finish his coffee and his cigarette. He flipped his pack open and said, "Smoke?"

"I don't smoke."

He winked at me. "Your father's gone."

I glanced up at my mother as she crossed the terrace like a soldier. "I mean ..."

"Your mother won't let you?" He chuckled. "Fair!"

He was still in his pyjamas. Folding his short legs and rubbing his belly, he said, "They took plenty of people last night." He exhaled a plume of smoke through his nostrils. "May the cowards never sleep."

Every time the army came, he would repeat the same sentence. I took it to mean the government and their spies. Although, sitting idle in our pyjamas, the word *cowards* fit us perfectly.

Remembering my conversation with Mustafa and his father, I asked my uncle, "Did you fight when you were younger?"

Rubbing his bald head, he said, "I threw rocks, if you could call that fighting. I wrote on walls. I did that once during a curfew. We were crazy!"

His eyes grew wide, as he described how everyone in Jerusalem knew that if the mosques were calling for the prayer when it was not time to pray, it was time to rally in the streets. Then the army's loudspeakers would announce early curfews.

"Whoever violated the orders was shot in the legs or tied to the hood of an army jeep. So people stayed in, drank coffee and tea, and made babies." He laughed at his joke, and then continued, "In the late nineties, just before the Second Intifada, when it was kind of peaceful, I helped reclaim Palestinian houses in Jerusalem. Many vacant houses—or those about to become vacant—had owners who lived abroad, or elderly, childless owners, or tenants without proper papers. The Israeli Absentee Property Law threatened those houses, so we needed to act fast and fill them with good people instead of fanatical settlers from God-knows-where, or greedy locals who would sell them to the settlers."

He patted me on the back. "That is how we got this house. Your father and I partitioned it into two apartments, and then you came a year later."

He pointed at houses with similar stories. Grease lined his fingernails, which shimmered under the rising sun. "We were a small group of young people supported by the Palestinian Authority during Arafat's time. The support was limited compared to settlers' organizations, which have foreign donors and billionaires who believe in the Promised Land and Armageddon."

"Did you like Arafat?"

"I did. I still do."

"Wasn't he a sellout?"

My uncle picked at the blanket, gently gathering the lint between his fingers.

"Wasn't he?" I repeated.

"Arafat tried to make peace," he said, tilting his head. "During the negotiations in 2000, Clinton told Barak and

Arafat: I have a good deal for both of you. What's below Al-Aqsa Mosque is for the Jews; what's above is for the Palestinians. Arafat refused. We could have had everything above, which is what really matters. Right?"

"No!" I said, and he flinched. I pointed toward the small chunk of the city wall jutting from behind the neighbours' roofs. "It's all ours. The whole sanctuary, the grey dome, the yellow dome, the underground Marwani Mosque, the trees, the fountains, the pigeons. Everything!"

Although my voice was loud, he did not shush me.

He cleared his throat. "This is what Arafat feared. He told Clinton, I can't sign off on this. My people would say I was a traitor—or a sellout, like you just described him."

"If he didn't sign off, why do people call him names?"

"He had surrounded himself with people who were not so clean. After he died, we were thrown to the wolves."

"It was Sharon who ruined things," I said. "By walking into our mosque."

"It was many things," he mumbled.

"War is coming," I said. "Then Arabs will stand together."

"You want more war? Don't you watch the news?"

"All the time!"

He shook his head. "You talk about wars and Arabs? They lost every war they fought. And then came the Arab Spring—riots and refugees for nothing. Poor Syrians! Have you seen them on the news? Who would have thought that people from the same house would kill one another, that women and children would get lost in the wilderness and open seas. God save us from all evils!"

"I'm talking about the big war," I said, losing my patience.

"The big war will save us all! The one in the Quran. You know what I'm talking about—unless you don't believe in the Quran?"

I was not used to talking to my uncle this way. But I did so now, and it felt good.

He grimaced. "You don't understand how these things work."

"Things like wars?"

"Yes, things like wars," he whispered, as though he and I were going to start a war now. He counted every war since the Nakba: 1948, 1967, 1973, 1982, the two intifadas.

"The war I'm talking about will not be like any other war."

"Third World War?"

"Bigger."

"We don't even have shelters."

"God is our shelter," I said.

He smiled.

"Why are you smiling?"

"Let me tell you something," he said, throwing his arm over my shoulder, and then into the air, "what we have now is worse than war."

"How?"

"My dear nephew, this is our situation: There is no war. But everyone is at war. You see my point?"

"I don't understand," I said, as he rubbed his eyes and looked straight ahead.

"Your uncle's eyes are garbage," he said. "I used to see ants and cockroaches on the neighbours' windows. Now, I can barely see the windows." Then he went back to his house.

On my way to school, I stopped by the bakery. I thought Yousef would know about last night's arrests. From his family's home on the third floor, he could see the spot where the army would assemble before marching down into the neighbourhood.

Abu-Yousef sat in the doorway.

"Salam alaikum, Hajj Abu-Yousef," I greeted him.

Although I used his favourite title, he did not respond. He rolled his eyes and scolded one of his grandsons, telling him to sweep the floor around my feet—a clever way to kick out people who were not buying. His grandson's broom brushed against my shoes, but I stayed put.

"What brought you here?" He fixed my face with a long stare. "If you're looking for my son, he's not here. Captain Moussa took him."

Night

The Dome of the Rock looked like a campfire. The inscriptions on the octagon's blue walls stood at attention like soldiers, ready to engage. Mustafa and I sat in the shadow of the dome and played with pine needles, breaking them and then trying to glue them back together with sweat from our hands. We were waiting. We did not know what for, but we were waiting.

Mustafa opened the back of his phone, flicked out a SIM card, and showed it to me.

"I have a new phone number," he said. I saved it in my phone. "You have to change yours," he added, pointing insistently to my phone.

A helicopter hovered over the sanctuary, the whirl of

its blades drowning out our words. He pointed to the sky. "Captain Moussa is watching, and this flying whore takes pictures. We don't want to end up like Yousef. Only Allah knows how he's doing now."

"Yousef has nothing on us," I said.

"It's the parade I'm worried about," he whispered.

I glanced at a line of people washing their arms and feet at the fountain in front of Al-Aqsa Mosque, then putting on their rubber slippers, dripping water from their elbows onto the stone floor before walking into the mosque, as though getting rid of all the filth they had collected outside and starting clean. A family of five—mother, two daughters, and two sons—walked past us carrying a pot of stuffed cabbage. Water leaked from under the lid, and I remembered my mother and Mustafa's mother, years before, walking ahead of us, swishing and clanking. They would bring us here to escape the packed alleys. We would sit on smooth rugs and pray, or pretend to pray. We would climb the stone pulpit in front of the dome and improvise funny speeches, telling our imaginary followers to listen hard because good things were about to turn bad and bad things to turn worse than ever. We'd climb trees and throw olives, spruce balls, and pine cones at each other, and then, when we got bored, we'd throw the same projectiles at boys we did not like and girls we did.

"Give me your phone," he said.

He had another SIM card in his pocket. He placed it in my phone, and then we recited, "'No evil shall ever touch them, and neither shall they grieve.'"

8

November 29

Abu-Hassan was released today. After the Maghreb prayer, Mustafa and I went to see him. Standing at the gate to his house, he looked like a seer returning from solitude.

We told him that he was glowing, and he smiled and said, "What can they do to me? My Paradise is in my heart. If they imprison me, it is seclusion; if they exile me, it is Hijra; if they execute me, it is martyrdom."

He squeezed us between his arms, and we were one with him. He had lost his only son, and we were his sons. People came from all over Palestine to console him, and we seated them. We placed rugs under their feet and handed them water and dates and unsweetened coffee. We sat in the front yard, flanked by fig trees and recited the Quran, cover to cover, all 114 surahs. A small fire stood in the middle, enclosed by boulders Abu-Hassan's friends had brought him as a gift from the sanctuary. Since he couldn't go to Al-Aqsa because of a three-month police ban, his friends had brought Al-Aqsa to him.

Behind his back, his friends said the nicest things about him. To hear more, I lingered while serving the coffee and dates. They said his videos on the internet had surpassed millions of views, reaching followers across the planet. They said he had memorized the Quran and spoke four languages and won every argument, even when he was interrogated by Captain Moussa. They said he could leave prison early every time because God had given him the wisdom. They said he deserved to give the Friday sermon at Al-Aqsa. Sadly, he could not because the cloaked and robed officials from the Jerusalem Waqf did not like him. They did not want the truth to shine over the pulpit.

Visitors rotated in reading the Quran. When it was my turn, I felt a load on the back of my neck. I looked down, avoiding the gazes of strangers who waited for me to start. All I could see was a cloud of calligraphed words with accents and commas. All I could hear were coughs and sneezes, whizzing like fireworks. Then a force from inside me directed my eyes toward Abu-Hassan's eyes. *Start*, they said. *Start with all our blessings.* The faint firelight covering the side of his face pushed my tongue forward. The holy words came out, and I sang.

"Mashallah, mashallah," Abu-Hassan said after I had finished. He asked me to introduce myself, and I remembered that I had never told him who I was, that I had only been watching him and hearing about him from a distance.

"Aziz," I said, unsure of the pronunciation of my own name.

"Beautiful name!" he said. "Aziz from Izza—sublimity, glory, power. May Allah bless and guide you. Stand up, brother Aziz. We need to see you."

As I rose to my feet, my knees buckled. Mustafa and Yousef, who were gazing at me from across the gathering of fifty people or more, sat orderly and comfortably. I wished to be like them. I turned to face the rose-stone house and Hassan's room, where a group of little boys and girls had been playing, opening and closing the window, running from his desk to his bed and back again. They were having the greatest time, and I wondered if Hassan's soul was playing with them, showing off the new software and new movies he had downloaded for free or very cheap. He did not have brothers, only sisters, five of them. They must be crying now. They must be looking at us through the dim windows on the second floor, wondering if we were talking about him, recalling his name.

"I am Hassan's brother and your brother," I said. "Aziz Omar Aziz."

LATER THAT NIGHT, ABU-HASSAN stood in the middle of the yard and cupped his face with his hands for the longest time. His whispered prayers left his hands and landed on the fig tree opposite Hassan's room. The broad leaves of the fig tree fluttered slightly, catching his prayers between their thick veins. Except for the soft rustling of the fig leaves and the buzzing sound of the cicadas, the yard was calm and quiet. The mourners had left. Only their footprints remained across the soiled yard. Only the date seeds and coffee grounds in the white plastic cups remained by the low chairs and the tree trunks.

We stood behind him. Only the three of us remained: Mustafa, Yousef, and me. Yousef had gotten out of jail the same morning. He looked tired, his face yellow, his eyes swollen. When I asked him about his time in jail, he told me it was easy. He was a peacock, even with something as dreadful as jail time.

Abu-Hassan waved us into his house. I glanced up at the decorated ceiling and breathed through my nose to smell old things. They came from a good family with roots going back to Prophet Muhammed. I had once seen the family tree in Hassan's hands. I tried to recall when we had been at his house together. Two times, maybe three. One time I had talked to his younger sister. She was nice and very smart. That must have been the last time I visited.

Abu-Hassan took us to his library—its own room, with books, pictures, and sayings calligraphed and framed like museum pieces. One of the sayings read: "The two armies that can never be defeated are the sincere heart and the righteous dua." He gave us books—Mustafa, a book of Islamic poetry; Yousef, a book about the Mujahideen in Afghanistan.

"I'm not sure what I should give you," he told me. "What do you like?"

My eyes drifted to the family photographs on the only wall without books. Black-and-white photos with serious-looking men wearing suits and holding canes. One of the pictures had a young man in a military uniform with a rifle.

"My grandfather," he said. "May Allah have mercy on him. He fought against the British."

Mustafa and Yousef fooled around, lifting their gifted books up and down like dumbbells.

"Careful, Yousef. This is not your fitness club," Abu-Hassan said, and we all laughed.

He told Yousef to give me a membership to his gym. "Every Muslim should have competence and integrity," he said. "Some we get from books. Some from iron and steel."

He mentioned a weekly gathering where young people like us would read books and talk about them. He called it the Circle of Sincere Hearts. I told him I liked the name, and he was pleased. I asked him about the books we would read and discuss and if he was going to test us and maybe give out prizes. His face beamed. He took me to a corner of the room and told me that I had an eager soul. Then he gave me two hundred shekels.

"This is for the iron and steel," he said. "And concerning the books I would like you to read, give me some time to think." He shook my hand, and his firm grip told me that he liked me.

"You remind me of Hassan," he said.

9

December 3

Yousef had turned the bakery's mouldy storage room into a gym with mirrors and pulley machines, and a large bathroom with four showerheads.

"Do you like it, my brother?" he asked me.

I nodded three times—because I liked it, because he had asked for my opinion, and because he had called me brother. We had been neighbours all my life, but I could not remember receiving anything from him except a scowling face.

It was just after the dawn prayer, but boys from the alley filled the carpeted gym and started lifting substantial weights. Their muscles jolted and twitched with every move. I could see their blood pouring through their arms and necks.

As if reading my mind, Yousef commented, "I promise you, my brother, if you listen to me, in three months—no, in two months—you will be bigger and stronger than these boys. Say *Inshallah*!"

I grabbed the list of exercises from his hand and did them all—the light, heavy, and medium levels. Then

I took a shower. The water was pleasantly warm and the pressure very high. On my way out, I stopped by Yousef sitting behind the counter. "From now on, I'm taking all my showers here," I said.

He laughed. "Of course, my brother. Anytime."

A sign with the monthly membership fees was nailed to the wall. "I owe you the fees," I said, feeling my pocket where I kept Abu-Hassan's money.

"This month is on me," he said, handing me a bottle of orange juice, also free.

On the counter, beside a notebook where he had written many names and phone numbers, I saw the book from Abu-Hassan about the Mujahideen. I asked him if he had read it.

"Not yet," he said. "I only got it two or three days ago. We were together, remember?"

"It's a short book. I could finish it in two hours."

"Two hours? Mashallah! Take it, my brother. You'll explain it to me later. You're smarter than me."

His praise made me happy, and since he was in a good mood, I inquired about the next meeting of the Circle of Sincere Hearts.

"Inshallah, soon," he said. "It will be at the Quran School. I will let you know when I hear back from our sheikh."

I rolled the book inside my fist and had a feeling that my hand had already gotten stronger. As I walked to school, my arms swung, ready to lift buildings.

IN THE CLASSROOM I SAT in Hassan's spot by the window. The cypress trees behind the basketball hoop were poking the clouds, but there was no rain and there was no sun. I opened the window a little and observed the folding and unfolding of the world. Now and then, I would open Yousef's book and read a paragraph or two. Books that talk about faith have a different touch and smell, a different feel. As though looking like books is their favourite disguise. Looking like books is their way to excite us, pulling us in and driving us to transcend and change.

"Why are you sitting here?" Ustaz Salim demanded, interrupting my thoughts.

"I need some air."

"That's fine," he said. He then noticed the book in my hand. "What are you holding?"

"Nothing."

"I teach you physics! This *thing* you are holding in your hands is not *nothing*." He snatched the book away, ripping off one of the pages, and told me to follow him outside.

I hesitated.

"Move it!" he shouted, and closed the door behind us. Dangling the book from one hand, he said, "Who gave it to you?"

"A friend."

"Do you understand what's written in here?"

"Yes," I said, though I had found some paragraphs hard to comprehend. I had marked them to go back to and reread slowly and carefully.

"Are you ready to defend it?"

"Defend it?"

"You said you understand it. If you understand it, you should be able to defend it. Right?"

He skimmed through the book. He was quick. He

pointed at a page listing miracles that happened to the Mujahideen while fighting communist Russians in Afghanistan. "Do you believe these lies?"

My eyes maintained their trajectory on the page, which was blurry now. "What lies, Ustaz?"

His finger ran over a header that said *Bullets Do Not Pierce Their Bodies*, then another, *Light Ascends from the Body of a Shaheed*, and another, *A Cloud Protects the Mujahideen*.

"These are ... these are miracles, Ustaz."

"Miracles?!" he shouted at me. "There are no such things as miracles."

I was afraid he would hit me. I took two steps back. Behind me was the railing of the long staircase. I grasped the top of the railing and looked over my shoulder. I saw the headmaster walking up the stairs.

"What's the problem?" he asked.

"Let me finish with him, and then I'll explain to you," Ustaz Salim said. "First he needs to understand his mistake, then he can go."

The headmaster did not like this response. "That's for me to decide," he said.

"With all due respect, I'm his teacher."

"With all due respect, I'm responsible for all of this," the headmaster said, spreading his arms toward the ceiling, the classrooms, and the stained windows at the end of the corridor.

The pages of the book about martyrs and miracles fluttered between Ustaz Salim's hands. The book was about to fly away and leave on its own.

"I caught him with this book. He was reading from

it during my class. I'll show it to you—all lies, the same bullshit they watch on TV and social media. These boys can barely understand how nature works. They can't tell the facts from the lies. It is my duty to teach them not to believe in stupid lies and superstitions."

The veins on the headmaster's forehead throbbed. "Wrong," he said. "Your duty is to teach them the curriculum."

"I want them to think for themselves. To be critical."

"That will come with time."

Ustaz Salim chuckled. "Only rot and death come with time."

Two students opened the classroom door and peeked out. The headmaster shouted at them, "Close the door and go back to your seats!" He raised his stick at me. "You, too!"

"Stay!" Ustaz Salim told me.

My throat felt like a prickly pear. I moved closer to the door but lingered in the hall, trying to please them both.

"Give me the book and we'll talk this afternoon," the headmaster said.

Ustaz Salim pulled back. "You need to support me," he told him. "You're the fucking headmaster! You need to act before the fanatics take over your school, your office, your moustache, the yard, the ceiling, the roof, our shoes and socks. You need to do something!"

Hitting the floor with his long stick, the headmaster yelled, "Salim! That's enough!"

I ran back to the seat by the window and waited for Ustaz Salim to return. He didn't. Had losing his house to the settlers done damage to his head? Or maybe he had been like this all his life. Part of me wanted him to burn in hell because he was mocking the acts of God; another part wanted him to find solace and peace.

Late Afternoon

It was Thursday, and East Jerusalem was out for the weekend. At the corner of Musrara Market and Sultan Suleiman Street, I bought falafel and huddled under a yellow awning. I bit slowly into my sandwich. It was hot and cold, typical of this time of year. My thin sweatshirt was not warm enough, and I folded my arms and watched journalists talk to random people. How depressing to watch those journalists! In their black vests, carrying black cameras, they looked like crows. They never cared who had been shot minutes before. All they cared about was making conversation with random people, turning and twisting their words.

Across the street from Schmidt's Girls College, buses pulled in and out of the station. Schoolgirls walked down the sidewalk, took off their uniform tunics, and tied them around their waists like a belt. They passed by the sidewalk peddlers and the newspaper stands, combing their hair and looking at the sun. Their tight blouses attracted the sun as well as the piercing looks of passing strangers. They checked the time, then they waited for the next bus, and the next. Crammed inside the buses, people from Silwan and Abu-Dis stared out the windows like prisoners' families on visiting day.

I stopped at a grocery store and bought a Red Bull and a pack of cigarettes. I was in the doorway when the shopkeeper pounced on me and pulled me by the shoulder. "You didn't pay!"

"I didn't?"

"No, you didn't," he said, mocking my voice.

I pulled the two-hundred-shekel bill out of my pocket and said, "I forgot."

"Sure, you forgot," he mumbled, holding the bill up toward a dangling light bulb.

I walked out, sat on the side of the road, and lit a cigarette. It tasted very good. I finished it and wondered if the second cigarette would taste as good. I lit it and puffed. It didn't. I tossed it on the asphalt and turned to face a line of tall trees growing beside a large hole that had been dug for a future hotel. A pool of sunshine lay at the edge of the hole, and the whole thing looked very sad, like everything does at the end of the year. I threw some rocks over the trees toward the big hole. I imagined a monster coming out and telling me to stop or else; then I would say, "Else!" and he would give up and ask me to make three wishes.

I called Mustafa. He didn't answer, so I decided to walk to the west side of the city. I went to the Mamilla Mall. Music piped through the stores as I browsed through expensive running shoes. They were not on sale, the Arab saleswoman said, then she helped me choose an olive-green jacket with wide pockets. It was on sale, and she said it suited me very well. I put it on and strolled down Jaffa Road, watching my reflection in display windows.

My feet took me to the spot where I had seen Hassan for the last time. I leaned against a leafless tree and smoked. I remembered his last comment about inhaling properly and smiled to myself; then I stopped smiling when a bird came over and started eating crumbs from the sidewalk.

A hand slapped me on the back. I flinched.

"Hey, ferret, what are you doing here?" It was Marwan. "I'm on my way to work. Are you hungry? It's on me," he went on, pulling me toward the café around the corner. "Wait for me here. One minute."

I stood in the doorway while he talked to a girl at the cash register. Stretching out his tattooed arm, he pointed to me and waved. She waved as well, and I hesitated—should I wave back, or walk toward them and say hello? I remembered her. She had given us the ice cream on that awful night. Yes, it was her.

Marwan disappeared inside the kitchen. He took his time. One minute became ten, twelve, fifteen. I wondered if he had forgotten about me. Customers came in and out, and I stood in the doorway like a fool, a stalker, a "terror suspect." Take your pick. The café did not have security guards, but what if the staff started getting ideas? Stupid Marwan! Browsing my phone, I found I did not have his number. I was trembling. My new jacket could not provide the warmth I needed.

I was turning around to leave when the girl at the register told me to have a seat. I sat down and watched as she tapped her long fingers on the counter and told servers what to do. It was too hard not to look at her—the almond eyes, the curving eyelashes, the hoop earrings. Cups and plates with sugar packets sat on the round tables as curious flies flitted around, licking at them. Like a fly, my eyes flitted and licked, and I was ashamed.

Does she notice my gaze? Will she have me arrested? How long would a gaze have to be to warrant an arrest?

Marwan came back with a sandwich.

"Not hungry," I said.

"It's free," he said. "Listen, are you looking for work?"

I shrugged. "I don't know."

"We need people," he said, handing me his number. "Dafna just told me so."

10

December 4

After the Friday prayer, I went to help Yousef clean and arrange his gym. I also exercised, and he said my muscles were growing fast. As it was getting dark, I was standing with him in front of the bakery when he pointed out a woman's silhouette down the road.

He whispered in my ear, "I see men going in and out of her house."

"Aunt Nuha's house?"

He snickered. "You call her *Aunt* Nuha? She's a whore!"

I winced under the weight of the word, but I remained silent. She was my aunt Sarah's friend, and my mother liked her.

He clasped my shoulder. "I know a whore when I see one."

Then Nuha was in front of us. "Salam, Yousef," she said in a singsong tone.

"Salam to the most beautiful woman on this earth," he said.

She blushed and turned toward me. "Give your aunt a hug."

I shook her hand instead, and she went into the bakery, her necklace with the letter *N* bouncing on her cleavage. She bent over a wooden tray and squeezed a few bagels. "Yousef, come here! I have guests from Ramallah. I talk about your bagels all the time. I want them to eat Jerusalem bagels, not some stale shit." She said the word *shit* like someone else would say *chair* or *table*.

Yousef ran to her. "How do you like your bagels?"

"You know what I like!" she said playfully. "Crusty but soft on the inside."

He told her to stand beside him, behind the counter, near the oven. "Pick what you like," he said, pointing at the tray with the hottest and freshest bagels.

She caressed a bagel from the middle, squeezed it where it curved, and pinched it at the line of soot.

Yousef danced around her like some wild animal. He was moving closer now, almost grinding into her. Ogling her from top to bottom, he hissed, "Try this one."

She laughed nervously.

He brushed his arm against her belly. "Touch it. Crusty enough for you?"

"Is what crusty enough?" she said, pulling back.

He whispered in her ear, flexing his arm under her eyes.

The bagels she was carrying fell to the floor. "Shame on you, Yousef. Shame!"

An old man at the end of the line tried to intervene and told her to calm down. "He was just joking," he said.

"Do you see me laughing?" she yelled at the old man. "Do you?" And then she spat on the floor and left.

. . .

WHEN I GOT HOME, MY father was sitting on my sofa bed. "Where have you been?"

"School," I said, "then the public library."

He got up and crossed the floor. "You're telling me the public library is open this late?" He stood zero distance from me. "I saw your teacher Salim. He told me what type of student you have become. Listen, if you hate school so much, why do you waste my money and your teachers' time?"

My mother told him to lower his voice because the neighbours might think bad things of us.

Then there was a knock on the door. It was Nuha. She wanted mint.

"Long time!" my mother said, kissing her on the cheek.

She asked her to sit at the kitchen table and told me to cut some mint. We had two planters outside—one with mint and another with peppers and basil. I cut a bundle of the mint and gave it to Nuha, who took it and turned to go. Standing in the doorway, my mother insisted that Nuha taste the lentil soup simmering on the stove.

"No time, dear. I have visitors," she said.

"They can wait," my mother said, and she served soup for Nuha and my father, who was about to drive to Ben Gurion Airport for work. He yawned and looked at his phone, then he sat down and started his train of jokes. He liked it when women neighbours visited, especially Nuha, who liked his jokes, including the dirty ones—especially the dirty ones. With every joke, her head moved like a bobblehead doll.

I stared at her. She was not beautiful—her face was big and her fingers round and thick. Why did half the neighbourhood drool over her, including my father?

"You know what this soup needs?" my father said, looking in my direction. "Hot peppers." I went out and brought back two hot peppers. "I handed one pepper to my father and the other to Nuha, who took a bite of hers and immediately began to squeal. My father laughed.

"Poor Nuha," my mother said. "Omar! Not everyone has your tolerance for spice." Then, handing her a glass of water: "Sorry, Nuha!"

"No problem," she said, struggling to catch her breath. "I like it. I used to eat hot stuff."

"Ramallah is making you soft," my father said.

She nodded, struggling to put words together. Her face was red, and she waved her hands near her mouth.

Unfolding my arms, I walked toward the door.

My mother said, "Where to now?"

"The mosque," I said. My father told me to pull my hands out of my pockets and sit down "like a man."

No reason to argue now, I thought. He was leaving soon.

He started talking about his trip to the airport.

Nuha moaned. "I don't remember the last time I travelled. I forget the shape of the sky." She was taking classes at the French Centre. "I'm not very good with languages, but I'm trying. Your sister speaks three or four languages by now."

"Sarah is good at everything," my mother said, tilting her head like she always did when her little sister's name came up.

Nuha scanned me. "Are you smart like your aunt?"

"As if life's troubles can be solved with brains," my father said. "At least a dozen people with university degrees are on my route. Can't find work, or their jobs are not enough." He hitched up his pants and walked toward me. "Before I go, I want you to call Ustaz Salim and apologize to him."

"For what?"

"For not paying attention."

"What did I do?"

"I'll tell you what you didn't do. Respect! Ustaz Salim is one of the smartest people in the city. A man of culture. Shame on you and your mates for treating him like that."

"Like what?"

Veins throbbed across his forehead. "The man has a doctorate in physics. He decided to come back to this city—this shithole—to teach you! He could have worked anywhere in the world, but he chose to come back here and teach you morons!"

My mother handed him a glass of water and asked him to relax.

"I had a book in my hand. That's all," I said, trying to calm him down.

He grabbed his phone from the table, pressed a few buttons, and gave it to me. The number was on the screen; I only needed to press the call button.

"He's crazy," I said. "Something is really wrong with his brain."

"Call him!"

Shuffling my feet, I looked up at the low ceiling. The room was tight and heavy; there was nowhere to turn my head. I could not bear my own gravity. The phone in my hand was wires and shock waves. I threw it. It went up, spiralled, came down, and bumped against Nuha's bowl. Soup spilled, dripped on her arm, and trickled onto the floor.

"Why don't you go to the airport?" I told him. "You're late. Go!"

Silence. It pricked like a needle.

"See? We raise him and feed him, and look what we get," my father told Nuha, who sprang up to wash her hands at the sink and thanked my mother for the soup. He saw her out, closed the door, locked it, and turned around. Digging his fingers into his belt, he came toward me. He dragged me by my sweatshirt. He hit me with his fists. I fell to the ground, and he hit me again. He took off his belt and struck me. The square metal buckle drummed against my skull, and I shrank into a ball. I felt light and numb.

My mother screamed, trying to pull him away from me.

"Allahu Akbar," I said. "You are evil. You're an evil man! Allahu Akbar."

More lashes.

"I will kill myself," I said. "I don't want this life. I will kill myself."

"Go kill yourself!" he shouted. "Take a pair of scissors and go to the next checkpoint. Dance with the scissors. Let them piss bullets on you. What do I care?"

He stood over me, panting. He slipped the belt back onto his pants. One loop at a time. One loop. Two loops. Three loops. Four loops. Done. He might have missed the fifth loop. Why tell him? He would not care.

He left, and I wiped the blood and drool off my face. Seeing blood spattered on the wall behind me, my mother fainted. I grabbed her perfume bottle from the cupboard and sprayed it around her head. She woke up and raised her hand to touch the bruise on my forehead.

"I'm fine," I said. "I swear to Allah I'm fine."

I waited until she sat down and looked like she was feeling better, then I left and ran down the stairs. I roamed from one dim alley to another before finding the Quran School. I went in, finished my prayer, and looked around. It was a renovated building, the smell of new paint hanging in the air. The lower floor was full of young people and well-dressed older people. There was no furniture, only Quran holders, a square carpet, a curtain, and a wooden door. The second floor had a metal door with a sign that said: *Zakat Committee.*

Abu-Hassan sat behind one of the Quran holders. He held a small prayer book and his eyes were closed. When he got up and started embracing everyone, I stood near the wooden door and waited for my turn. He was leaving with visitors who spoke a mix of Arabic and English. They were taking him to be interviewed by Al Jazeera. He was showing them around and said similar schools would be opening soon across the city.

He saw me, and his brow furrowed. "What happened to you?"

"Checkpoint around the corner," I said.

He rushed over to a small refrigerator behind the curtain, brought out two ice cubes, and told me to sit down. He laid the ice against my forehead and said, "How nice to see you, brother Aziz. Last time, I could not set a date for our meeting, but you have come on your own, and I am pleased."

Then he clutched my arm. "Come tomorrow at dawn. Let's pray together."

Night

I sat for some time on the doorstep of my uncle's house. Then I knocked on the door.

He opened the door and looked right and left. "About time you visited your uncle! What am I to you? A Jew?"

I took off my shoes and sank onto the couch. He was watching a football game. Aunt Amal was happy to see me. She made tea and served carrot cake.

"Don't be shy," my uncle said, pointing to the piece of cake in front of me.

"Thank you," I said, holding a cushion and drumming on it.

"You are so polite I sometimes forget you were raised here," my aunt said with a smile.

They kept asking if I wanted anything else. I could have asked for anything I desired. They had no children, and I liked to think of them as my spare parents.

"It's strange to have carrots in a cake," my uncle said, swallowing the last bite of his cake, "but I like it! Your aunt did not have to force it on me. What I don't like is maqluba with broccoli. I hate that thing!"

My aunt was a vegetarian. "Broccoli is more nutritious than cauliflower," she said.

I pulled out my phone and saw my mother's number. She had called several times. I gazed at my untouched carrot cake and remembered her low opinion of my aunt's food.

"Your parents are not feeding you well," Uncle Fahmi said, caressing his flabby belly, then poking me in the stomach. "Shame on them."

"Shame on them," I said in a firm voice, and he laughed loudly.

I took a bite of carrot cake, but then I started coughing. My aunt handed me a glass of water and took my uncle's empty plate to the kitchen. I gulped the water and my legs shook.

"What's going on?" my uncle asked in a whisper. "Trouble with your father?"

"No," I said quickly. "I was just wondering if I could sleep at your place."

He folded his arms, waiting for me to say more. As I looked down at the shiny carpet, ideas bounced around in my head. I shifted my hair with my hand to hide the growing bruise on my forehead. I stared at the door, considering other sleeping arrangements: Mustafa's place, though with the construction their living room was messy. The sanctuary, under a tree. The night was warm.

"Of course you can stay!" my uncle roared, pulling me into his lap in a wrestling move and tickling my armpit. "You're visiting your uncle."

We drank tea, ate roasted nuts, and watched the football game between Real Madrid and another team from the Spanish league. A staunch fan of Real Madrid, my uncle owned T-shirts and key chains with their logo. My father supported Barcelona, and they quarrelled when their teams played each other.

"I should call your father," he said.

Don't you dare, I wanted to say. Then the doorbell rang.

Uncle Fahmi opened the door. "We should have mentioned a million dollars!"

"Talking about me?" my father said. "Try now. I'll hide. Mention two million this time."

In his hands, he carried a box of baklava. He dropped it on the table, sat down beside me, and cupped my knee with his hand. What did he want from me now? I recoiled and went to the kitchen to help my aunt with the dishes. Remembering the sound of his belt against my head, I scrubbed viciously, wanting to wipe off his face, his voice, his touch. I splashed water on myself and on the ground.

"Be careful," my aunt said, then she patted me on the back. "Your mother raised you well."

When Ronaldo scored a goal, my uncle pounded the table and danced up and down.

"You bought the referee," my father said.

"Envy is going to kill you," my uncle told him.

He unwrapped the box of baklava, ate two pieces, then threw his arm around my father's shoulder in approval. He had diabetes, but he liked his baklava.

Sticking her head out of the kitchen, my aunt said, "Sugar is going to kill both of you before anything else."

After the football game, they played cards. I stacked the scattered cards for them, shuffled, and gave them two cards at a time. I then recorded their points as they accused each other of cheating. They cursed but still laughed and cheered. *To have a brother is a very nice thing*, I thought. Being my father's only son bothered me.

I wondered if it bothered him as well. My mother had not been able to give me brothers or sisters.

My uncle claimed me for the night and walked his brother to the door. I closed the guest room door behind me and sat on the floor. Wet laundry had been hung on foldable racks, and the smell of detergent bumped up against the scent of fermented olives in yellow gallon containers, all harvested from the fifteen olive trees our family owned in Silwan.

I got into bed and tried to sleep. I couldn't. I tried to think of a list of nice things: sheep, cats, puppies. The sound of my uncle scratching his back on the other side of the wall did not help. He scratched himself so harshly it sounded like his flesh was about to come off.

Peering under the bed, I saw a swollen suitcase. Maybe winter or summer clothing. Maybe money. Smiling at the thought of my uncle saving his money inside a large suitcase, I opened it. Instead of money, I found books. Stacks of books. Old and mouldy. They smelled bad and large spiders nested in their spines. Now I started scratching myself, and I pushed the suitcase back under the bed. Not in the mood to read now. Not in the mood for bugs or mad spirits.

I lay down and tried not to think about the fight with my father. Only nice things now. Only new things. The dawn prayer was approaching.

11

December 5

Abu-Hassan embraced me tightly. I could smell the musk on the collar of his dishdasha. His hand lingered on my back, and I had a feeling that he had known me for so long. I had a feeling that he had missed me, that he had been missing me since Hassan's death.

"We will have breakfast together," he said, and we left the Quran School and walked quickly, like arrows. He was my father's age, but he moved like an arrow, talked like an arrow.

A boy was standing by the traffic light, selling bagels and falafel and oven-roasted eggs. Abu-Hassan gave him fifty shekels and told him to keep the change, which was a lot. He ruffled the boy's hair and told him it was God's money.

"The son of a martyr," he whispered in my ear, and I stared at the holes in the boy's pants.

We were walking in the middle of the road leading to his house, when a truck with oranges and clementines honked behind us. Without thinking, I yelled at the truck driver.

"Praise the prophet," Abu-Hassan said, pulling me to the sidewalk. "Strong is the one who controls his anger." He then gave me a small blue book. "Keep this with you. Read from it whenever you have time."

It was a prayer book. I held it between my thumb and index finger. "Whenever I am angry?"

He grinned. "Whenever. There are no limits to God's doors."

We sat in his front yard, at a plastic table between the loquat tree and a broken fountain. He walked over to talk to his wife, whose shadow vibrated in the doorway. She carried a teakettle and glasses. I wanted to say something to her about Hassan. I stood, then I sat. When she went back inside, I was in between sitting and standing.

"Bismillah," Abu-Hassan said, grabbing a bagel and opening it from the middle. "Let's eat!"

He noticed I was looking at the fountain's basin and the rusty pipes. "Do you like it?"

"I like fountains," I said. "Pity it's not working."

He put his hand on my shoulder. "Brother Aziz, I'm going to tell you something not many people know. This fountain used to work nicely, just as God intended. I built it with my own hands, laid the pipes, constructed the basin, and purchased the tiles from an Armenian shop. I sculpted a statue of a woman and painted it."

"You did?"

"I used to follow my desires," he said, covering his eyes. "But then I received God's blessing. Until the Day of Judgment, I will be asking for His mercy and forgiveness."

He pushed the teakettle toward me, and I glanced at his delicate fingers.

"Hassan, bless his soul, did not like tea," he said. "Mint, sage, chamomile—never liked it. His mother would try and try, but he was stubborn." He took a sip.

"He was very smart," I said, glancing down at the steam coming out of my cup to mix with the morning mist. "He taught me many things."

Abu-Hassan's eyes went again to the fountain. "He wanted to fix it."

"I can fix it for you," I said quickly.

He frowned for a second, then grinned. "Brother Aziz, may Allah guard you with His eyes. It is a blessing that I have you now. Allah has compensated me with you and your brothers—Mustafa and Yousef, and Mahmoud and Samer and Khaled and"—he counted on his fingers—"mashallah, so many. I need more fingers."

I helped him collect the dishes, and he headed to the door and returned with a stack of books that glistened under the sun. "A wise man once said, 'The learned men are the lights of the ages.'" He dropped five books in front of me. "I picked these especially for you."

Bringing the books close to my chest, I thanked him and started telling him about my reading habits and the types of books I would borrow or buy. I mentioned Islamic philosophy by Ibn Tufail and Ibn Rushd and worldly stories by English and French writers.

"May Allah forgive you," he said, shaking his head. "I don't want you wasting your time on Western hallucinations."

I understood what he meant. "I'm very careful. I stop reading when—"

He interrupted me, "Don't touch that filth! This is how

the devil gets to you—'I'll stop in a minute, a few pages won't hurt, one song is not the end of the world, one movie is fine as long as I look away when the actors jump on one another.'"

He rubbed his eyes with both hands. "That sort of thing, my son, is the source of all sins! Stay away! The West bombards our youth with messages that glorify the material world and disrespect the word of Allah: books, movies, games, chit-chat. They want us to doubt our values and principles. You know why? Because, deep in their hearts, they know that Islam is the remedy to the sickness and suffering of this broken world. They talk about freedom, but in truth, they want our women to disobey their men and our sons to challenge their fathers and our daughters to wear revealing clothes. I lived in the West. I know them. I know them very well. They think they are better than us. Certainly not!"

He asked me if I was in the scientific or literary stream at school.

"Scientific," I said.

He said that in his time he had also been in the scientific stream but changed later because he loved geography and history. "I went to study in London," he said. "In my eyes as a boy, London was a city of wonder, beauty, civilization, truth. Biggest lie ever told. Westerners think they are the wisest of all people. They say, 'We bring civilization to the world,' but then they ban our sisters from wearing hijab, tear up our holy book on the streets, insult our prophet. That's not civilization. That's aggression. Then you find deviant people from our flesh and blood following them like the blind follow the blind. They preach democracy and free speech, and then what happens? Cast your ballot for Islam, and they say, 'Game over!' They don't want Islam to rule. They won't allow the word of Allah to prevail. They want to impose their rules and evil desires. Some of our people help them, knowingly and unknowingly. Can you imagine that, brother Aziz?! You are an avid reader, I'm sure you know about this."

I thought of Aunt Sarah and her obsession with everything Western. I told him about a documentary she had once told me to watch.

"What was it about?"

"Animals," I said.

He snickered, and I added, "They respect animals more than humans."

"Not even that, my son! They tell you they respect animals, but they respect nothing. You already know that. You are smart. Mashallah, you are very smart." Moving his chair closer and bumping into my knees, he said, "People who are beneath you in knowledge and wisdom will never be able to teach you. You should refuse to let them teach you because, otherwise, they will show you their mistaken path. Don't let people beneath you in knowledge lead you onto their mistaken path. You understand?" He paused. "Is she married, your aunt?"

"No."

His nose wrinkled. "She lives on her own?"

"Maybe. I don't know."

"Are you close to her?"

When she lived here, years back, she had been my

second mother, giving me money and taking me places. I did not tell him that.

"We do not choose our families," he said, "but we can always show them the path. Because when Doomsday comes, judgment will be pronounced on everyone in accordance with their deeds."

He looked at the time and then pointed to the books that I was holding. "Read them. They will give you clues about who you should trust or fear. Do not ever forget that the only reason we ruled the world from China to Spain is that we guarded our houses and our families."

"I read about miracles in Yousef's book," I said. "My heart was throbbing with every story."

"Well said! My heart feels the same. Allah will never leave His people. It is the truth. It is a promise. Believe it or not, our victory is near—in Iraq, in Syria, and soon here in Jerusalem. When I look at you and Yousef and Mustafa, I see it. You are special. You have a responsibility. You are carrying the first flags on behalf of more than a billion Muslims!"

His eyes were moist, and he rested his right hand on my chest. His hand was soft and warm. When he took it away, I could not look directly into his eyes. I turned toward the gate, closed it behind me, and walked up the road. I was tired from lack of sleep but could have reached China or Spain if I really wanted to. I could have reached the unseen lands of the jinn and the high mountains of Gog and Magog if I really wanted to.

The hills of Jerusalem overlapped, and the clouds touched each hill and moved to the next, like runners in a relay race. I walked fast, arms swinging, hands open.

I wanted to hug every hilltop, every foothill, every rock and pebble. I wanted to touch every cell inside me and tell the smallest part of my being—*I am a flag bearer, a true Jerusalemite, one of a billion!*

WINTER 2015–16

12

December 17

Every Thursday, after the Maghreb prayer, we ate dinner and read dua from the blue prayer book. We were about thirty brothers—men and boys and little boys, whom we called Baby Lions. We met on Thursdays because that was the day Hassan had gone to heaven. Or because it was the day before Friday. I wasn't sure, but I liked to associate Thursdays with Hassan.

Abu-Hassan called us the Circle of Sincere Hearts. The idea had come to him from seeing Muslim youth fight against one another and lose themselves in meaningless pursuits. He had seen Jewish and Christian seminaries pop up across the land, and he thought, *How come other religions are more concerned about their youth than we are? How come they protect and treasure their source of pride while we ignore it and treat it like an old rag? How come they mock our religion while we follow them inch by inch, even as they sink into the deepest holes?*

After the prayer, Abu-Hassan would give a lecture in which he talked about everything from the history of Islam to how to be a good Muslim in a fucked-up world. He never said the words *fucked-up*, but that's what he meant when he said *deviant*, *heathen*, or *apostate*. Sometimes what he said seemed like riddles, but I wrote everything down in my notebook. All the serious words he told us, I wrote down, enunciated, and repeated at home, threading them into speeches that I would deliver one day.

We ate chicken and hummus and roasted potatoes. It was a big meal; I gave half to Mustafa. When he noticed I was done with my food, Abu-Hassan called me to sit beside him. "You have an eager soul," he said. He saw something in me. Something special!

Some in the Circle of Sincere Hearts knew the Quran by heart, but I didn't. Still, he chose me to lead some of the prayers. "You have water in your voice," he said.

I did not get how my voice could hold water, but I believed him. That night, I led the Isha prayer. My brothers stood behind me and listened to my recitation, and when I said, "Allahu Akbar," they repeated after me. And when I bowed and knelt, they bowed and knelt behind me. I coiled vowels and consonants and *mims* and *noons*, then unleashed, coiled, then unleashed, then glided and soared with the holy verses—a holy roller coaster from first standing to last salutation, among hanging gardens with canals running between lush trees. I had water in my voice!

After the prayer, Abu-Hassan asked our brothers to come closer because he had something important to say. He told them about an essay I had written about one of the books he had given me to read. It had been published in a local newspaper and shared by hundreds on social media. He showed it to them on his phone, which moved from one hand to another through the Circle. Grinning through the whole evening, he told everyone to follow my lead: "Look at what your brother Aziz has done. Look and learn!"

He saw something in me, but I knew I could improve. I could do more, especially with small talk. Because while I only said a few words when he and I talked, my brothers told the most entertaining stories. Also, while I only called him Abu-Hassan, they called him more suitable names like Amir, Sheikh, or Maulana.

Standing outside the Quran School afterward, we wore white dishdashas and hugged one another and talked about truthful things. People glanced at us in admiration. We reminded them of the times of the prophet and his disciples. Their admiration was kind and sweet, and we could feel it from far away. Now I understood how Mustafa had felt on the day of the parade. Now I was on the right side, not the wrong side—the gaping, staring side.

December 18

Our martyr's blood is a debt around our necks until the end of days.

I was panting and humming Islamic songs when Yousef's shadow fell near the dumbbells. Laying his hands on my lower back and pinching my shoulder, he said, "This has to thicken and harden."

He was right. I wanted a hanger for a shoulder, a hook, an anchor.

He arranged the dumbbells on the rack and said, "Don't lose count if you're looking to build size and strength. Count loudly so you keep track of your progress. Talk to yourself. When you talk to yourself, you're in control. Don't be shy. Shout if you like!"

He handed me a bottle of apple juice and a cigarette. We went outside to smoke.

"Listen," he said. "Abu-Hassan likes you. He can't stop talking about you. He keeps saying, 'Aziz is something else.' You see, my brother? I'm the sheikh's nephew, and he never talks about me." Looking right and left to check no one could hear us, he told me the Circle of Sincere Hearts was something grand, and not every passerby could join. "Only the chosen ones," he said. "You think the sheikh would waste time and free food if he didn't like you? He picked you because he likes you, and because he likes you, I will take care of you."

The wind carried the cigarette smoke into his eyes, and he rubbed his face.

"You're already taking care of me," I told him, flexing my biceps.

"My brother, I mean you will be under my hand, my responsibility. I will be your leader, and you'll receive assignments from me."

The sound of hurried steps came from behind us.

"Salam," Mustafa said, giving us one-armed hugs. He took to the corner by the door and unzipped his fly.

Yousef waved him away. "Inside, Mustafa. Inside! My wall is not a pissery."

"I have an assignment for you today," Yousef told me. "You might find it too easy, but only you can pull it off.

Because you have this thing—Abu-Hassan mentioned it to me. I forget what it is."

"An eager soul?"

"An eager soul!" he repeated after me. Then, resting his hand on my neck, he pointed at people walking up and down the alley. "Take a look at these people. Do you know any of them?"

I shrugged.

"Do you know what they want?"

"No, I don't."

"May Allah open the doors to Paradise for you, Aziz. Excellent. You just said it. We don't know these people. Some belong here. Some don't. See, my brother? That is your assignment."

"I don't get it."

He leaned over and whispered, "All I need from you is a list of suspicious people."

We stopped talking as Nuha walked past us and into the bakery with a guy who had a man bun and wore a leather jacket with chains dangling from the sleeves.

"You see?" Yousef said. "You're smart enough to see these things."

"Is she sleeping with him?" I said without thinking.

Yousef folded his arms. "Maybe. This ponytail boy could be anything: drug dealer, realtor, antique smuggler, pimp, traitor, homo, or Captain Moussa himself in disguise. You said it: we don't know. I want to protect our neighbourhood. Your job is to help me. I want you to record names and conversations and take pictures. Nothing should happen without you taking note. Everything is important to me and to our sheikh."

There was a short silence. "You understand me now?"

"I thought I would be given another kind of assignment," I said.

"Like what?" Yousef asked, but then his phone rang.

I wanted to be Abu-Hassan's right hand, working with him directly, helping with office work, organizing his schedule, running his social media accounts with videos and quotes. If he already had someone else who did that for him, I would be honoured to make his tea with the right amount of mint and sugar and his coffee with the right amount of cardamom.

I looked up and down the road, trying to make sense of my assignment. When Yousef finished his call, I asked if he was giving the same assignment to Mustafa and if we could share responsibilities.

His face changed colour, and he growled at me, "Don't worry about Mustafa! And never talk about this to anyone. Got it?"

"Got it."

Afternoon

Bells clanged and fell silent as Mustafa and I walked through the Christian Quarter. A large, decorated spruce tree stood in front of one of the monasteries. The tree was covered with yellow stars and bells with bow ties, and beside it, Christian girls swung their hair and blew soap bubbles at Christian boys. They wore the nicest clothes and had the brightest smiles and chatted loudly.

Few tourists had come for Christmas this year. Not safe, their embassies had told them. There were some

Romanians and Bulgarians and Russians, who, after lighting the candles and kissing the marble slabs, followed their tour guide quietly and talked to nobody. Everybody missed the Americans. They were big spenders and generous tippers.

Mustafa was looking for work. He scanned the tourists, throwing an English sentence here and a French or Italian sentence there. His foreign tongue wasn't great, but he was brave with words and he had a happy face, which drew tourists to him like white candles drew pilgrims. His work at the car wash was temporary, only to save cash so that he could enrol in a one-year tour guide program in Tel Aviv. The program taught history and archaeology and how to talk to foreigners. When he was a boy, his father would leave him with guide friends who took him on air-conditioned buses across the country. When they gave him the microphone, he told jokes in Arabic. The tourists loved his rhyming jokes and tipped him and sometimes even requested that he come with them on the next trip.

Among the tourists were Palestinians who had emigrated years ago and come back for a short visit to show their children and grandchildren their old doorways and balconies and the neighbours they had left behind. They were also big spenders and generous tippers, and they smiled and told jokes and sometimes cried when they walked into a shop or stepped through an archway from their childhood.

We spent most of the afternoon asking souvenir shopkeepers if they had connections at hotels or travel agencies. Mustafa knew some of them by name, through his father or because he had brought them tourists, receiving a commission.

"Come drink something with me," Abu-George called as we passed his store.

He looked funny wearing a Papa Noel hat with his twirled moustache and red nose from the arak he drank all day.

"Coffee or the other stuff?" said Mustafa with a wink.

Abu-George laughed. "God forbid. You want your father to kick my ass?"

"What's with the hat, Abu-George?" I asked him.

"Boredom, habibi, boredom," he said, snatching two hats from a tall stack beside him. "Want to get bored for twenty shekels?"

"Let me hear some other deals," Mustafa said, browsing the carousels of postcards. "You know how much I love you, Abu-George. You got contacts? I need greenbacks, euros, anything."

Abu-George pointed at the shelves behind him. "Look around. Come inside and take a look. The Tax Authority came the other day and made a mess. Did you see them? They made an awful mess, the bastards. They started at Abu-Kamel's shop by the monastery and ended here at my doorstep. I swear to al Adra, the life of dogs and cockroaches is better than ours."

Walking on down the alleyway, Mustafa remained silent.

"You know what's wrong with our shopkeepers?" I said.

"What?"

"Every time tourists buy something, they want to sell them something else. They wear them out. But if you think about it, tourists want everything for free—falafel for free, bagel for free, knafeh for free—and when you tell them the price they say, 'Too expensive,' like we're ripping them off."

"You know nothing," Mustafa said, looking straight ahead. "I feel sorry for the tourists. All shopkeepers are liars. I hate them, and the worst of them is that pig Abu-George." He kicked an empty can down the road. "That shithead! Last year, I used my connections and my father's to bring him a busload of tourists. Now he's making up stories, treating me like a child!"

"He's not making up stories."

"He is. Just like he makes up prices. Next time—tomorrow—I swear to Allah, I'll stand in front of his shop and direct all the tourists to the neighbouring shops. Mark my words."

"Why do you need the money, anyway?"

He raised his voice. "The new roof is breaking me."

"Isn't Marwan helping? I thought it was his house."

He threw down what remained of his cigarette and stomped on it. "My brother is a loser. I can't stand him sometimes."

"You can always work overtime," I said, "or with him at the café. They pay more than the car wash. Talk to him. They're hiring."

"How do you know they're hiring?"

"Marwan told me and gave me his number."

He scoffed. "You call him! You'll be able to buy your own cigarettes instead of bumming from me all the time."

I slapped him on the head.

We leaned against a church wall across the street from

a restaurant that sold alcohol to tourists and juice to locals. Mustafa pulled out his phone and showed me pictures of municipality employees and informants who'd come to his neighbourhood and taken pictures of the new roof.

"I wasn't there," he said. "A neighbour took the pictures and sent them to me. They walked casually, pretending they were only passersby. Had I been there, I would have taught them a lesson."

"What could you do?"

He gritted his teeth. "Let them come again, and you'll see what I can do."

Then he showed me pictures from last week of Yousef and him riding horses at Abu-Hassan's winter house in Jericho. "Arabian horses," he said. "They come with real birth certificates. The sheikh showed us a picture of the old certificate with an Ottoman stamp and everything."

He talked about how sensitive and gentle his horse had been and how the littlest noise would startle him. "Yousef taught me all the commands," he said. "The gaits, orders of speed, and how to get into their head. Because your horse can tell if you're afraid or dishonest. If you have doubts, he'll react to your uncertainty. If you're strong, he'll react to your confidence—"

I interrupted him, "Did he talk to you about an assignment?"

"Who?"

"Yousef. Did he talk to you?"

"About what?"

"Nothing," I said, and watched the juicer across the street squeeze half an orange down to the skin.

13

December 18
Evening

When I got home, there was no electricity. My mother sat by the back door folding the laundry by candlelight. My father sat at the kitchen table fanning his face with unpaid bills.

"First thing tomorrow, I'll talk to them," he was telling her.

She sighed, and the candlelight by the stack of underwear flickered. "It's not the first time, Omar," she said. "I thought you paid them."

He went to the hook on the wall by the side table, reached into his jacket pocket, and pulled out a crumpled fifty-shekel bill. "This is all I have!" he said.

"What should I tell the neighbours?" she said. "I borrowed from all of them. What should I tell my sister who lives God knows how far away from us—across oceans."

"I told you not to borrow from your sister. I don't want her money."

"You don't want her money? You should be grateful!"

He started shouting and cursing. She stopped arguing. He began to smoke.

I kissed my mother's head and went to search for the flashlight. I opened the back door and squatted to look under the solar heater, where loose things found a home. I bent down and swung my arms. I found the flashlight and opened the battery case. It was empty, and rust and white powder had spread throughout. I went back inside, shuffling my feet slowly so as not to bother my mother, whose body sagged as though it needed electricity to function. She had not been feeling well since receiving the news about my grandfather.

He had been complaining about his back—cancer, the doctors said. Ninety-nine percent, cancer. They scanned him with X-rays and an ultrasound, taking images of his organs, putting needles in his back. They found a tumour in his kidney the size of a turnip, they said.

"Close the damn door!" my father yelled, and I jumped to close it—or I thought I closed it, but it opened again.

"Your son can't close a door properly," he told my mother, and she looked in my direction as though consoling me.

My father fidgeted with his key chain, his fingers nervously twisting it around. "Nothing is working for me," he said, raising his arm and dropping it. "Everything is blocked, not only the roads. Everything! Wherever I go, blocked. Whatever I do, blocked! Blocked! Blocked!"

"But you go to work," she said. "You leave at dawn and come back late—"

He threw his key chain on the floor, then followed it with something else—an onion. It hit the wall and rolled underneath the table. "I gamble, Khawla! I waste my money in casinos at the Red Sea. Is that what you want me to say?"

She ignored his sarcasm, but her hands were shaking. "The house is cold," she said.

The muscle in the corner of her mouth was twitching. She was about to cry. I caught her eye, and she grabbed a clean towel from the stack in front of her and hid her face with it.

"Let's leave this place," my father suddenly said. "Rent it out and go live in Shuafat or Beit Hanina. You have friends in Shuafat, no?"

She shrugged. "I used to."

"People envy us because we live here," I said. "They dream about living near Al-Aqsa."

He squinted at me. I wondered if he had registered my words or only the sound of them. He turned to my mother and said, "Aziz is right. I have a better idea. Let's sell the house. That should solve all our problems."

Her eyes traced our swimming shadows on the peeling walls. "Too small," she said. "Nobody would buy it. Too small and no air, no sun to keep the bones straight."

"It doesn't matter," he said in an excited tone. "For a place like ours, people pay cash."

"Nobody pays cash these days."

"Some do," he said, pacing between the refrigerator and the side table, almost tumbling over the dying candles.

Resting her chin on her hand, she said. "These days, it's hard to know the good from the bad."

"Who cares?" he said. "Only God knows what's in people's hearts."

The conversation was going to a frightening place. "You need money?" I said. "I'll get a job. I'll work and pay the bills. I'll pay the debts. Everything."

"Where could you get a job?" my father asked in the same sarcastic tone he used with my mother.

"Jaffa Road."

My mother slapped her own face. "My son wants to kill me. You are not going to work there."

"Why?"

"Because people get killed. Remember your schoolmate? What was his name?"

"More people get killed in the Old City than Jaffa Road," I told her.

"You are not going to work there. I won't allow it."

"I'll work with my uncle then."

She raised her voice. "You are not going to work. Period."

I glanced at my father.

"Nothing will happen to him," he said.

Night

A pot of water sat on the three-legged kerosene stove on the bathroom floor. Fire danced between the two metals as I took off my clothes. I dipped my thumb in the water. Cold. I took a shower, instead of bathing in the tub. Colder, but faster.

The showerhead spat on my head as I thought about faith. I ran my fingers through my hair. *They say hair continues to grow after we are dead.* I scrubbed my chest with a loofah and thought about the anatomy of hearts.

Hearts are wrapped in envelopes and bound by ligaments. They are better protected than any other organ. They must be fed to refill the necessary fluids for the rest of the body. I had learned that from the book about the barefoot, bare-chested boy who was left to fend for himself on an island.

After the shower, I went to my parents' room and locked the door. They let me use their room to study. I sat on the bed and set my backpack in front of me. I pulled out notebooks, pens, pencils. Flipping through my notes, I saw only gibberish.

On my father's side of the bed lay a pack of Marlboro Red. I stood over the pack. It was full. He must have forgotten it. I grabbed it, squeezed it, seized one cigarette, but then returned it to the pack with the rest of the fake leaves and fake wrappers. The room smelled of my father: tobacco, sweat, and cologne. The three smells ran around the bed like ghosts. They ran and laughed, and I tucked my head between my knees and wept.

December 27

On my first day of work at the café, my mother tried to convince me that all I needed in this world was acne cream and an amulet.

"This is to protect you," she said, hanging a necklace around my neck. "Don't throw it away. I made three more, for your father and your grandparents."

My fingers ran over the silver chain and the black leather triangle attached to it. The amulet was sewn with thread. Leaning over the sink, I grabbed a dirty knife and tried to open it.

"Have you lost your mind?" she said, snatching it from my hands. "These are expensive."

"This is something pagans do. Not halal!"

"There's Quran inside," she said, placing the chain around my neck again.

"We protect ourselves with prayer."

"This amulet is my prayer," she said, following me to the door. She kissed me on the forehead. "Promise me you'll quit work when the winter semester starts. Promise! We don't need money. Don't listen to your father. Sometimes, he's angry—"

"He's always angry."

"But also kind and sweet. I want you to focus on school. He wants the same, believe me."

I said I would get her the jelly-filled sufganiyot she liked from West Jerusalem, and a smile bloomed on her face. Cold air came in through the open door, and her hair flew; I reminded her to wear her hijab because passersby were glancing up at the doorway.

"They could see everything," I said.

Her eyes went blank. "Your father wants good things for you," she said. "His troubles with money will end soon, inshallah. I pray day and night. I could work and help him, but he won't let me. This morning he drove Nuha to work. She knows people from the Palestinian Authority in Ramallah—they need drivers. She told them about your father. Allah is generous! Allah is generous!" Her eyes grew wet, and she closed the door behind me.

I arrived on time for the evening shift and walked through the back door into the kitchen. The floor was wet, and I tiptoed in slowly.

A man with bushy eyebrows and an open shirt stormed in. "Yalla! Yalla!" he said to Marwan. "We have people to feed." He gave me a quick look. "You know what to do with him?"

Marwan told him not to worry, then introduced me to the kitchen boys, whose hands were wet from the mopping and the washing. I shook hands with their clean and dry elbows. They explained how the dishwasher worked and how to empty and fill the bins and racks, and I joked about drowning in soap bubbles. They were all Arabs, and I was relieved I only needed to work in the kitchen and speak my language.

Hours passed, and I got bored with the sink. I went to take a look at the dining area and the customers as they ate and drank and chatted or sat alone with their computers. Servers wiped tables, putting out shiny plates and returning with those streaked in tahini and ketchup. Now it was my job to clean the dishes. Strange how I was needed now. Strange how this place felt now compared to previous times I had been here. *My place of work*, I kept saying to myself.

A waitress turned around, and I remembered her curls and her wide, chatty eyes. The coffee boy called her name—"Dafna"—and my heart sank. He told her a joke that I didn't understand, and she laughed. I smiled to myself for no reason.

Marwan tapped me on the shoulder, and I helped him lift and shelve boxes of Coke and Sprite. Then we huddled in the back area by the dumpster, which had been gathering garbage since the beginning of time.

"Who's the guy with the eyebrows?" I asked.

"Uri? He's the owner," Marwan said, scratching the hair on his chest. "He's happy as long as you do your job. He likes new ideas that can bring in cash. When I started, their meals stank—shakshuka, salads, sandwiches, everything stank. I threw away the skillets, the cutting boards, the ladles, turned the kitchen upside down. Now people come from Eilat and Nahariya to eat my shakshuka, my avocado salad, my tabbouleh, my fattoush.

"But Uri doesn't like it when kitchen boys go in the dining area or shout from behind the kitchen wall. And don't talk to the customers," he warned. "Big trouble! One time, one of the boys got arrested because he told a customer not to use the toilet. He'd been cleaning and thought the customer would mess up the floor. Stupid!"

"Not his fault, though."

"Doesn't matter. The customer made a scene, especially after the boy told him to shut up. He was a security guard at one of those art galleries down the road. He had a gun on his waist."

"Did he shoot the boy?"

"No. Uri intervened and called the police."

Marwan gave me one of his cigarettes and then scanned my shirt. "You need to change your look," he said. "I know a good place that sells very nice T-shirts. Name brands. Also, change your haircut. You look like a West Banker."

"What's wrong with West Bankers?"

"You're very young, a year younger than my brother, right? But you look like a married man. You see how I look? How Itzik, the waiter, looks? Go to this place." He showed me the address on his phone. "They have a discount. Beseder?"

"Beseder. Now, tell me more about Uri."

He laughed. "Why do you care? You won't see him much. Keep your head down and do your job. That will keep him happy. When Uri's in a good mood, he'll give you a nod—two nods if he's feeling generous. Then you know things are fine. When he's not nodding, you're his worst enemy. He can be an asshole sometimes. It's his business, right? We all need to please him. He is number one; Dafna is number two."

14

December 31

The Hour of the Sincere was a time for private talk, during which the members of the Circle spoke about their troubles in front of everyone, or alone with Abu-Hassan. It replaced Abu-Hassan's lecture on the last Thursday of every month. Because the last one landed on the last day of the year, it was a special hour.

The evening was cold and damp. An electric heater with orange rods stood in the middle of the room, too far from any of us and barely heating itself. Mustafa sat across from me, beside Yousef, and they whispered and giggled.

Abu-Hassan looked annoyed. "Share your jokes with your brothers," he said, holding a notebook.

Yousef was startled. "I was talking about foreigners who rent rooms in the Old City and stink them up with alcohol and bitches"—he corrected himself—"dirty women."

Abu-Hassan scolded him for speaking inappropriately. He pointed to Mahmoud, who had just come out of jail, inviting him to speak. He was Uncle Fahmi's age, one of the leaders of the Circle, like Yousef, and he worked in the souk selling T-shirts and wallets.

"They wanted me to inform on my brothers," Mahmoud said. "I played dumb, told them I'm just a schoolboy, and I hurt nobody."

There were other schoolboys among us, but I felt as though Mahmoud's comment was directed at me because, compared to my brothers, I had spent the least amount of time in jails. I took it to heart. My shoulders drooped, and I shrank. He must have thought I was dumb because I was also the least talkative, because I spent my time between home and school, or because, other than Mustafa, I had no friends. I gazed down at the carpet, listening to my loud thoughts, and I only started to calm down and forgive Mahmoud when he sang nasheed. God had blessed him with a wonderful voice, like Wadih El Safi. He even looked like the singer—big voice, big head. Mahmoud used to sing old fellahin songs at weddings and special occasions. Now he only sang Islamic songs.

"If you have a sincere heart," Abu-Hassan always told us, "everything you do should be Islamic, even the air you breathe."

"Did you sing nasheed in your cell?" Mustafa asked Mahmoud.

"I did," Mahmoud said with a hint of a smile. It was a rare sight. The joke was that he would not show his teeth as long as Al-Aqsa was occupied.

Swathed in a brown abaya, Abu-Hassan's arms crackled with static as he moved. He liked Mahmoud but did not nod after he spoke like he always did. Something was troubling him.

"There are two kinds of enemies," he said. "The easy and the difficult. For example, the Jews are our easy enemies. You might think they are difficult, even impossible, to defeat. But Allah has promised that their fake country and fake glory will be gone in seven years, maybe ten. What worries me the most is the enemies who live and breathe among us. They eat with us and sleep in our beds. Their hearts have hardened. They stab us in the back when it is least expected."

Abu-Hassan moved from one subject to another with the speed of light. When I could not understand him, I felt small. I could see it in his face, on his fingers, at the hem of his abaya. He was in pain. Which also caused me pain. I frowned because he frowned. I ached because he ached.

"Have you seen the tree that stands in the Christian Quarter?" he said. "It's an ugly tree, but our Muslim brothers and sisters stood there and shook hands with Christians and wished them a merry Christmas. Our Muslim brothers and sisters brought their children to glorify the cross. Shame! Do you know what that says about us? What does it say, my brothers? I want to hear it from you."

He pointed at us randomly. When it was my turn, I stammered and borrowed somebody else's answer. Abu-Hassan gave me a strange look.

"Bring more people to the Circle," he said. "Bring them out of the darkness. Show them the path. How will Allah bring His power and His nations to support us if we cannot get the support from ourselves? How?"

When it was Mustafa's turn to talk, he said he had written a poem about Hassan. I got excited, everyone did, and we hunched forward and listened as he recited line after line, remembering Hassan's qualities and things he had said or done at school or on the streets.

The last line was "We are sorry, Hassan."

I held in my tears and looked up toward Abu-Hassan, who took one deep breath after another and rubbed and rolled his beads between his fingers. He leaned back and glared at Mustafa.

"Don't ever say you are sorry. Sorrow is for women and unfit souls." His eyes hovered over us. "Who among you was allowed into Al-Aqsa today?"

I was able to get in, but I recognized many faces who hadn't.

"Most of you could not enter the mosque," he said, pointing at Yousef and Mahmoud and others. "The ones who could enter were only permitted during the week. Not on Friday or Saturday and Sunday. Was it fine with you not to be able to walk into your own mosque? When the police pushed you away, did you feel sorry for yourselves?"

Full of embarrassment and shame, we slumped and slouched. We knew that many of us couldn't step inside the mosque because somebody behind a desk said so. Somebody with a screen that showed pictures from a million cameras sprinkled across the city.

"I was angry," Yousef said. "My blood was boiling."

"Angry, humiliated, crushed," Abu-Hassan said. "When you find these feelings in your heart, you'll know that Hassan needs nobody to be sorry for him. My son is in Paradise. Is there something more precious to Muslims than Paradise?"

Night

Mustafa left after the Isha prayer. He needed to wake up early for work. I walked with Mahmoud, who gave me Islamic stickers to distribute among classmates, friends, and family.

"They're free," he said. "But if you can make money off them, it's all yours." He said nice things about what I had posted on social media—Abu-Hassan's quotes and snippets from his lectures.

"My generation is caught up in stickers and flyers," Mahmoud complained.

"What matters is the intention," I told him.

"Wise thing to say, my brother," he said.

The night was dry and dark except for the coloured light bulbs dangling from Christian houses and the reflections from televisions erected behind windows overlooking the alleyways. People who did not celebrate the new year stayed home and cracked melon seeds and watched Lebanese trivia shows. People who celebrated walked along the road, dressed up and perfumed.

A woman in a see-through black dress walked in front of us, and we passed her quickly. Mahmoud cleared his throat and told me stories about when he was my age, distributing flyers telling men not to go to bars and shady coffee shops and restaurants, telling women to wear decent clothes, telling women who wear decent clothes not to walk or talk with women who wear indecent clothes, or they would both go to hell.

"Now it's easier," he said. "You just post a few things or share a picture online and thousands of people see it and like it and spread it."

He pointed toward the Qattanin Market, also called the Dark Market because it only had six holes in its high ceiling, barely letting in any light, though during Ramadan and the two Eids, it shone brightly as though cuddled by the whole solar system.

"My shop is this way," he said. "I only sell halal merchandise. You will never find a cross or a kippah in my shop. I don't look for money. I just want what Allah is willing to give me."

I nodded, and he continued. "I need someone like you to help me. Someone I can trust. You would print pictures and logos on T-shirts and stand at the counter when I'm outside on business."

I apologized and said I was busy.

"With school?" he asked, leaning closer.

I was about to say "Working at a café in West Jerusalem," but remembering his comment about schoolboys, I thought he would give the same unkind response.

"Yes, school," I said.

He nodded, got on his motorbike at the side of the road, and left.

It was a quiet night, and I kicked empty cans to make noise and drown out the buzz in my head. At the turn to my house, I heard a woman's laughter. She was talking to the soldiers down the road, asking for directions.

"It should be there," she said in English, pointing up toward my neighbourhood.

The soldiers asked her where she was from.

"France," she said, laughing again, and one soldier blabbered something that sounded French.

Soon I heard the clicking of heels. I turned. She was behind me.

"Excuse me," she said. "I'm looking for a friend who lives in this area."

The smell of perfume drifted from her bare neck and long arms. She wore high boots and a heavy necklace. Trying to be a good Muslim, I stared at my shoes.

"Do you know someone called Nuha?" she asked.

"Come, I will show you," I said, leading the way.

As we stood in the middle of the courtyard, there was enough light to see her face. She had a soft face, and her eyes were bright blue. She glanced at the sky above her head, the walls surrounding us, the staircase to our house on the upper floor, and the cistern, its stone opening and its rusty cover.

"This is nice," she said.

I pointed. "See that lemon tree? Nuha lives behind it."

I lingered until I heard Nuha shriek, "You're finally here!"

When I opened our door, my mother was sitting on the sofa, watching a Turkish drama.

"Waste of time," I said, and she told me to take off my shoes and move out of the way. Music came from behind the back door. "New Year's party," she said. "Nuha invited me, but I don't think I'll go."

"Good. I don't want you involved with her."

"Live and let live," she said.

I went outside, crouched down at the end of the terrace, and looked down at Nuha's open front door. There was a lot of noise and a lot of light. Her guests were chatting and dancing behind the purple curtain and in the corridor, on the mosaic tiles with stars and crescents. I knew her house.

For Yousef's assignment, I had read *The Art of War*. The best of spies, the book said, should be bright and strong of heart but, on the outside, unnoticeable. I sat in the dark and remained quiet. Nuha came out with a fancy glass in her hand. A man in a leather jacket followed her—the same man I had seen before, but his hair was loose. Their arms swayed and tangled. I counted her guests and the words on their lips. I measured the steps her cat, Lolo, took meandering between bare legs. Between songs, Nuha looked at the time. It was not midnight yet, but her body swayed like a pendulum. Unable to hold her knees together, she pressed her fingers against the man's chest, and he grabbed her waist.

She noticed me and waved. "Zizou! Come down! Come meet my friends!"

The Art of War said a spy should be immune to seduction.

I smiled to be polite. "Thank you. I can't."

She was holding a cigarette and reaching toward me with her arm. "Smoke with me!"

I scratched my head.

"I won't tell your mother," she said playfully.

I climbed down and joined them. I took the cigarette and smelled it, like always when she gave me things. There was a long silence. Then I heard her talking about my aunt and my mother and how we had been neighbours for years. Her guests' eyes lashed at my back. When her French friend recognized me, she serenaded me with praises. She said I was "gentil." The air was sour as they talked. Alcohol stung my nose, and I went to the kitchen and started washing dishes and glasses. This way, I could listen without breathing in their offences.

Soon Nuha appeared at my side. "Yalla!" she said in a sleepy tone. "I don't want you to wash my dishes."

"I don't mind," I told her. "This is what I do for work."

"Your parents let you work? I can't believe it," she sulked.

"I always help my mother anyway, so I may as well make money from it."

"Not the same thing," she said, leaning against my back, trying to grab glasses off the upper shelf.

I reached up and gave them to her.

"Such a gentleman," she said, then she paused. "I just can't believe Khawla is letting you work. You should stay in school. You're a smart boy."

"Boy?"

"A man!" she said, laughing. "A smart and handsome man!" She slapped her hand into mine. "You've grown. Your fingers are still small, though. Small and thin!" She traced my pants with her eyes. "You need new pants. The style now is tight."

"Tight is for girls."

"Tight is chic," she said.

I turned to face the sink. I placed the dish soap on the counter, and my eyes lingered on the bubbles in the drain, which had inflated until they became a giant mound.

When a strand of Nuha's hair fell on my arm, I almost exploded. I grabbed another glass to wash, but she pulled me by the arm and told me to stop. She was holding a drink with a slice of lemon on top. She sucked her teeth and asked if I wanted lemonade or Coke.

"I want something else," I said, throwing myself onto her. I kissed her neck. I licked her cheek like a dog. I tried to kiss her on the mouth.

She pushed me away and glanced up at the kitchen window. Her guests were all outside or in the corridor. I fumbled with her breasts.

"Animal!" she yelled.

Her friends hurried into the kitchen. "What happened? What happened?" they said in many languages.

I panicked and stormed through them and into the alley. I squatted in the nook of a pissing wall and laid my head between my hands. The smell of piss made me dizzy. Like Nuha and her friends, I was drunk, but without alcohol, without music, and without the magic of the midnight hour.

Strange music played in the air—a mix of Nuha's darbuka—*dum tek tek dum tek*—Mahmoud's nasheed, and the adhan. There was the sound of stray dogs. There was laughing and crying mixed together. I could not stand that mix of sounds anymore: the wounded and hungry with the strong and joyful, the laughing and crying at the same time, taking the same breath, trying to say the same thing.

15

January 1

My mother called me at work. "Come home," she said. "There was an attack on a café in Tel Aviv."

"Tel Aviv is far away," I told her.

"Aziz," she scolded, "I swear I will be mad at you until the end of days."

Putting her on speaker, I asked the kitchen boys to joke and sing. "See?" I said. "It's good here. Very good."

Few customers showed up, and I took my time with the dishes, studying patterns of ketchup and oil and mayonnaise. Better this way. When shootings or stabbings happened in the city, or even in Tel Aviv or Haifa, we remained silent. When we ate in the kitchen, we lowered our voices and chewed slowly. We toned down our jokes and laughter. Any stupid gesture could be used against us. The Jewish boys and girls in the dining area knew us well, and Uri sometimes gave us leftovers to take away, but when bullets flew and daggers dropped, we kept our heads down, did our job, and then went home. Marwan's advice. He wanted us to stay safe.

In the evening, Dafna came to the kitchen and took me to see Uri.

He ran his hairy hands over the shiny top of the coffee machine and shifted a toothpick around his lips. "Marwan told me you're good with coffee," he said, then, seeing well-dressed customers in the doorway, he rushed in their direction.

I waited for some time, shifting my feet, my gaze fixed on the doorway. As Uri walked by, he wagged his finger at me. I wiped sweat off my forehead and thought about quitting. I could quit. It wouldn't be the end of the world if I quit right this minute.

Then Dafna's voice came again. "Are you ready?"

She slipped in behind the coffee machine and told me to stand close and watch. "What's your name?" she asked me.

"I'm the new guy," I said in Hebrew. One of the few sentences Marwan had taught me to avoid being asked to do difficult things.

"Sababa," she said with a grin. "New guy, do you have a name?"

"Aziz Omar Aziz," I said, and she grinned again. Her lipsticked mouth was small like a rosebud.

Marwan walked by and said, "Take care of my boy."

She ignored him and pointed to the list of drinks and sandwiches on the whiteboard. The list had no alcohol, so I felt at ease. She babbled instructions, and I gaped at her and fumbled with the five or ten Hebrew words I knew before she interrupted me, "Marwan said you spoke the language."

I started shaking.

"Don't worry," she said, pulling a piece of paper from her back pocket. She wrote the list in English, and over the next hour turned the handles on the coffee machine clockwise and counter-clockwise and taught me how to make espresso, cappuccino, and latte.

Finally, I retreated to the back area to smoke with Marwan. I asked him about the lies he had told Uri and Dafna exaggerating my skills, and he said that was the best way to get me the job.

"You don't want to keep washing dishes forever, do you?" he said. "You deserve a promotion. You work like a mule."

He went back inside, and I pulled out my phone to check the news. Three people had been killed in the Tel Aviv shooting. One of the casualties was an Arab taxi driver.

My heart raced, and I called my mother. "Where's my father?"

"Here," she said. "At home."

January 2

In Jerusalem, people forgot how to walk straight. Barricades blocked all entrances and exits. As I walked to work, I picked at my dry, cracked lips until they bled. The winter sun was intense.

I was approaching the coffee machine when Uri ran toward me. "You were supposed to be here a half hour ago," he said.

"I was in the kitchen," I lied.

"What were you doing in the kitchen? Your job is to make coffee and keep this machine clean. Then, when you're not busy with the machine, you wash dishes. You understand?"

"I thought—"

"You thought? Are we going to have a debate? You want some coffee so we can talk?"

I grinned at the thought of Uri bringing me coffee so we could discuss business or politics like the roundtables on Al Jazeera and Channel 12.

"What's wrong with you?" he said, his voice bursting. "Are you crazy?"

"It won't happen again," I said.

Six bins of dirty dishes stood in the kitchen like a pillar of doom. The dining area was short on cups and plates. Uri wanted them ready in one hour. Thirty minutes later, he came to check on me. Only two bins of dishes had been washed. He was not happy. I asked the kitchen boys for help, but they could not leave their stations. I searched for Marwan, but he had taken the day off.

I crouched down behind the sink and cupped my face with my hands. Working here was a big mistake. I could have worked at Mahmoud's shop, selling wooden camels and fake leather wallets, or at my uncle's, toying with wrenches. I aimed one of the wet plates at the dumpster.

Dafna came out of nowhere. "What are you doing?" She pulled a piece of cardboard from the garbage and sat on it, folding her legs Arab style. "Don't be shy with Uri," she said. "If he tells you to do something difficult, just say no, or 'I need help.' Or come talk to me. You understand?"

I hated it when people said "You understand?" I hated

it in all languages. From her, though, it sounded different.

"I'm missing Marwan," I told her.

"Are you related?" she asked.

"Friends," I said in Hebrew, and she corrected my vowels—*chaverim*, short *a* and *e*, long *i*.

I asked her if Olga, a grumpy waitress who only smiled at Marwan, was a friend of hers, and she said she only had two friends. I told her I also did not have many friends.

"Marwan's fun but loud. I prefer quiet people. Like you," she said. "You don't talk much, and when you do talk, you whisper. The kitchen boys roar like beasts. They shout and make balagan."

I liked the sound of the word coming out of her mouth. "Balagan, balagan," I mumbled. "This is my new favourite word."

She laughed and slapped me with a towel. When she got up, I glimpsed a hamsa tattoo on her calf—a hand symbolizing protection against the evil eye. I had seen the same symbol in the souk, I told her.

"They come in all shapes and sizes," I said, "but this one is the nicest."

Evening

I was cleaning the sink and getting ready to leave work when Yousef called. I didn't answer. He called again. "I have to see you immediately," he said.

It was midnight when I knocked at the gym's door. The gym was empty, and smoke hovered in the air.

"They arrested Mustafa," Yousef said, jamming his cigarette into a wooden ashtray.

I slapped my head.

"Where have you been all day?" he asked.

"School, you know," I said.

He nodded and dangled another cigarette from his mouth but did not light it. He glanced down at one of the heavy dumbbells, pointed at it, and told me to roll it back onto the opposite wall. I rolled it back, then sat beside him.

"This afternoon," he said, "every Israeli officer from the river to the sea paid a visit to Mustafa's house. They climbed up to the roof. One of the officers gave him a notice of demolition, or whatever they call it. Mustafa took the notice with one hand and punched the officer's lights out with the other. They grabbed him and knocked him to the ground, hit his head against the concrete walls, the bricks, the cement bags. His blood was everywhere."

"Everywhere?" I said, fear filling my lungs.

Yousef tapped my arm and went on. "He's fine. You know Mustafa. He's a monkey."

"Did you see him?"

"I didn't see him. I didn't have to be there. Your brother has eyes. If Captain Moussa has a thousand eyes, your brother has a million."

He reminded me that I had skipped a few days of exercise. I told him I had been at work, and he narrowed his eyes. "You work? Where?"

The rope of lies is short, they say. Now I had to tell him the truth.

"Jaffa Road, with Mustafa's brother."

He pulled back. "And you didn't tell me?!"

"Did I have to tell you?"

"I am your leader," he said, pounding his fist on the carpet. "You need to tell me everything, from when you wake up until you go to sleep. How am I going to protect you when things go bad?"

"I thought it wasn't important. I mean, it's just a job."

"Everything is important," he said. "Besides, Abu-Hassan is not going to like it."

"Why?"

"You said it's a café, right? What do they serve there? Why do you work until midnight?"

"All halal. I swear, Yousef. No alcohol, no pork. You know Jews do not eat pork."

"What's this?" he demanded, noticing my amulet. "Get rid of this garbage and go clean the toilets."

"My parents are waiting for me," I said. "Tomorrow."

"Tonight," he said. "I like order in my place."

The toilets smelled of goats and rabbits put together. Worn rags and forgotten undershirts and underpants lay on the tiles. There was piss on the floor, on the toilet seats, and on the walls. I tried to erase the graffiti behind the toilets, first with a rag, then with my bare hands. Holding the mop, I made quick strokes at every solid surface in front of me. With every sweep, I was about to vomit.

I came back out and sat beside Yousef. He gave me a cigarette and lit it for me.

"There is another reason why I called you," he said. "The list. Are you done with my list?"

"I'm working on it," I said.

He stared at me. "I'll visit you tomorrow," he said.

"Where?"

"Your house," he said.

January 3

I waited for my father to leave for work and my mother to go to the hospital to see my grandfather, and then I called Yousef. He walked through the living room and darted onto the terrace. His steps were automatic, as though he lived with us. He ogled the line of coloured underwear on Nuha's roof.

"Is she home?" he asked.

"She left early," I said, and he jumped onto her roof. He leaned against the wobbly railing, the water tank, and the clotheslines.

My head spun 360 degrees to locate prying eyes, then I jumped after him. "Tell me what you want, and I'll help you."

"I'm doing your job," he said dismissively.

He strode to the far corner of Nuha's roof and sank his arm deep inside the garbage bin. He waved to me. "You should see this."

I folded my arms.

"I said you should see this. Come quickly!"

Empty wine, vodka, and arak bottles made a mound inside the stinking bin. He joggled some of the bottles, his face alternating between serious and silly. I looked away, trying to block out memories of Nuha's party. Not only Nuha's lips and the sweat on her neck, but also the pissing corner, the cries and laughter, the dogs.

I jumped back to my house. He followed me and went inside to wash his hands.

He came back out quickly. "She had *visitors*," he said, stressing the last word. "She had a party. You didn't tell me. Who was there?"

"Friends—"

"Friends who piss on the blood of martyrs," he said. "The whore is working for Captain Moussa."

Our neighbours sat on their roof peeling oranges under the sun. I waved to them, and then whispered to Yousef, "Praise the prophet, Yousef. Nuha is strange sometimes, but she's clean. You know her. It's not like you don't know her."

"Don't defend her," he said, wagging his finger.

"You're exaggerating—"

"Leave it with me," he said, walking toward the front door.

His eyes caught on the straw basket on top of the refrigerator. He pulled down the basket and grabbed my books one by one. "Did Abu-Hassan give you these?"

I shrugged.

"Where's my book about the Mujahideen?"

"On the roof," I said. "I'm not done with it."

He rubbed the tip of his nose and said his fingers smelled like alcohol. Washing his hands again, he cursed Nuha, her family, and her friends.

"Listen, Aziz," he said. "A person who remains silent in the face of wrong is worse than the devil. Do you know that? Don't ever defend rotten people. Stay away from her. She will disgrace you. She will shame your whole family. Stay clean. Abu-Hassan asked me to test you, and I vouched for you. Don't betray my trust."

"I don't want to watch people," I said. "I want to do something else."

He folded his arms and told me to wait for his orders.

16

January 15

After Yousef's visit, I stopped talking to Nuha. I also spied on the neighbours and the neighbours' neighbours up to the seventh house. Sitting by the back door or in the bathroom, I listened to stories my mother's friends told her—the neighbour woman who ran away with her employer; another neighbour woman who hid dark magic in the cemetery to block babies from her sister's womb; a construction worker who brought AIDS to his house through sleeping with women of the streets in Petah Tikva; the neighbour who rented his basement to tourists and one night found his daughter in bed with one of them.

Yousef enjoyed hearing the women's stories. Sometimes I could not understand his orders. Sometimes I forced myself to obey him out of respect to Abu-Hassan. Sometimes when he was unhappy with me, when I was being "stubborn" or "difficult," he would tell me to clean the toilets or collect sesame seeds from underneath the bakery's refrigerator. And I would do what he ordered me to do. He said I should use my hands instead of the dustpan because sesame seeds stick better to fingers. What else loved my fingers? Old candy, ants, cockroaches, splinters, and once, the tail of a scorpion.

"This is for your own good," he would tell me. "One day, you will become a leader, like me. Then you will remember this and thank me."

"No problem," I said. "We need to know our friends from our enemies."

He seemed to have forgotten about Mustafa. When I reminded him, he said, "Our friend's case is very complicated. Tell his brother to find him a good lawyer."

THE POLICE STATION WHERE Mustafa was jailed was on my route to work. Passing by the fences, I imagined him being tortured, cuffed to a metal chair, slapped on the head and face. Nodding in his direction, toward his cell, the one I imagined, I said, "Patience, my friend. Patience."

In the kitchen, I held a cup of tea in both hands, and the warmth of the cup reminded me of Mustafa's cold and dark mornings in prison. I threw the tea down the drain and chased after Marwan. It was a busy afternoon, and he strode between the refrigerator and the prep table, pulling out avocados and tomatoes, slicing them, throwing them on pita bread, then sending them out onto warm tables, into warm hands.

"Have you found a good lawyer?" I asked him.

He nodded, but I knew he was lying. Good lawyers were hard to find.

"You should get him a good one," I said. "You don't

want your brother to spend ten or twenty years in jail."

"We don't talk about this kind of stuff in here," he said, twirling a sharp knife between his fingers. "Nobody talks politics here."

"Listen," I whispered. "I could talk to Abu-Hassan. He could lend you money."

"Lend me money? From his own pocket?"

"From the Zakat money. He is the head of a Zakat committee. He helps the poor."

"We're not poor."

"You know what I mean."

"I don't want your sheikh's money."

"It is God's money," I said.

"If it's God's money, then he is a thief."

"Watch your mouth," I told him. "You're belittling a man with a great heart and mind. A man who would give his own life for our people."

"Is that what he told you?"

"I know it because I use my brain."

He scoffed. "I heard about your sheikh. Seems like your little brain likes the sound of his words. You know what they say about men with big words: The strong fart comes from the weak donkey."

He laughed, and I clenched my fist and prepared for a fight. The kitchen boys tried to guide me back to the sink, but I refused.

Marwan went on. "Before you get too angry, listen to this. Just listen and use the brains you have. Okay? Just to make sure we're talking about the same man. You're talking about Abu-Hassan, owner of the grocery stores at Musrara and Beit Hanina, right? He's so rich he could give fifty shekels and a juice box to every man and woman in the city and his mountain of money would not decrease an inch."

"So what?" I said. "May Allah give him more and more."

"More and more, huh? Do you know that your sheikh is going to make money out of his own son's death? He's suing the government."

"Good for him," I said. "He's smart."

"He's making money out of his son's blood. You call that smart?"

I refused to stoop to his level. "You're sick with envy. Whoever told you this lie is sick with envy."

"Why would I envy him? I have everything I need."

"You have no dignity," I told him. "You don't care about your brother—who's in jail because he was protecting *your* house!"

"Shut your trap," he said. "You don't know me. Let me tell you something, just so you know that you and your sheikh are not the greatest of all people. I know jails very well. A while ago, I was imprisoned, and it took me years to clear my name and get this job."

One of the servers came into the kitchen, and Marwan stopped talking. I walked over to the sink, and when the server had left the kitchen, Marwan went on. "Here's another one," he said. "What about the charity money your sheikh receives from abroad for each house that gets demolished in the city? Don't tell me you don't know about that. Would you also call that smart?"

I turned around, about to throw a wet plate in his face. "Don't push it, Marwan. Don't push it! I can take you! I swear to Allah I can take you."

He laughed again. But it was a nervous laugh.

"Let's go outside," I said.

I could take him easily. He would be under my shoes in no time, not because I lifted weights but because alcohol and weed made him weak and pathetic.

"I don't have time for you," he said with a foolish smile.

He kept cutting vegetables with a knife as sharp as his tongue. I was about to push him against the sink and punch his smug face, but the kitchen boys grabbed my arms and separated us.

January 21

Abu-Hassan told the Circle of Sincere Hearts about the benefits of Zakat. He asked us to write the names of poor families we knew who lived only on pita and zaatar. I looked up at the ceiling and thanked God for this unbelievable chance. My sheikh and I were communicating on the same wavelength, as though he were summoning my hopes like a place of solitude would summon a Sufi worshipper.

He sat in a corner, skimming his coil-bound notebook.

"May Allah reward you, Abu-Hassan," I said, shaking his hand. "Zakat is very important."

"It is not *important*," he said, raising his eyebrows. "It is one of the five pillars of Islam." He disliked it when we used different words from the Quran and the traditions of the Prophet Muhammad.

His eyes danced across his notebook, and I knew I had to speak quickly. "Mustafa's family needs help. They're looking for good lawyers. You know—"

He interrupted me. "Good lawyers? They are everywhere."

"I mean, my sheikh, since you hired a lawyer for martyr Hassan—"

"Brother Aziz, what are you talking about?" He rested his hand on my back. "Lawyers? You talk about lawyers during the time of worship and heart cleansing? Praise the name of Allah and go mingle with your brothers."

January 25

After the holiday break, I went to see Ustaz Salim. He was an educated man—sometimes foolish, but educated—and he knew people. I peeked into the teachers' lounge. He was not there, or in the yard. When his class began, another teacher came in. I knew then that he had been fired. It took the new teacher some time to get the classroom in order. He scribbled on the whiteboard and mumbled to himself, then drew circles and arrows—charged spheres and electric fields.

I raised my hand and asked, "Can we apply this kind of science to politics?"

"Politics?" he said, squinting in the light coming from the window. "What do you mean?"

"In the news, they keep saying the ball is in this court or that court. If Gauss's law could tell us where the ball is, that would be useful, no?"

There was winking and snickering. The teacher lifted his stick and walked toward me.

I continued musing. "I mean, one day, they say the ball

is in the Israeli court. Another day, the Palestinian court. Where is the ball exactly?"

"Up your ass," said a student in the back, and I took off my shoe and threw it at him.

The two of us were sent to the headmaster, who sat on a swivel chair and scanned us from top to bottom. "Your teachers aren't here to entertain you," he told me. "You are one of our smart boys. Leave jokes to jokers."

Afternoon

I visited my grandfather at Hadassah Hospital. He shared a room with two people. His bed was on the brighter side of the room, overlooking the valley and a row of pine trees. A sickly smell filled the air, and my mother sprayed air freshener near his bed and toward the ceiling. A nurse told her to stop, but my mother was not convinced and they argued.

I looked out the window, then gazed at my grandfather. "Look, Sidi." I pointed to the trees. "They planted them especially for you."

He was frail and weak. He knew I was treating him like a child, but he smiled and nodded. My mother sat on the edge of his bed and told him he looked *very* healthy. She was also lying. This made him sad. When people visited, he would open his palms to show the size of his tumour. He would look up at the doorway and cry. He called Aunt Sarah and wept on the phone. She could not come. She said the security services at the airport might interrogate her, and there was a possibility they might confiscate her ID card and travel document.

My mother shifted the pillow from behind his neck and poured pomegranate juice into his cup. He pushed her hand away. "I will take a nap," he said.

Feeling useless, I took the elevator to the ground floor. I went outside and sat under one of the pine trees. Cars were pulling in and out of the parking lot. Some visitors held flowers, some held bags filled with treats, and some came with a big frown. Some chatted and smiled as though they were going shopping or to the movies. I collected a number of pine cones and started breaking them open and looking at them from the inside one by one. I found no seeds. The birds had eaten all the seeds. Or they were hiding like a sneaky tumour. Or maybe the cones had grown seedless because some other types of trees were supposed to be here.

Aunt Sarah had told me this once. That the forests of Jerusalem had never been forests before the Nakba. There had been fields of olives and figs and pomegranates, and the fellahin used to harvest them and live on them the entire year. She was smart, my aunt, but also foolish and selfish. I pulled out my phone and checked social media. There was a picture of her sitting in a restaurant. In the caption, she called it a restaurant, though it looked like a bar or a nightclub. A blond man sat beside my aunt. He sat too close; I could not see one of her arms. *Her boyfriend?* She was wearing a black dress with holes in it. I scrolled down and saw similar pictures—one from the fall said *My new religion: Stand tall, smile, and live as you please.* Her other posts were pictures of flowers and wild animals and quotes about inner peace.

I pushed the phone away, almost breaking it into

pieces, like a seedless pine cone. *Is this what keeps her too busy to visit her dying father?*

Taking up my phone and browsing my aunt's face again, I saw it was not the same face I had known. It was not the face I had chased after during our long and tiring walks in Ein Karem and Jericho, laughing and chatting about the wild lives of plants and trails and stone walls.

"Only the pure can make it in this city," my grandfather had always said.

She did not deserve to live in this holy city. She did not deserve to be here, with my grandfather. She did not deserve to be part of this family.

I ran my thumb over the screen. I gave her face a final look—then *tap tap tap*, and she was gone.

Night

I could not sleep. I walked aimlessly. Sadness filled my head and my legs, and I did not know what to do or where to go. I found myself standing in front of Abu-Salim's house. I glanced up at the balcony where he used to sit, waving to random people and tossing out jokes like fireworks. The flag Mustafa and I had drawn, or half drawn, was gone now, erased. Two dogs barked at me from behind the fences, and I hurried down the road and squatted in the shadow of a stairway.

Peering out, I saw a beggar in the distance. One of those who wandered between the Isha and Fajr prayers, silently waiting for a shekel or two, a cigarette or two. This one, though, shouted in Arabic and Russian. Neighbours peeped from behind their curtains. An older passerby told him off. "Shut up, you donkey. They will shoot you," he said, pointing at the balcony. Then, when he saw me hiding, he said, "You too."

"Mind your business," I told him.

The beggar was walking in front of me now. He wore a formal suit and a wool hat and walked slowly and clumsily, rubbing his face with the suit's long sleeves. When he removed his wool hat, the settlers came onto the balcony, flashed their lights, and readied their guns. Then, like at the circus, where spotlights follow the elephants and clowns, the full moon followed the beggar.

I could not believe my eyes. He had a beard now, but he also had the same slouching shoulders and the same thick glasses.

My heart fell to my feet. *Is it really him?*

Ustaz Salim held a can of gasoline and a rag, almost invisible under his long sleeves. "Curse your God! Curse Allah! Curse every God on this cursed planet!" he screamed. "Curse everybody!"

17

January 28

Weeks had passed since Mustafa's arrest, and my brothers at the Quran School would not bring up his name when we talked. He would be out soon, they must have thought. For some of them, going in and out of jail was as normal as walking up and down the street. Trying to think like them, I felt pain in my stomach.

Tonight everyone left after the meeting of the Circle except Yousef and Abu-Hassan, who walked up the spiral staircase toward the Zakat office on the second floor.

I lingered at the bottom of the stairs. "I have a question," I said.

"You always have questions," Abu-Hassan said, half smiling, half frowning.

He and Yousef stood on the first landing and spoke in hushed, quick voices. They were talking about money. I also wanted to talk about money. In my front pocket, I carried two thousand shekels—money from overtime work that I had not told my parents about. I had been planning to give it to Marwan, but then I kept it. I could not trust him. Abu-Hassan, however, could give it to a good lawyer as a first payment, and then I could pay him the rest in installments.

I climbed up the winding staircase and smiled at Abu-Hassan, but he did not return my smile.

"It has come to my attention that you still read deviant books," he said.

I gripped the railing. "Deviant? No. Who said so?"

He took my hand in his and looked me straight in the eye. "Tell me the truth. Do you still read books that I warned you not to read?"

My heart was racing, and I stared at Yousef, the snitch, the mother of all snitches. "No. Never."

He patted me on the shoulder. "Brother Aziz, do you want to be one of those who cannot tell good from bad, even if the truth is right before their eyes?"

"I swear to Allah and the Quran—"

"I don't want you to swear," he said. "I just want the truth."

I was about to cry. My throat was dry and my heart had stopped racing. It was too heavy to race now. Too heavy to care for my trouble.

"We are people who have been dignified by the love of Allah and the next life. Not this lowly life. Do you agree with me, brother Aziz?"

I sniffled. "Yes, I agree."

"Do you think heaven is a big market where everyone can walk in and stroll up and down? Do you think heaven is a souk?"

I shrugged. "No. God forbid. No."

"Heaven is heaven and souks are only souks. Right, brother Aziz?"

I could hear Yousef mumbling "Right" behind my red ears.

"Right," I said. "Believe me, my sheikh. I—"

He interrupted me. "I believe you."

"I swear—"

"I believe you," he said again, and when Yousef muttered something about the books he had seen in my straw basket, Abu-Hassan raised his hand and told him to leave us alone.

Staring at my sheikh's serene face, I remembered his words from that cold December morning, as the sun travelled up the sky: "Don't let people beneath you in knowledge lead you onto their mistaken path."

From now on, he was my only guide, my only path.

Night

When I got home, all I could think about were Abu-Hassan's words: "I believe you."

He believed me. Did I believe myself?

I grabbed the straw basket from on top of the refrigerator. I jumped onto the roof and dragged the crate down onto the terrace. I threw my deviant books on the ground and arranged them in a pile, a pyramid. To avoid having second thoughts, I flipped them face down. I tore several pages from one of the large books and shoved them into the middle of the pile.

All I needed now was a spark.

One of my father's lighters lay on the kitchen table. I snatched it and adjusted it to the highest flame. I sat close to the pile of books. At first, there was a little fire. Then the wind came and killed it. I tore more pages, rolled them in the shape of a cone, and went inside. Pulling the kerosene heater toward the back door, I dipped the paper cone inside the kerosene tank. I then went outside and lit the cone and the pile. The books were catching fire now, and I sat silently and watched. My deviant books were disappearing—pagan gods, always angry and vengeful; rules of love, always fake and unreal: a girl receiving letters from a mysterious and confusing philosopher, a boy starting a long journey that he would never finish, and a man who left his home and went into the mountains to enjoy solitude. He went crazy in the end. He must have been crazy right from the beginning.

What had I gained from all these books except foolishness and stupidity? Ask me what I had learned and I would not have an answer. Ask me now! Say, "Aziz, explain to me five rules of love, three, two, one rule." Ask me how any stupid journey had ended and I would not be able to answer. How pathetic was that? Abu-Hassan must have known that I deserved better than being slapped around by useless fairy tales.

My books did not make me happy. They were the reason why I was mute, and when I talked, I stuttered. Let them burn. All of them. Even *The Art of War.* My kind of art of war should be taught by my own teacher.

They were burning now. They were burning with their bookmarks—quotes, sketches, question marks, coloured stars. Drums and a sad choir played in the back of my head. Fragments and sparks flew over the roof and floated away. The neighbours, whose clotheslines held white underwear and white socks and white bedsheets, complained about my singed confetti. They yelled, but I pretended to be somewhere else, at some unheard-of war, under invisible rubble.

An hour later, my father came home and complained about the smell.

"Garbage," I said. "Our neighbours just burned their garbage. Nasty stuff."

"I brought dinner," he said, throwing a bag of shawarma wraps on the table. "Your mother is not coming home tonight." He looked different—face shaved, hair combed. He wore the cologne that he only wore on special occasions.

I gave him his cut from my salary, and he pursed his lips and counted the money.

"Are they happy with you?" he asked.

"I think so."

"Can you work while going to school?"

"I think so."

"Keep working then," he said. "Six hours a day won't kill you."

"How's my grandfather?" I asked.

"Nothing new," he said. "He's dying."

He went to his room, and I lay on the sofa bed. An hour or so later, I opened my eyes, and my phone was on my chest. I had dozed off without noticing. I got up and opened the back door. In the dark, at the far end of the terrace, my father squatted under the branches of the lemon tree.

I turned on the light, and he waved his hands. "Turn it off! The settlers are on their balconies!"

I kept the door ajar and stood behind it, gazing at his cigarette as it burned like a glow-worm. He finished it and pulled out another, and it flared up and danced between his fingers. His arm leaned against the thickest branch; he plucked a lemon and tossed it between his hands. The leaves hissed, and he hummed, and a faint purple light came from Nuha's kitchen. Her kitchen light turned off, and there was a soft giggle, then another and another.

January 30

In the morning, the settlers' dogs barked in the road and birds chirped in the misty lemon tree. They chirped loudly, louder than the dogs barking and louder than the zipping carts in the souk. Walking slowly toward the edge of the terrace, I wanted a closer look at the birds, but they flew away. Dozens of them suddenly flew. The tree shuddered, and I gazed down at Nuha's yellow door as it opened.

It was my father at the door. I pulled back slowly while trying not to miss anything. Nuha stood so close to him, holding a thermos.

"Grip it firmly," she said in a sleepy voice. "Don't spill it like last time."

He said something in a whisper. Then they went away. I could only hear her high heels clicking in the lower courtyard. I went back inside and texted my mother to see when she was coming home. *Inshallah soon*, she texted back.

My father? What did Nuha see in him? The pools of sweat under his armpits or his foul mouth? Maybe his foul mouth. She loved his jokes. Now he had all the time in the world to tell her jokes, all the way to Ramallah. And if the road was blocked, all the better.

The clown, the cheater, the adulterer.

Inshallah, when? I texted again, fingers shaking.

Less than an hour later, I met my mother in the stairwell. Coming back from a long night at the hospital, she smelled of Dettol and drugs.

"How is my grandfather?"

"They are going to take out the tumour," she said.

"When?"

"He's old. They have to make sure his body can take it."

Her scarf made marks on her forehead, and she checked my face to see if I had cleaned the sleep from my eyes and brushed my teeth. She asked about a stain on my shirt—streaks from the labneh sandwich I had made for breakfast. I spat on the stain and scratched it.

"I'm late for school," I told her. "I'll be back later tonight."

"Later tonight? Why?"

"Work."

She had lost track of how my father and I spent our time. She slapped her face. "We said no work after the holidays. I told you we don't want you to work."

"My father can't carry the load alone," I said.

She took another step up the stairs. She kissed me on the cheek, her face wet with tears, and I told her not to cry.

"Did you take care of your father while I was gone?" she asked.

I cringed and looked away.

The entire day, I calculated my next move. Hours

passed, and I channelled my anger in all sorts of directions—smoked fifteen cigarettes, shouted at the kitchen boys and at myself in the mirror, masturbated three times.

I thought of Nuha every time, but she had another face. She had to have another face.

February 1

In the early morning, I rolled down the stairs. The neighbourhood was deep asleep. Nuha's house did not overlook the street, but the neighbours knew that metres behind our wall lay the lemon tree and the yellow door and the kitchen window with the purple curtain.

I shook the spray can. I was not wearing a mask. This time my target did not require one. I wrote one sentence and then went home.

When the neighbours woke up, they saw my anger.

Nuha is a traitor and a whore.

Noon

I texted Yousef. *I took care of her.*

He did not respond.

Night

After work, I went to see Yousef. He was teaching nunchaku. "Watch me," he kept saying. "Look at my hands. Only look at my hands." The sticks in his hands hissed as the boys he was training swung their heads like windscreen wipers. They were scared, and he was enjoying it.

He looked at me from the side of his eye. I threw my backpack against the wall and sat down to wait for him. Now the boys were becoming bolder. They held their arms up, asking to try. Yousef was loving the competition. He told two of them to step closer, and then he gave the sticks to the one with steady hands. He swung fast, almost slashing the other boy's face.

Yousef laughed. "Good enough for now. We will continue tomorrow."

He threw himself on his swivel chair. "You see these Baby Lions?" he said, pointing to them as they spread out between pulley machines. "If I told them to jump off Al-Aqsa's walls, they would."

"Why would they jump off Al-Aqsa's walls?" I asked, and he looked at me sideways.

"They are brave," he said.

I looked the other way.

"Today, the toilets need extra cleaning," he said.

I stared at him, as though weighing his worth. He saw the contempt in my eyes.

We went outside, and he leaned close and whispered, "Listen to me. What you did last night was foolish. This time, I will give you a pass. Next time, we're done. You're out."

"What do you mean?"

"You heard me. If you make one more mistake, you will be out."

"Out?"

"Yes, out!"

"Out of what?"

"Out of the Circle."

"No."

"Yes."

"Why?"

"Because you don't listen!"

I was listening. I was listening hard. At once, I felt dumb and sad and angry. "Isn't this what you wanted?" I shouted at him.

He puffed out his chest. "I already told you: Leave it with me! Wait for my orders! But you don't listen. It's like you're deaf or stupid."

"You're the one who's stupid. Maybe I don't listen to you because you're stupid."

He pushed me. "Go home and stop embarrassing yourself and your family."

"My family?"

"Your father and Nuha are like this," he said, crossing his fingers.

"No, they are not."

"They are." He chuckled. "I thought you were smarter than this. I gave you clear orders. I put you in charge of the whole neighbourhood, and you can't even watch your father!"

Pulling away from the door, I shouted, "I don't need your fucking orders! My sheikh is Abu-Hassan, not you! He's my leader, not you!"

He raised his arm to knock me down, and I ran.

18

February 10

The day Nuha moved out of the neighbourhood, the sky was shifting between blue and grey. The door leading to the lower courtyard was flung open, and she stood on the threshold, hair unkempt and eyes swollen. She had not told anyone about her destination, but people assumed she was going to live in Ramallah.

The writing on the wall had done more damage than I had expected. It made our neighbours look at her sideways and mumble things. I had erased the words the following night, but loads of people had snapped pictures of my judgment, and now they were asking themselves if the writing on the wall was the truth.

Her mirrored closet and metal bed frame lay in the middle of the courtyard, while her kitchen table rested upside down over the mouth of the cistern, surrounded by four sturdy chairs. I grabbed two of the chairs and was about to haul them out when she called my name.

"I need to talk to you," she said.

My heart leapt inside my chest.

"What are you doing?" she asked me.

"Helping."

Her face looked dim, very dim, and I decided not to let her see my own dimness, my guilty eyes. I looked down.

"Do you really want to help me?" she said.

"Of course."

She glanced back at the suitcases and rolled-up carpets laid against the lemon tree.

"Who did it?" she said.

"Who did what?"

She just looked at me.

I opened my mouth, but she leaned closer as though asking me to shut up and listen. Her cold hand landed on my shoulder. "I swear to Allah I don't care," she said. "I have been thinking about leaving this stinky neighbourhood for a while. Now, I can leave with no regrets."

We were standing at the foot of our staircase, in a spot where it was always dark, even if you dangled a megawatt bulb from above.

I turned and was about to climb up to our house and disappear inside when she said, "Was it Yousef?"

"I don't know."

"I have a feeling you do know."

"I don't know," I repeated. "I told you I don't!"

"Why are you so upset?" she said in a soft voice.

"I'm not upset," I told her, though I was upset, because I was not innocent, and because Yousef was not innocent. She was not innocent either. She said she had no regrets, but she was about to steal my father and wreck our family.

"By the way," she whispered. "I'm not mad at you."

I remained silent.

She went on. "Because of what you did at my house on New Year's Eve."

"I'm sorry," I mumbled.

She nodded and walked back toward her front door, where her friends were waiting for her to tell them what to pack and what to throw away.

Then, Yousef came into the courtyard. "My tractor is outside," he told her, pointing to the road. "You can load anything you like."

He started directing her friends on how to lift and place fragile objects. He called them "brother" and "sister," which was ridiculous, considering what he had called them before—traitors and homos and dancers on our martyrs' blood. He did not talk to me. We did not even nod at one another; it seemed our relationship was going back to those good old days when I hated him without pretending.

As her friends loaded her things in carts and wheelbarrows, I sat up on the landing by the jasmine tree. I made sure Nuha could not see my face or my shadow, though I wanted to help her. My heart was aching to help her. It pained me that she was leaving without knowing the truth. But perhaps she knew and wanted to leave the truth hanging in the air like a clothesline, sagging under all kinds of burdens and in all kinds of winds.

February 14

On Valentine's Day, I did not masturbate or buy a red rose. When waitresses at the café arranged candles and free chocolates on decorated tables, I did not feel a thing.

When lovers kissed, I did not feel a thing. And when I lowered my gaze and saw fancy shoes and sandals and hands caressing bronze skin from the knee up, I did not feel a thing.

In the evening, Jewish boys and girls came for alcohol, and we told them: "No alcohol. Café policy." That drove them mad, especially when I said it in Arabic.

"If they start selling alcohol, I'll quit," I told Marwan.

He laughed at me. "Like they'd care."

"Ahava Ktana" played all day behind the counter. Dafna grabbed a steaming pitcher of frothed milk from my hand and nudged me. "Do you know this song?"

When I shrugged, she said, "Everybody knows it. The whole planet knows it!" She gave me a piece of chocolate with the imprint of her teeth in it. I ate it and then I felt bad—the excited kind of bad.

"Ahava Ktana" played on and on. I understood every word of the song. It was about the pain of love when it starts, or the pain of love when it ends, or both. My Hebrew had improved significantly since December, though Dafna said I spoke like a news anchor. True, because while Marwan and Mustafa spoke the Hebrew of the street, I spoke that of newspapers and talk shows.

Dafna roamed the café with a rose behind her ear. Now and then, she pushed her curls away from her eyes. Sweat trickled in front of her ears and along her upper lip. It was late in the evening, and I wondered what she was doing after work. What her boyfriend was planning for the rest of the night and why he never came to visit or pick her up. Did he live far? Was he a student? A bodybuilder? A singer? A dancer? Was he in the army?

Thoughts like these would come and go. I knew they were all based on false desires. And because I knew, pain floated in the top of my stomach and stayed there. Marwan gave me something for heartburn—a small tablet he tossed in a glass of water. It fizzed, dissolved, and disappeared.

"Gulp it down," he said. "Works like magic."

I was not sure if I should trust him. The word *magic* felt sinister. I was having a hard time forgetting our last argument about hiring a lawyer for Mustafa. I remembered stories about people spiking drinks. They came in so many forms, those spikes—capsules, pills, powders, rocks. Not long ago, a neighbour had guzzled something where he worked in Tel Aviv. His family had to take him to an exorcist to kick the jinn out of him. But the jinn (or the spike) had never left his body. Now he walked and talked funny, and people called him all kinds of names.

Fingers on the glass, I lingered with my thoughts until Marwan snatched it and opened my mouth for me. "You want your mama to give it to you?"

So I drank it, and he told me to return to the sink because I looked like a rag. But I stayed at my lookout behind the coffee machine, watching customers as they loved one another. Arab boys and girls also came. I saw hijabs and overheard Muslim names, like Muhammad and Fatima. They did not kiss or touch each other like the Jewish boys and girls, but I saw kisses hovering over their tables, waiting to be caught.

"Watching people is hard work," an Arab poet said, centuries ago.

Or maybe he said it like this: "He who watches people dies of worry, and to the bold belong the thrills."

There were customers who came in every day and ordered the same thing. One was a friend of Uri's, a businessman who worked at a nearby office building. Today he came for a quick coffee. I prepared it while keeping an eye on him. He was special. He would come every day, twice, sometimes four times. Most of the time, Dafna made his coffee. The moment he came in, she would ask whoever was at the machine to switch, and then she would grace him with her specialty coffee, with the right amount of espresso, the right amount of foam, the right amount of her attention. This time she wasn't around, and he kept asking for her.

When my arm reached over to give him his order, my foot skidded, I lost my balance, and the coffee flew and landed on his nice suit.

He clutched the fabric of his pants. "Oy!"

I apologized, Hebrew words emerging slowly and thickly as though I had never spoken the language before. I gave him a rag, and he looked at it in disgust, then threw it in my face. "Dirty! This is dirty. No brain! No brain!"

Dafna appeared and seated him at a table. She came to take my spot, but I could not move from behind the machine. She pushed me gently while my hands trembled, chained by invisible cuffs.

The man was watching me the entire time. His eyes pierced through me. "Filthy Arab! Take him out of my sight!"

One customer grinned and another gasped and asked him to behave. Then Uri showed up. His eyes sent sparks across the café, and he asked Marwan to take me to the kitchen. I was dragged out like a dirty plate. As I leaned against the sink, the kitchen boys stared at me.

"Relax," Marwan said, throwing his arm over my shoulder. "Nothing happened. Don't let these people get under your skin."

Shortly after, Uri came in and told the boys to get back to work. "Bad customer," he said. "Now, tell me, are you okay?"

I hid my face behind my hands. I could only hear the clattering of dishes and frying pans. My mouth twitched, and I did not know what secrets my face held—embarrassment, gratitude, fear, fury, contempt, or all of them at once.

February 15

I took the day off. The entire day, I lay on the sofa bed and watched a gecko resting in the corner of the living room where our short wall met our short ceiling, and where spiders came and went as they pleased. His triangular head pointed toward me, and I squinted at him. Then I got up and squinted more. He was so ugly I went through killing routines in my head—a book to flatten him, a broom, a frying pan, a flying dagger. I wondered if he would look better in another corner, if he was a chameleon pretending to be a simple gecko just for fun. I pulled out the broom, and my mother followed me. She grabbed other things I could use as killing tools. She wanted me to finish him off quickly.

I called him names; I swore at him. My mother's patience was running out, and she tried to steal the broom from my hand, but I had a tight grip. His ugliness was annoying me, but I admired his silence. He deserved respect. Contrary to other creepy animals that hid in holes and crevices and broken outlets, this one was out in the open. I told my mother that human fetuses grow lizardlike hands that the body later absorbs, and she said I was crazy because God created humans in His image. She then said that in the past, a gecko, or the father of all geckos, had told the infidels about the hiding place of Prophet Muhammad.

"You should know this," she said. "It's in the Quran."

"It's not in the Quran," I said.

"It is."

"It's not."

She opened the back door, and I waved the broom at the gecko's tail. I hit the ceiling several times and she yelled, worried I might hit the television, the family pictures, or the Quality Street container filled with coins and keys and sewing needles. It took about ten minutes to move the stubborn gecko ten centimetres. But soon he listened and made it out.

My mother went to the kitchen and made sage tea. "I'm not happy about your health," she said, swirling the dry green herb in my cup. "God knows what you eat at that place. You look like a ghost ever since the damned day you started working."

Two crates of vegetables lay beside the stove, and she peeled potatoes and eggplants and chopped them into little pieces. The knife in her hand flowed smoothly on the surface of each potato, and she hummed a romantic tune.

Seeing the sweat on her forehead and the mound of vegetables covering the kitchen table, I went to help her. I tried to grab the large knife from her hand, but she clutched it in both hands.

"Careful," she said. "This knife needs stable hands."

"I have stable hands."

She shook her head and kept cutting and slicing and humming.

Why did she bother to feed someone who was betraying her? She should not cook for him. She should keep an eye on my father instead of putting me in her crosshairs. I wondered if she had been spying on him. When she had said goodbye to Nuha, the stretch of her smile could be seen from the Mount of Olives.

I turned on the television and watched footage about hunger strikers in Israeli jails. I pointed to one starved prisoner who had been transferred to the hospital. He looked weightless. When I cursed, my mother told me to watch my mouth.

"Is this the language you learn at your café?" she said, sweeping vegetable peelings off the table.

"This man has eaten nothing for a hundred days," I said. "A hundred days! Can you imagine? And we stuff our faces with food day and night. Disgusting!"

"What is disgusting?" she asked, eyes wide.

"Food."

She laughed, and I walked over and sat beside her by the kerosene heater.

Resting her moist hand on my head, she said, "Has Mustafa been released yet?"

"No," I said.

"May Allah set him free. He's your only friend."

I nodded. Then, looking at the number of vegetables she was cutting and arranging into open trays, I said, "Isn't this too much?"

"I'm not making this dinner for you," she said, rolling her eyes. "Your grandparents are visiting tonight. We are going to celebrate your grandfather's medical results."

"Is he cured?"

"His body could not handle surgery, but the pills are working, his doctors said. Inshallah, good news. Inshallah, ya rab!"

Evening

My mother stood in the doorway and waited for my grandparents. She had dishes on the stove and dishes in the oven, and she held her phone with the tips of her fingers. She called my father, who had left two hours before to pick them up.

"Where are you now?" she asked him.

She frowned, and they argued. She was asking him questions and biting her nails, which were already very short. After the call, she slipped the stuffed potatoes out of the oven.

"This life is not worth living," she said. Covering her face with half-scorched oven mitts, she started to cry.

I did not know what to do. Then Uncle Fahmi and Aunt Amal arrived.

"Omar could not make it to my parents' place," she said. "He could not drive through their neighbourhood. The army had closed off the road."

When I told her I could go bring them over with my uncle, she said, "I'm visiting tomorrow. I'll take some food with me. It won't be the same, but..."

Seeing her mood had improved somewhat, my uncle asked me about school.

My mother turned to face me. "We're hoping for good marks this year."

"You need many things to make it in this city, but school is not one of them," my uncle said. "Believe me, here, the shitter and the reader are all the same. They have the same value. Didn't your father tell you this already?"

"Stop putting ideas in his head," my aunt told him while serving tea.

"I'm telling the truth," he said, almost jumping in his seat. "School will ruin his brains. He's smart. I'll train him to be the best mechanic this city has ever seen. I'll mentor him. Everybody knows Fahmi and what Fahmi does."

My father walked in. "Is Fahmi here?"

They laughed and hugged, and I left my chair so they could sit side by side. Then we had dinner. My uncle left the vegetarian food to my aunt and dug into the moussaka with beef. He licked his fingers and wiped his mouth with the back of his hand.

"What's in these eggplants, Khawla? Strange flavour."

"Tomato sauce—" she said, tilting her head.

"That's it?" he interrupted her.

She added with a grin, "And basil and hot peppers from the terrace and olive oil from my parents' trees."

"Nothing beats local!" he exclaimed.

Putting his phone aside, my father said, "Strange, Fahmi? You would eat it even if it was cooked in tar and oil."

"Only advanced full synthetic motor oil," he responded, and everybody laughed.

There was a lot of laughing, and to match it, firecrackers exploded outside. My mother got up and looked through the front door's small window. "Ya Allah, give us patience. How annoying to hear them all the time."

Aunt Amal nodded. "I only relax when I'm out of this neighbourhood. Fahmi and I go to a new place every week, every other week. Good for the nerves."

A dry smile covered my mother's face. She was about to say something, but then she didn't. Although my father was a taxi driver, he loathed going places that weren't on his route, loathed driving for pleasure, contrary to my uncle, who plowed through the country, north to south.

"Fahmi has money," my father would tell my mother. "He has time. He has no kids. His wife works." To which she would respond, "Let me work then," and he would say, "We have enough. Only greedy men let their wives work."

My uncle and aunt had just returned from a camping trip to Mitzpe Ramon in the Negev desert. He showed us photos of them hiking, driving, and eating inside a tent, their faces shimmering under the sun and sparkling under moonlight.

"You have no idea, Khawla," Aunt Amal said. "The sunrise in the desert, Khawla—unbelievable! I woke up to a fresh breeze, opened the tent, and the sun was on its way up. Everything around us was shining like silk."

My mother loved the photos. "Look, Omar! Look at the stars in the sky! We should go!"

My father looked down and picked at his food. She waited for him to say something, but he didn't, and she got up and opened the front door. The smell of rain came in with the sound of firecrackers. The noise grew louder. The cold air drifted in, and he told her to close the door and bring more bread. She was not listening. She breathed in and out, in and out, as though she were alone in the middle of a faraway oasis, standing barefoot, forgetting everything, said and unsaid, done and undone, everything about folding the blankets, everything about sweeping the floors, everything about cooking and cleaning, everything about cooking again and cleaning again.

19

February 15
Night

Outside, there was a burst of voices, then bullets. My uncle ran down the stairs, and I followed him. We hurried up toward the bakery, where people were gathered, speaking loudly, praying, cursing, shaking their heads. Up the road, there was a line of soldiers. A line of settlers peeked from behind the barricades and the soldiers' flak suits. It was raining, not daring but timid, the kind that leaves bugs in your veins.

I shuffled my feet, carefully at first, but then I elbowed my way through the crowd to stand beside my uncle. Abu-Yousef joined us.

Somebody yelled, "Where is the ambulance?"

On the ground lay Ustaz Salim with his fist curled under his cheek like a baby. He wore the same tattered suit, and his blood trickled on the stones.

"Four bullets," a neighbour said, her hijab sliding down to her neck. "I did not hear the first bullet, but the second struck him right there, in the middle of the road. He held up his arms and asked them to stop, but the pigs did not stop." She was holding a bottle of water and her body shook. "He crawled away and then started knocking on our door. He called out his father's name, 'Yabaaaa. Abu-Salim. Yabaaaa.' He sounded like a goat. I heard him say 'Yabaaaaa' ten times. When I opened the door, he asked for water. When I came back, he was like this... We leave it to Allah."

Up the road, guns waved to the passing sun. The ambulance waited behind the barricade.

Without thinking, I called Yousef's name. I searched for him in the crowd and then marched into the bakery. He was unloading sacks of flour from a three-wheel cart. He patted his knees, releasing white dust.

"I need your cart," I said. "The road is blocked. We need to put Ustaz Salim in a cart and take him to the ambulance."

Yousef chained the cart to a hook on the floor.

I jiggled it back and forth. "The man is dying!" I shouted.

He brandished a broomstick in my face.

"You helped Nuha before," I reminded him.

"It's not the same."

"Allah is the judge, not you!" I said.

He pushed me, and I pushed back. Three times he pushed, and I pushed.

"Why are you defending him, anyway? He sold his house to the Jews."

"He didn't."

"He did. And after they got the house, they dumped him like garbage."

"These are all lies. Fear Allah, Yousef!"

Abu-Yousef came over from where he had been chatting with my uncle and unchained the cart. He rolled it down to where Ustaz Salim was gasping for his life.

"May Allah have mercy on your father," said Abu-Yousef. "May Allah have mercy on you. May Allah have mercy on us."

With two neighbours, I hoisted Ustaz Salim into the cart and pushed it down the alley. A thousand little boys followed. Ustaz Salim was mute but breathing. His ears pressed against the sesame seeds in the bottom of the cart, making dunes and ripples. Behind us, the boys chattered like angry birds. One of them was pointing at the small bottle of alcohol inside Ustaz Salim's jacket and asking his friend if he would die an infidel.

That evening, after we dropped off Ustaz Salim at the hospital, the army shut the gates of the Old City, and tear gas made clouds below the clouds. The soldiers chased after us. We ran together, then split off into a thousand alleys. No exits in sight.

Later, I crouched in a corner and asked myself if I wanted to throw one more rock, one more bottle, one more curse, and then get the gunshot that would turn my brains into sesame seeds.

It rained, the daring kind. Then it got dark, and the darkness was thick. Walking home, I could not see the outlines of our stairs. I could see nothing, as though nothing wished to be seen.

February 16

I woke up to water dripping from the ceiling into a bucket behind my pillow. My mother stood nearby, looking up at a damp patch on the ceiling above the television. Another patch was above my sofa. I got up and brought a second bucket from the bathroom.

"Not this one," my mother said. "This I keep for our baths. Bring the blue bucket from the terrace, by the planters."

Suddenly my father came in. He was talking quickly and we could not understand a word. Then he said, "The taxi. My taxi is gone. They smashed the glass and slashed the tires."

My mother told him to call the police. He hesitated, and then he called. His Hebrew was not very good, and he put the phone on speaker for us to help him. The policewoman pretended not to understand him, and he nodded.

"They can't see you nodding, Omar!" my mother told him, pointing at the phone.

He went out to the terrace. The policewoman said she could not hear a thing. I walked behind him and quickly took the phone from his hand. I started talking to her, but when I said the word *settlers*, my father took the phone back and pushed me away.

Two hours later, the police came to the parking area near Damascus Gate. They took pictures of the car and made my father sign some papers. He came home and showed us pictures of the smashed windshield and the dented doors. The police had told him to go to the station that afternoon for further questions.

"Questions?" I said. "Are they accusing you of damaging your own car?"

He looked at the time and asked me if I had school. I nodded.

"Get out of my sight," he said.

Evening

I was smoking on the terrace when I heard the back door open, then close. I threw away the cigarette and stood up, almost knocking my head against one of the solar heater pipes.

"What are you doing?" my father asked, and I gazed down at the lost cigarette.

He went back inside, and I followed him. He took off his shoes and sat down on the sofa. "Where's your mother?"

"I don't know."

"She told me she was home," he said. "My wife is a ghost. I swear, I'm married to a ghost."

He opened the oven. No food. He opened the cupboards one by one and peered in. No food. He opened the refrigerator, drank milk, and cursed at edible and inedible things. I wondered if he had ever cursed at Nuha. I looked at his confused face and wondered if he was still seeing her. The amount of cologne he wore was suspicious, toxic.

I got up to go to the bathroom, and he told me to sit down.

"I need to study with a friend," I lied.

"Who?"

"You don't know him," I said loudly. I just wanted to get out of the house.

"So you're a man now and you can speak up? When I say sit, you sit!"

I sat on the floor, clasping my hands tightly, hoping to hide my trembling.

He started searching for something other than food. Not his smokes because they were on the coffee table with his wallet and keys. He snatched his jacket, sending the hanger to the floor. He slipped a small piece of paper out of a pocket and waved it in my face.

"Captain Moussa wants to talk to you," he said.

I recoiled. "Why does he want to see me?"

"You tell me. Tell me what you're up to, besides smoking like a bum."

I remained silent, and he went on, "Let's start with Facebook and shit like that. How many times did I tell you not to get involved in politics?"

"I just share whatever other people post."

"You are not other people. I raised you to be smart." Hunched over the coffee table, he stared at me. "Since when do you know Abu-Hassan?"

"He's my friend's father."

"He's a crook!"

"He is not a crook. He lost his son for our cause. His only son!"

"What cause? I told you not to get involved in politics!"

"We don't talk politics."

"What do you talk about?"

"He teaches us how to be good Muslims. How to be responsible."

He chuckled. "Responsible? You?"

I raised my voice. "Yes, me! I'm responsible before God for your soul, my mother's, my grandparents', my uncle's and aunts', and my neighbours'."

He opened and closed the refrigerator again, then he moved in my direction. His soiled shoes stamped the carpet as I rolled myself in a ball and remained quiet. He collected his things from the table, and the key chain hit the buttons of his jacket with an ominous sound. The note fell from his hand, landing between my knees.

"When the time comes," he said, pointing at me, "I want you to go to the police station. I want you to tell them what they want to hear. Tell them you want peace. Say it clearly. Don't mince words the way you always do. Tell Captain Moussa that you have no involvement in anything against any of his people."

He gave me his back, the way he did to passengers. He gave me his back as though we were strangers, as though I were paying him for a quick ride. We would spend a few minutes together, and then each of us would go his own way.

20

February 23

Mustafa was released. Marwan and I had planned to pick him up, and then go somewhere to celebrate, but Marwan went alone. I did not want to raise alarms, waiting by the police station's doors, under the eyes of interrogators and spies, coming in and out with notes and names. Captain Moussa's note remained in my pocket, wrinkled and smudged. In twenty days, I would have to sit in his office. I had missed the Circle's last meeting and cut myself off social media. Fear was eating at me.

February 24

Mustafa and I met at the Musrara Market. We hugged and sat on plastic chairs in front of a falafel shop. I bought two wraps, one with hot sauce for me and one without for Mustafa. We always joked that spice was already built into his system, in the blood.

"You've lost weight," I told him.

He nodded and chewed slowly. He had grown a beard.

It was spotty, but from a distance it looked full. His phone rang, and he pushed cancel.

"Work?" I asked.

He ate in small bites. "They fired me when they knew I was in jail."

I scanned his face and arms for bruises and scars. "Were you tortured?"

"They did their thing," he said.

"What do you mean?"

He pointed at his sandwich. "Let me eat!"

Taxis pulled onto the shoulder of the road. I recognized two or three drivers, friends of my father's. One of them waved at me, and I nodded. I folded my arms and counted passengers arriving and departing. I registered their faces, the singsong greetings, the laughs, the jokes, the touches, the holding of hands, the pats on the back. I should have picked up my friend; I should have been there at the station's entrance when he got out, like a friend, a true friend. Was it my fault or my father's, the man who had passed down to me his weak genes?

The owner of the falafel shop came over and asked us to leave. He was closing. Mustafa did not like the owner's tone. He stretched out his legs and ignored him, but then I suggested walking would be better to discuss things nobody needed to hear. It was warm and Sultan Suleiman Street buzzed with people. I took off my jacket and tied it around my waist.

"So what was it like in jail?"

"When they say jail is for men, it's the truth," he said. "Inside, I met guys our age from all over Palestine. Only inside you could see real heroes."

Every time he said the word *inside*, I cringed.

"They're on another level," he said. "They laughed at me when I told them I wrote on walls. They said I must be five years old. When I said my house might get demolished, they said their houses had been demolished at least three times. When I said I punched a soldier in the face, they told me their mothers and sisters did exactly that every single day."

I gasped.

"They told me many stories, so many heroic stories, and I asked how I could join them. Too bad they weren't recruiting."

"Are you sure they were real resistance fighters and not asafir? Did they ask you why you were in jail? Because that's how they get information from you and then—"

He slapped me on the neck. "Don't be silly. I saw them with my own eyes. I talked to them. There are things I cannot share. You and I are nothing compared to these heroes. We should only wish we were laces on their shoes and threads on their keffiyehs."

I squinted at his face. Despite having lost five to ten kilos, he looked heavy, and I wondered if a few weeks *inside* were enough to cause this much heaviness.

"Are you still working with my brother?" he asked me.

I didn't answer.

"You're brooding," he said.

"Sorry I didn't come to pick you up," I said.

"No problem. Yousef came."

I cursed Yousef under my breath. We talked about our families and the conversation felt as though I were pulling the words from his mouth, from the deepest corners of his mouth.

His phone rang again. "It's Marwan," he said. "I have to go."

"Are you coming to the Circle tomorrow?" I asked him.

"No, I'm busy," he said.

February 25

The Hour of the Sincere came again. This time, the special hour of the month was one-on-one, ten minutes for each brother. When it was my turn, Abu-Hassan and I sat in a corner.

"Yousef is your brother," he said with a long stare. "You should not fight."

"We didn't fight," I said.

He raised his right eyebrow, the one he raised when he was annoyed. He wanted to tell me that he knew.

"Yousef would not help a Muslim in need," I said.

"You mean your drunken neighbour Salim? You call him a Muslim? Have you learned nothing from my lectures, Aziz? Have you learned nothing here?"

"I mean, he's my neighbour, my old neighbour, and my teacher."

His eyes widened. "Your teacher? I am your teacher."

"I mean, he was. I mean, he's hanging between life and death in the hospital."

"I know what happened. You don't have to explain to me."

I tried not to look at him directly, out of respect. "His family lives in the streets because of the settlers. I wanted to talk to you about giving him Zakat money. It will be a blessing from Allah if he receives Zakat. It will be a great blessing. You know, I grew up with his kids—"

"I don't care."

"Their mother is Russian, but she wears hijab."

He raised his hand as though to hit me. "Enough! Your *teacher* does not deserve money or mercy. A blow to the head, maybe."

Laughter broke out behind us.

"Maybe he is not right in the head—" I said, still looking down, still avoiding Abu-Hassan's irritated eyes.

He scoffed. "He has never been right in the head, even in his good days."

"Allah forgives. Allah is merciful—"

He interrupted me again. "Listen, boy, your imagination is running away with you. Maybe *you* are not right in the head."

The *you* boomeranged across the lower floor, which was packed with my brothers, who were waiting for their turn. I ducked my head. I wanted to kiss Abu-Hassan's hands and feet so that he wouldn't say more mean things to me, wouldn't humiliate me in front of my brothers. But he did, and they saw it on my face, the humiliation.

After he had finished with me, I sat under the spiral staircase, where nobody could see me or feel my presence. I was watching him now, scanning his face as he whispered to my brothers, and as they nodded and then went back to lean against one of the four white walls.

When it was Yousef's turn to chat with Abu-Hassan, I observed them as they exchanged words and smiles. Now and then, Yousef would look over his shoulder at one of our brothers and say something. He seemed to be gossiping, telling secrets. Abu-Hassan was giving him his ear, tilting his head and raising his eyebrows. They had the same eyebrows and the same head. How come I was noticing this for the first time? They were relatives, of course. But now, looking at them, they were not only relatives. They were twins. Identical twins.

This observation sent shivers down my spine.

Everything around me started to shrink and thorns grew on the edges of the floor, the walls, the ceiling, and the spiral staircase. A giant prickly pear had grown in my lap and was stinging me. I had to leave. I had to get out.

Night

A faceless man trailed me. He jumped me and started choking me. I let him. I thought he would go away if I let him. But he did not, and I woke with a start.

I went up to the roof. The earth below was too far away to see. I tried not to look at my hands. I tried not to look at my feet as they walked over the growing mounds of clutter and pigeon shit. I sat far enough from the edge not to tumble over my shadow. I slapped myself awake. Anger brewed inside me: at my parents, who were fighting constantly; at my neighbours, whose silly stories I knew by heart, though I could not tell real from fake; at my classmates, who were studying for exams as though they could save the world.

I was angry at myself, at Abu-Hassan. I had gone to Abu-Hassan to untangle my tongue, but now my tongue was still tangled and my head ached. Was I right in the head? Was I not? Something was not working for me. Was the world conspiring against me? But who was I to deserve the world's attention? A tough riddle was hovering over my head. It had to be cracked open and solved. But how?

Across the street, the neighbours were celebrating a wedding. It was three in the morning, and they were still going. They had erected a tent and crammed it with chairs. Straddling one pair of shoulders after another, the groom threw his arms up in the air and whirled like a helicopter. His friends climbed up on the chairs and on the scaffolding of the stage. Throwing sugar-coated almonds in the air, their arms chased after the groom's helicopter. I wanted to whirr and howl like them. Not because I was happy—because I was alone.

I couldn't be that boy who was left to fend for himself on an island but trusted his heart and the animals who raised him. I couldn't be any of the characters in my books, because they had been burned with the books. What had not been completely burned was resting deep in the cistern of muddy water by Nuha's lemon tree.

The oud player sang folk, romantic, patriotic, Islamic, everything. A song I really liked went, *To be stabbed with daggers is better than being ruled by a scoundrel.* The singer sounded drunk, especially when he stretched *ya lail* and *ya ain* and *ya habibi*.

You know Doomsday is around the corner when people talk and walk funny.

"You see them drunk, but they are not. But your god's torture is so severe."

God almighty has spoken the truth.

Nuha's house stood silent, the kitchen window staring blankly into the night, the tight corridor collecting spider-webs and mildew. Would the settlers take over Nuha's place? Who knows? Nobody knows anything these days.

Abu-Yousef's bakery was still open. Three settlers from Abu-Salim's house stood outside; they nibbled on bread and patted one another on the shoulder. Neighbours who had been dancing at the wedding or awoken hungry in the middle of the night manoeuvred around the settlers, keeping their distance like a caravan of ants blocked by a finger.

I collected pebbles and tossed them down. They were light and harmless, but the way they whizzed down like a giant's piss cheered me up. I wondered if those settlers had their own Abu-Hassan who sat with them on Thursdays or Fridays or Saturdays to untangle their tongues. I wondered if they were seekers of religion or seekers of the world. Did their hearts beat fast when they saw a sleepy cat or a warm bagel? Did they feel bad for the misery of a stranger? Did they have families? I had never seen them walk with their children or parents or grandparents. Did their mothers wish them a safe and quiet day every morning? Or a calm evening after they had rested their rifles on the dinner table?

21

March 11

I did my Friday prayers alone, and my other prayers and recitations also alone. I only walked to and from school and work, and I turned off my phone. I did not see Mustafa and I avoided Yousef. When my mother asked me to buy bread and groceries, I bought them from another bakery on Salaheddin Street. More expensive, but better than seeing the snitch. If the two angels sitting on my shoulders were busy registering my good and bad deeds, they would do so because they were under the authority of God and God alone.

As the workday drew to a close, Marwan pulled me aside to complain about Mustafa. "I want to yank his beard from the roots," he said. "Every time I talk to him, he tells me a story from the times of Muhammad. He does not like how we eat, how we sleep, how we fart. My uncle's wife visited the other day, and he did not shake her hand. Forbidden, he said. His aunt!"

"Being a good Muslim is hard work," I said.

"What about the rest of us? Are we bad apples? Old shoes?"

"Allah tests His people. Why do you think there is heaven and hell?"

"Heaven?" he scoffed. "I don't believe in heaven. Do you really believe in rivers of honey and wine? Why would we have wine in heaven if it is not halal here?"

"It has no alcohol."

His laughter reached the street. "What's the use of a river of wine with no alcohol?"

Olga came into the kitchen and asked why he was laughing so loudly. He told her, and she made fun of Muslim beards, and I got mad. I told him he should be ashamed of himself, sharing this kind of joke with an outsider.

He pulled her close with his long arm. "Muslims and Jews are cousins. Right, cousin? Besides, we also make fun of the Haredim. Olga, what do you think of the Haredim?"

She made horns with her fingers. "They can go to hell," she said.

Evening

Mustafa barged into the café and sat at one of the big tables.

I went to him and said, "I'll make you the best cappuccino in town."

"I don't want your cappuccino," he said, folding his arms and scanning the customers.

We chatted as though we were both patrons. Marwan came and told him he needed to order something.

"I'm waiting," he said, still scanning the customers. "Is there a law against waiting?"

His loud Arabic was bothering Uri, who was sitting at a corner table doing bookkeeping. Uri scowled and looked at Marwan, who drummed his hand on the back of Mustafa's chair. "Listen," he told his brother. "I'm off soon. Take my car and come back in an hour."

"I changed my mind," Mustafa said. "I do want a cappuccino."

I was about to go make it for him, but Marwan stopped me. "On my mother's soul," he said, giving him the keys, "go now, and I will get you whatever you like when you come back."

Mustafa grabbed the keys and got up, kicking the leg of one of the chairs on his way out.

Night

I was cleaning the counter when Dafna came out of the kitchen. She was rubbing her eyes.

"You need a coffee," I teased.

"Absolutely," she said, rubbing her hands together. "Arabic coffee?"

I nodded.

She sat on the stool behind the counter and unhooked the buckle of one shoe, slipped her heel out, massaged her ankle, and then slipped it back in.

"Aren't you hot?" she asked, pointing at my corduroy trousers. "You should wear shorts. Arab boys don't wear shorts. I find it strange."

"I wear shorts," I said, gazing down at my knees as they

bumped against the drawers. From one of those drawers, I pulled out a coffee pot and a bag of ground coffee.

"Ha!" she said. "You have your own coffee machine?"

"The machine and the fuel. Marwan and I make our own, but it's not the same when it's made on an electric stove," I said.

She looked over her shoulder. "Marwan is a joker," she said. It was only us in the café, besides Marwan and Olga, whose laughter was coming through the kitchen wall.

"He makes girls laugh," I said. "Are they together?"

"Olga and Marwan? No!" She paused. "You know what? Maybe. They're both crazy!"

I focused on the water in the pot as it started to heat up and bubble.

"Tell me about yourself," she said.

"What do you want to know?"

"What's your school like?"

"Boring."

She grinned. "My school is also boring. But do you have a favourite subject?"

"No."

"Very short answers," she said, and furrowed her brow, imitating me.

"I don't look like that," I said, slapping her arm.

The touch felt natural, and she returned it with equal force. My heart plunged in my chest like falafel in a frying pan on a Ramadan night. The water steamed, and I gave it my attention again. She hummed, and the heat welled up inside the pot and inside me, and I was unsure how to control both. Slowly, I dispensed the ground coffee. I shifted the mounds of coffee and watched them sink into the bubbly water, where they darkened.

"Why are you doing that?" she asked, leaning closer.

"To make foam. I like foam."

When the coffee swelled, I scooped the thick layer of foam with a spoon and laid it into her cup. I did the same with mine.

"My Yemenite grandmother knows how to make this kind of coffee," she said. "But she never taught me."

I slid her cup toward her. "Your grandmother makes Arabic coffee?"

"She taught me some Arabic, though, a few good words. I'm learning the dirty words from Marwan."

She poured a sugar packet down her throat, and I gritted my teeth.

"It gives you a good rush," she said. "You should try it."

I tried it, then spat a mouthful in the empty bin.

"Balagan," she said, handing me a napkin. "Habibi, moshkel, balagan!"

I covered my mouth with a napkin and waited for her to speak more Arabic, the language of her grandmother's family. Half of her was from Yemen: native land of coffee and Arabs. History said so, not me. I looked at her once more—*How nice to be near her all day, how good she is to me, how smooth her skin must be, how nice it would be to—*

Across the street, a car flashed its headlights and honked. Mustafa was back. Putting on my jacket, I called Marwan, who came out from the kitchen.

He winked. "Yalla!" And I followed him.

Dafna grabbed my arm. "Next time I want you to get me coffee."

Confused, I responded, "You want more coffee?"

"No," she said, laughing. "I mean ground coffee. From the Old City. Like the kind you and Marwan drink in secret."

I nodded, and she leaned against the counter and smiled her smile—like the sun at five in the morning, shy, but radiating enough colour and energy to tell the world: *I am here.*

OUTSIDE, MUSTAFA WAS PARKED illegally. A police car was approaching as we got in, so Marwan told him to pull up at a construction site around the corner. Mustafa pressed the gas, disappearing in a flash. He did not have a driver's licence but could drive a tractor-trailer if he put his mind to it.

I lay flat on the long back seat. Marwan wanted to go to Bethlehem to smoke nargileh and play cards, but Mustafa wanted to eat. He drove south, then he made a U-turn. "Forget Bethlehem. Let's grab something on the road." We pulled into a pizza shop in Baka, bought a large pizza, and ate quietly. Mustafa left the crusts, and Marwan and I ate them.

Mustafa opened the car windows and turned on the Quran station.

"Turn it off," Marwan said.

He turned it up instead. "Relax."

Marwan shook his head. "Mustafa, don't start! Put on something lively."

"Like what?"

"Anything! If Nancy Ajram is too suggestive, play Umm Kulthum. She's dead and unfuckable."

Mustafa turned the volume up to the max. "You should thank me," he said, swinging his arms. "I'm helping you expel the devil in your heart. Get out, devil! Get out!"

"You get out!" Marwan yelled. He told Mustafa to pull over near Damascus Gate, kicked us out, and drove away. There was a long silence as Mustafa and I snaked through the empty roads, a cold breeze stinging our faces.

"Why are you still working at the café?" he finally asked me.

"To help my father," I said.

He gave me a look. "Were you talking to Dafna while I was waiting outside?"

"I don't know. Maybe I was."

"And?"

"And what?"

"Did you fuck her?"

I reared back. "Kiss my ass, Mustafa!"

He scanned me with angry eyes. "Marwan told me you flirt all day with that whore. Is she teaching you Hebrew? Is that it? You're brushing up on your Hebrew?"

I spread my arms out across the narrow road. "Don't ever talk to me this way. Don't act like you don't know me. What's wrong with you? What's wrong with everyone? Every fucking second, someone points a finger! Every second, someone wants to say they're better than me. You are not better than me!"

"I did not say I'm better than you," he said.

"You did."

We turned into his neighbourhood and stood in front of his house.

"You're too sensitive," he said. "I was at the Circle today. Abu-Hassan wanted to see me."

"He wanted to see you? He does not care one inch about you."

"Why do you say that? He's always been nice to us, especially to you."

"I don't care."

He patted me on the back. He wanted to say something, but then he started coughing. It was a long and painful cough. He must have caught something in jail. Or his jailers must have messed him up, broken his ribs, or his lungs. He spat, and I looked down to see if there was blood. I ran to his house to get him water, but the door was locked.

"Don't worry," he said, spitting yellow phlegm and clearing his throat.

He pulled me into a hug. "You know, Aziz. You are my backbone."

"I miss the old days," I said, almost crying on his shoulder.

We crouched down and smoked. A wooden plank jutted out of their roof, and I asked him, "Are they still going to knock it down?"

"I don't know," he said. "They might keep it locked up forever or fill it up with concrete. I have a lawyer looking into the case."

"I have money," I said, handing him another cigarette. "How much do you need?"

"You know what? Sometimes I feel like bringing down the whole thing with my bare hands. I don't even want to finish it anymore. I don't care. I'm done. What purpose does it have anyway? My brother's head is elsewhere. My father—I don't see him. He's living his Sufi life, going on long trips to mosques in the middle of nowhere. I wish he was like Abu-Hassan. I wish there were more Abu-Hassans in this world."

"Abu-Hassan is a father like any father," I said. "Don't be fooled."

"He loves us."

"He only cares for himself."

He narrowed his eyes. "What changed your mind? You used to think he was the new caliph. Maybe my brother got to you, or is it the Jewish girl?"

"No, I just thought about it. I saw the light."

"The light? You sound like my father."

"Yes, the light! Think about it. Abu-Hassan is all talk. Did he help you at all? He's rich, very rich. He runs the Zakat. Did he give you money? He knows good lawyers. Did he hire one for you? I begged him for help, but he did nothing. Yousef did nothing to help you. Your brother, Marwan, did everything he could. I was there. I was worried he would not, but he did. He got you out."

"My family is doing nothing for me."

"I just told you, Marwan helped you get out. You already know that."

"The least he could do for me," he said.

I shook my head. "Abu-Hassan did nothing for his own son."

"The whole city marched in Hassan's funeral. It was a great funeral."

"I mean during his life. Again, think about it! Do you remember when we would go out or watch movies on

Hassan's computer? Do you remember how frightened Hassan used to be? Always afraid to get caught. Do you remember how many times he changed his password so his father couldn't pry? Do you remember our last night together, his face, talking on the phone? He was arguing with his father at that moment. I swear, Abu-Hassan was on the line—"

"Only God knows."

"It's the truth."

"Only God knows the truth."

"Listen for a second. Abu-Hassan runs a Zakat committee. You think he gives all the money he collects to the poor, like he says? What did he give you? What did he give me? And listen to this. Listen! There is a rumour he has received money from rich Arab countries for every demolished house in Jerusalem. He was supposed to give the money to people like you, but—"

"I don't believe it."

"People talk."

"Fuck people."

"I'm just saying, Abu-Hassan is not what he seems."

"Abu-Hassan is not our enemy."

"I did not say he was. I'm just telling you things I've heard. Some say he received money from the Israelis as compensation for Hassan's death. His lawyer was able to prove Hassan's innocence and got him hundreds of thousands of shekels."

Mustafa covered his ears. "Stop! On Hassan's life, stop! If you love Hassan at all, stop!"

"I'm telling you this for his sake. For our friend's sake."

I started to cry. Mustafa threw his arm over my

shoulder, and we glanced up at the neighbours' roof, their laundry, their faint lights leaking from the small square windows and then spilling down across the alleyway.

"The only reason I joined the Circle was because of Hassan," I said. "And now I'm through with it, because I feel—"

"You feel that we are not doing what we are supposed to do, right?"

"Maybe."

"On that I agree with you. The lectures and the readings and talk of the caliphate—maybe Abu-Hassan is all talk, as you said. We don't need his lectures anymore."

The neighbours opened, then closed their window across from where we were sitting. It was just after midnight, and we must have annoyed them with our conversation.

"Does Hassan visit you in your dreams?" Mustafa whispered.

"Only during the day. His face appears to me on many things."

"When you see him, does he look happy?"

"Not happy, not sad. Why do you ask?"

"He visited me once when I was in jail. It was a dream. He hugged me like you and I hugged a minute ago. Then he asked for revenge."

22

March 14

The time came for my appointment with Captain Moussa, and Mustafa told me not to go.

"You'll be eaten alive," he said. "Names will be picked from your tongue like loose screws, faces grabbed from your memory in bulk, like fish from a net."

Instead, we went to Ramallah. Mustafa was not working. He needed a police clearance after his time in jail. He had no money, so I gave him five hundred shekels. We sat at the back of the bus. He said we would be meeting people at Al-Manara Square. He told me not to ask questions until we had finished. I promised not to talk at all.

In Beit Hanina, two policemen waved down the bus driver. They hopped on and screened everybody. They were looking for people who'd entered from the West Bank without a permit. A boy two rows in front of us had his left eye bandaged, and his mother scrambled to get her documents from a large green purse. One of the two policemen pointed his gun at her face. The woman had a medical permit. The policeman nodded and didn't ask whether the boy's eye was infected with a germ or shrapnel.

After the police left, Mustafa looked out the window and pounded the seat in front of him. The traffic had jammed, and there was a lot of honking.

"The fucker," he said, referring to his brother. "He left the car to collect dust. We could have been at Qalandia by now."

"Good thing you didn't drive in the end," I told him.

"Why?"

"Because of this mess."

"It's a mess because we're stuck in this shitty bus," he said, looking out the window at cars hopping the curb and driving along the sidewalk. "We should have had a car to arrive early at our meeting."

I was going to say "What will happen in the meeting?" But I had promised him not to ask too many questions. At times, knowing less is better than knowing too much.

He noticed me fidgeting and told me to recite after him, "'My Lord, I seek refuge with You from the prompting of the devils. I seek refuge with You, lest they should come near me. Amen.'"

"Amen," I said three times.

A million energies seeped into my legs, and I jumped onto the seat by the opposite window. The tall and winding separation wall ran alongside the road, and dark clouds covered the sky. Approaching Qalandia checkpoint, the bus slowed to a crawl. Light rain came down as boys with plastic bags on their heads knocked on car windows selling tea and coffee. It took a while for the bus to move along. The rain turned to wind, and then everything became dry, and I could only smell the concrete barriers and the rusty iron that kept the concrete together. I watched cars get stuck at the checkpoint, and others drive away. I watched soldiers hide behind steel and concrete and sunglasses.

I went back to sit beside Mustafa. He was looking at the graffiti sprayed across the high separation wall—balloons and ladders and make-believe curtains. We talked about our unfinished flag on Abu-Salim's wall.

"We were stupid," he said, as we remembered juggling four spray cans of different colours and a slingshot while trying not to get caught.

An hour later, we were in Ramallah. We ran across Al-Manara Square, past the lion statues, and then huddled under a narrow awning. The rain had resumed, and we were not dressed for the weather. I went into a store and the shopkeeper gave me two garbage bags for free. We wore them as ponchos and waited by the side of the road. Mustafa's phone was dead, so he used mine to make a call.

No one picked up, and he was annoyed. "They're expecting my number, not yours," he said.

When my mother called, he hung up on her. "You can call her later."

A military vehicle carrying the logo *Palestinian Naval Police* stopped across the street and soldiers with machine guns stepped out.

"Naval Police!" Mustafa laughed and pointed at the men in uniform as they drank coffee and watched pedestrians cross the street. "Waiting for the flood!"

"There is no war in Ramallah," I said.

He nodded, still looking at the Naval Police. "They carry machine guns only for show. People here watch the news about Jerusalem and Al-Aqsa like foreigners watch the news. They have their own lives—big buildings, big cars, big companies."

"Ramallah is our capital," I joked.

He chuckled. "Capital of my shoes! Jerusalem is our only capital."

The rain continued, and men and women in suits and skirts strolled past us, jumping to avoid the muddy rivulets. They hurried toward tall buildings with shiny flags on the roofs. From up there, they say, on a clear day, if you're lucky, you can see the Mediterranean.

One of those buildings had an expensive restaurant. Nuha had mentioned it once to my mother. Everyday salad—tomato, cucumber, and parsley—cost sixty shekels, without tax and tip. Life in Ramallah could be very expensive. In Jerusalem too, but if you were poor in Jerusalem, you would always find a neighbour or a family member to take care of you. In Ramallah, I had been told, it was every man for himself.

Glancing up and down the road, I thought, *What if I run into Nuha?* Images from our past together poked me in the stomach: When she asked me about school, gave me advice about girls, told me things I didn't know about Aunt Sarah—their life as students at Birzeit University, how they cooked together and smoked nargileh in the evenings. Then I remembered the time they took me to a demonstration along Salaheddin Street. The police had blocked the roads, and the three of us had to hide at a clothing store, inside a fitting room. This was years ago.

Now I wished I could meet Nuha again on this potholed sidewalk. I wanted to lay my head in her lap and ask her to come back.

Mustafa nudged me. A white compact car was flashing its headlights. The driver, his mouth and nose wrapped in a keffiyeh, wound down his window and pointed to the next corner. He drove slowly, head rotating in all directions. We chased after him, water dripping from our garbage-bag ponchos. He stopped at the turn of the road and reached out the passenger window. Mustafa slipped an envelope out from under his shirt and threw it on the passenger seat. The driver nodded and sped down a side road.

Mustafa and I stood still. "Khalas. We're done," he said.

The rain had stopped, and I took off my poncho.

Walking into a warm and dry coffee shop, we forgot to scrape the mud off our wet shoes. The owner was upset. He told us to sit in one of the corners. Mustafa ordered tea and nargileh, and I got sahlab. The moment my lips touched the thick layer of cinnamon on top of the hot drink, my head lit up.

"I thought we were supposed to have a meeting," I said.

Looking out the window, Mustafa said, "We just did. Now we only need to wait. Inshallah, they give me what I want." He extended his hand for my phone.

"What do you want now?" I said, guarding the phone with both hands. "I know I promised not to ask questions, but can you explain what just happened?"

"I will." He grinned, holding his arm out. "Your phone, please."

I handed it over.

"The service in Ramallah is killing me!" he said, swiping the screen right and left.

"What was in the envelope? Money?"

He said nothing. Then he gave me my phone back. "Here!"

"Here what?" I looked at the screen. "You're joking. Tell me you're joking."

He shifted in his chair, and it screeched. "This time I'm serious. What did you expect?"

"Not this! I don't want this!"

"There is no other way."

"There is. There is!" I shouted.

One of the coffee boys told us to keep it down or he would kick us out.

"It goes against what I stand for," I whispered.

"Listen to yourself! What do you stand for? The Palestinian Authority and its policemen, directing traffic instead of fighting? You stand for selling out?"

"Listen," I said, flipping the phone on its face as people passed our table. "I agree with you in principle."

"*In principle!* For Allah and His prophets' sake, stop using words from Al Jazeera."

He sat an arm's length away, yet it felt as though he was moving toward a place where I couldn't follow him.

"We can always do what we used to," I said.

His fingers curled as though holding a spray can. "I'm done with kids' stuff."

"It's not kids' stuff."

"Aziz, if you want to back out, tell me now."

I lifted the phone, pulled it closer, inspecting the bits and pieces of what looked like a gun, or a cross between a handgun and a machine gun. It had a name: Carlo.

"Don't make me regret I showed it to you," he said calmly. "We've been talking about Hassan for months. All we do is talk, talk, talk."

"Listen," I said. "You need to be honest with me. Did Yousef have anything to do with this?"

He shook his head. "It's all my idea."

"What about Abu-Hassan? Does he know about this?"

"Forget about Abu-Hassan. He's behind us now."

"Behind us?"

"Yes, behind us. He showed us the way, like the people I met in jail showed me the way. Now you and me have our own path. You understand?"

My chest was burning. "I'm more confused than ever."

He put his hand on mine and whispered, "When you're confused or upset, do like I do, and think about our martyr friend."

"I think about him all the time," I said.

"Think about him this way," he said, spreading his arms wide. "Three in this world; three in Paradise!"

The Carlo was still on the screen, and he gave it another look.

"Are you disappointed because it's not the real thing? It's second-hand, but it works. They told me it works. They swore on it."

March 15

Mustafa didn't call. The Carlo people did.

I didn't answer. I knew it was them because I had saved their number under a fake name. I brought the screen close to my face and waited. What would I do if they called again?

Uri came to check on me. I was holding a pitcher of steaming milk. Inside the pitcher bubbles expanded and collided.

"Move it, Aziz," he said.

I finished the orders quickly and ran to the bathroom. I sat on the toilet for two or twenty minutes. I called Mustafa. His phone rang and rang, and my heart pounded and pounded.

He texted: *Meet me at Mahmoud's shop.*

I told Marwan I was sick and ran out. Before long, I was walking through the Qattanin Market, trying to find Mahmoud's shop in the hundred shops and stalls crammed with children's toys and scarves and T-shirts and candy. It was late afternoon, and most shops were closed or half-closed. Strolling through the dark market, I looked for T-shirts and leather wallets and scarves, things Mahmoud had told me he sold.

Then I saw Mustafa. He stood under a faint light bulb that dangled above his shaved head. He was emptying a wobbly wooden stall, bringing all the clothing and souvenirs and toys inside a little hole in the wall. He saw me and said nothing, then he went in and started folding things and shoving them onto tight metal racks. He was alone.

"You work with Mahmoud?" I asked him.

"He offered to help until I find a job," he said, stretching his arms to align the stacked shirts and scarves according to their print and size.

I leaned over the counter. "The Carlo people called," I said.

He looked right and left, then whispered, "Not here!"

"Where then?"

He grabbed me by the arm and walked me outside. "Later," he said. "We'll talk later."

Evening

The call to the Maghreb prayer sounded, and "Allahu Akbar" came from nowhere and everywhere. I walked to Al-Aqsa and sat outside, under a tall tree across from the mosque's widest door. Holy lights came from the Dome of the Rock, and I sat up and hung my cap on my knee. Holding my breath, I raised my thumb, extended my index finger, and moved it repeatedly, imagining a target.

On a slab of stone, I lay flat. I looked up, and a hundred pine cones dangled above like a chandelier. A breeze blew over my nose and pine needles pricked my face from above.

This is it, I told myself.

SPRING 2016

23

March 18

My grandfather died. On the first day of mourning, the women of the family sat on his bedroom floor, tears rolling down their swollen cheeks. My cousins and I served coffee and baklava. My aunts glanced up at us as we hurried past the half-open door.

"He could not live to see them grow and become men," they said. "He could not live to see their children."

I set the kettle by my mother's feet and was getting ready to leave when she called me to her side. She blew her nose, kissed me, then whispered to the woman beside her, "This is my son."

A small fern grew in the corridor. I sat beneath it and watched the news on my phone—*Latest clashes in Jerusalem and the West Bank: Four dead, twenty wounded*. Names and faces appeared, then disappeared across a medley of pictures. I had a feeling I was on that list. Was I wounded? Was I dead? Then I remembered a movie about a young man who watched himself die. He followed his body as it was wrapped and placed in a box, dumped into a hole, then talked about on the news. He could not believe it at first, but in the end, when nobody paid attention to his cries, he knew he was dead.

The men squatted on low stools across the living room. I went to sit down with them. They swallowed coffee in small amounts, like cough syrup, and read verses from the Quran. At the end of the evening, they started telling jokes and stories. It is good for the soul of the dead, they said. It stretches the borders of the grave.

"One night, a long time ago, when light bulbs and streetlights had not been invented," Uncle Fahmi began, "this handsome cousin of ours finished work in the fields and went down the Kidron Valley. He felt like something was trailing him. He turned but saw nothing. The thing was hiding behind a rock wall. He would turn, and the thing would hide—turn and hide, turn and hide—until a jinn woman jumped out and started walking toward him. She walked with a limp and had long hair, bushy eyebrows, and nails like blades. She shrieked, 'Habibi! Habibi!' Her shrill voice struck his wits, and like a rogue wheel, he ran down the valley. He made it to his house but could not speak for a month, could not go to the fields or use his hands. He had to leave the country. He never came back!"

"He did come back, maybe twenty years ago," my father corrected him. "It was a short visit. He was very old. He died in America, far from his family. God bless his soul."

Then it was my father's turn, and he told a joke about a Palestinian man describing heaven to his children. "So this simple man goes, 'Heaven is something else. It has mountains of spinach and lettuce, forests of zaatar and mallow and Akkoub, pillars of mint and sage, olives and figs in brimming sacks, just waiting to be hauled off by donkeys standing as far as the eye can see.'"

People laughed until they lost their breath, but a man with a grey beard said their laughter was inappropriate. "God prepared for the believers what no eye could see and no heart could perceive."

My father narrowed his eyes. "Praise the prophet, Hajj. We're only joking."

The man with the grey beard pursed his lips and looked right and left at the others.

My father stared at him. "Our religion is wise and gentle," he told him. "The holy Quran says, 'It is by mercy from Allah that you were gentle with them. Had you been rude, hard-hearted, they would have dispersed from around you.' God almighty has said the truth."

The line of people sitting across from my father nodded, and a well-dressed man said, "Mashallah. Abu-Aziz knows his Quran." Then he said, "It was like heaven when we were kids. We would go down to the spring of Silwan, forage cheeseweed and watercress and eat figs and hunt birds with our slingshots. Abu-Aziz was a great hunter!"

My uncle nodded. "He sure was!"

The man went on, "He and Abdullah competed for the highest number of bulbuls and swallows they could gather in their wooden cages. You remember Abdullah?"

My father shrugged.

"Sheikh Abdullah—Abu-Hassan?" the man said. "He owns a grocery shop in the Musrara."

"One shop?" Uncle Fahmi interjected. "You mean, at least five. The smallest is the size of this house. You know, my brother and Abu-Hassan would never invite me to their games when I was a boy."

My father wriggled on his stool and then roared, "Fahmi! Stop your silly talk! Let's read some Quran and remember our dead."

That night, my parents stayed over to keep my grandmother company, and I went home with my uncle. It was about one in the morning when we drove home, and he honked and swore at children crossing the potholed, half-paved roads without paying attention. "Why are they even awake?" he kept saying.

When my uncle parked his car, I asked, "Is it true that Abu-Hassan and my father were old friends? I find it hard to believe."

"Why is it hard to believe?"

"They're so different."

"Why are you asking me about this?" he said. "Talk to your father."

March 20

On the third and last day of mourning, I left my grandparents' house and trekked through the hills of Silwan. The sun was in the middle of the sky as I climbed up one of the steep hills and walked across a field of poppies. I trod gently so as not to harm the soft flowers. I sat on a cluster of rocks and tried to smell the poppies. They were odourless, or maybe I was losing my senses. I pushed my nose inside one, and a bug tickled me and flew away. The bug was smaller than a bee, so small, almost invisible.

I carried a long stick and went up to the peak of a massive cave. With the stick, I poked rusty cans of pickles and sardines and flung them into the mouth of the cave, which carried almond trees on its shoulders. The almonds were in bloom, and I walked around them; like in Mecca at the pilgrimage, I circled seven times and caressed the blossoms.

I was late for work. When I walked through the kitchen door, Marwan said not to worry because Uri was on vacation.

"Who cares?" I said.

"Tough boy!" he said, flexing his muscles. "What's up with Mustafa?" he asked.

"All good," I said. "Why are you asking?"

He put his hand on my shoulder. "He came home late last night, and the night before. I thought he was with you."

"He was with Yousef," I said without thinking.

I had not heard from Mustafa for almost a week. I had called and texted him a few times. No answer. But Marwan didn't need to know this.

He interrupted my thoughts. "Is my brother working for him at the bakery?"

"No, he's not," I said.

I went to see Dafna, who was standing in the doorway.

"I need to go home," I said.

"Why?"

"My grandfather died."

Her eyes widened, and she gave me a hug. My arms stiffened as she patted me on the back.

"When my grandfather died, I walked through the Ein Karem forest," she said.

I was about to tell her about my walk on top of the mighty cave, but it felt like another conversation. Moving from forests to cans of pickles and fish bones would be a slap in the face to good manners.

"I'll walk through the souk," I said. "It relaxes me."

"Is today market day?" she asked.

"Every day is market day," I said. "Friday is market day, Saturday is market day, Sunday, Monday, Tuesday ..."

We were blocking the doorway when she leaned closer and said, "Can I come with you?"

"With me? Where?"

"The Old City."

She waved to Olga, and they talked for a couple of minutes. Then she went to the washroom and changed her clothes. Before I knew it, we were walking out of the café together. At first I walked behind her, but then she told me to hurry because she had to be back before six. I looked at the time. It was five.

"Do we have enough time?" she asked me.

I nodded. "Most shops close by six. People do their shopping early and then go home."

Going down the many flights of stairs to the Old City, her baggy pants swished and whistled. Browsing her phone, she turned and looked up at the path we had taken, and then at our downhill trajectory. She could not make sense of the map on her phone.

"Your phone won't help you," I said.

"This will be my first time," she said with a confused look.

"Don't worry, you can ask me whatever you like," I said. "You should see the tourists start shaking when it gets dark because they're afraid to ask questions. They forget there are thousands of people who live here, and they will always help."

"Like you?"

"Of course. Everybody does. But we laugh at them first, then we help them."

"You should not laugh at them," she said, making a face.

She brushed against embroidered dresses hanging from the ceiling and cushions left out to soak in the passing sun. She ran her fingers over figurines of camels and shepherds. She bent down to kiss the camels' humps. We went into a store in the Christian Quarter, and she bought a gift for her mother, with whom she lived near Ein Karem. Her parents were divorced. Her father lived in Haifa with his new wife. She did not get him a gift.

Standing by a juice shop, I looked around, then at my phone. She looked at hers. "You're right, this Google map is useless," she said.

"I am your map," I said, and she grinned, her dimples showing then fading away.

When the smell of coffee with cardamom wafted from one of the stores, she went in. The coffee grinder revved behind the shopkeeper as his eyes rested on Dafna's wondering face. He asked what kind of coffee she wanted. One kilo—ground, half blond, half dark—I told him in Arabic, and then I told her in English it was the way my grandfather used to say coffee should be.

The shopkeeper handed me the coffee. Dafna leaned over the package of ground coffee, sniffed it, and her eyelids fluttered shut for a moment. "I came here because of this," she whispered. "Because someone promised to get me coffee and then forgot."

The shopkeeper asked where she was from.

"Holland," I said quickly, and pulled her outside.

"Why Holland?" she asked as we went down Al Wad Street.

"For your safety," I said, carrying her purse. "I mean, pickpockets and the like."

Barricade railings covered the two sides of the road, and the gridded windows above our heads were silent. We were standing metres away from the police barrier at the Chain Gate outside Al-Aqsa and I thought it could be dangerous for her to speak Hebrew. At this hour, as tourists and villagers made their way out of the walls, the neighbours might think she was a settler, or the police might think I had kidnapped her.

"You don't make any sense," she said, shaking her head.

I nodded. "Most of the time I don't."

It was already six o'clock. "You're going to be late."

"It's okay," she said. "I'm hungry now."

I bought her green plums. We sprinkled salt on them and ate until our stomachs ached.

"I want to eat something that's not green," she said, hand resting on her belly.

We walked into a restaurant with an arched ceiling and angular stones jutting like crooked teeth. She lingered under the ceiling fan, her eyes drifting across the rough walls, while I stared at the corner table. She went to the toilet, and I took the seat in the corner. Glancing up, I saw the blades of the ceiling fan were full of dust and spiderwebs. The greasy tabletop had hearts and arrows scratched into it. Everything was the same as last summer when the three of us had come here after exams. Hassan had ordered Perrier for his stomach, and we gave him a hard time. Mustafa announced he was not coming back to school and told us that our days of living off hummus were over, that after every paycheque, he would invite us for shawarma and ice cream.

The waiter took our orders: two hummus plates, falafel, and mint tea. He came back with our food, and Dafna's mouth opened in disbelief. It was the first time we had sat face-to-face, looking at one another closely, talking, smiling, winking.

"Hey, listen," she said. "Tomorrow we're having a party for Olga's birthday."

"Are you inviting me?"

"Of course."

"Who else is coming?"

She started counting on her fingers. "You, Marwan, Itzik, the girls."

"And the kitchen boys?"

She scoffed. "The kitchen boys don't drink."

"I don't drink."

"But you're cool," she said with a smile that could melt stone.

I shifted in my chair and looked up at the ceiling. I stopped watching her smile and kicking the table's legs. She had said I was cool. She said it in English, the language we both chose when we wanted to say things that were harder to say in her language or mine. The word did not sound right: *cool*. It sounded like *clown*.

She played with her disposable cup, squeezing it and then biting the rim. She tapped the table along with the Egyptian pop music that was playing and said she recognized the singer. She tried to come up with a name. I could not help her. She threw around Arabic names and then asked about the meaning of my name. Hers meant laurel trees, a symbol of victory, she said.

"Mine means glory," I said, and she laughed.

"You don't look so glorious," she said. She wriggled in her shoes and hummed with every bite. "Madhim, sababa."

Local customers were watching us, and then a hand landed on my back.

"What are you doing here?"

I turned. "Mustafa?" I said it loudly, as though yelling at myself.

He glared at Dafna. "This is Mustafa," I told her. "Marwan's brother."

She seemed not to remember him. She smiled faintly. He didn't smile back. My legs shook under the table, and I told her I had to talk to Mustafa in private. I got up and stood with him in a corner where she could not see us.

He clutched my wrist. "Why is she here? Are you taking her on a tour?"

"I met her by accident," I said. "I was coming home from work and bumped into her in the Christian Quarter. I swear to Allah."

It was a lie, a very small lie, though, because I had been on my way home and had not intended to take her on a tour. He didn't believe me. I could see it in his eyes.

I grabbed his arm gently. "She's eating. She will be gone soon."

He whispered, "Get her out of here and then come back. I'll wait."

"Tamam, no problem," I said.

When I went back to our table, Dafna said nothing about my conversation with Mustafa and ate slowly, enjoying the food. I wondered if she had understood anything. She must have thought we were just two good friends talking loudly.

Mustafa sat at the table behind us and ordered hummus and Coca-Cola. His plastic chair screeched against the tiled floor. It was difficult to talk now.

I pulled out my phone. "My mother texted. I have to go."

"I'm not finished," she said, pointing at her plate and the remaining falafel balls.

Outside, two Haredi men trotted down toward the Jewish Quarter.

"Go to the kotel," I said, pointing toward the Western Wall.

"I'm not religious," she said, laughing uncertainly.

In my head, I was running. I could not tell where to, or when I was going to stop. She grabbed her purse, and we got up. We strode out of the restaurant and up the road toward the juice shop where we had stopped earlier.

Showing her the path toward Jaffa Gate, I took her hand and squeezed it in mine. She grinned. My fingers stroked hers, and hers mine, and fire went through us.

"Until next time," I said.

She tapped me on the chest. "Go see your mother!"

24

March 20
Evening

When I got back to the restaurant it was closing—the tables wiped, the chairs stacked, and the kitchen boys clean and tidy, swapping jokes.

But Mustafa was still eating. "Sit down," he said.

I sat down as the sounds of incantations descended from the minarets.

Mustafa signalled with his chin toward the alleyway. "Is she gone?"

"No," I said, patting my front pocket, "she's here."

I was trying to make him laugh, to add humour to what had happened minutes earlier. Minutes that had felt like hours. He chuckled and scanned me from top to bottom. "I would expect Marwan to do something like this, but you? You of all people?"

"What?"

"What are you doing with Dafna? What, in Allah's name, are you doing?"

"I told you I ran into her by accident."

"How did you end up here, in this restaurant?"

"She was lost and—"

"Hungry?" He snorted. "So romantic! Did you also take her to Al-Aqsa? Did you take pictures with her in front of the Dome?"

He talked as if I owed him something. His bossy voice reminded me of Yousef's, and he folded his arms like Yousef.

"None of your business," I said.

"It *is* my business. You're my friend." He wrinkled his nose. "You should be ashamed of yourself, bringing her here. Have you no respect for anything? Have you forgotten our friend?"

"You're talking nonsense," I said, looking up at the dusty ceiling fan. It remained silent, but the blades and the screws still looked as though they were about to fall on our heads. I looked back at him. "I didn't forget," I said.

He drummed his fingers on the dirty table. "You know what? I'm regretting now that I took you to Ramallah, that I told you about my plan. I'm regretting everything. How stupid of me. How stupid!"

"Praise the prophet," I said, leaning closer.

"I don't want to praise the prophet," he said. Then, shaking his head, he repented. "'Our Lord, we have believed, so forgive us and have mercy upon us.'"

He had finished his hummus and Coca-Cola, but a shred of pita was left on his plate, soaked in olive oil.

"I want us to take an oath now," he said calmly. "An oath for our martyr friend."

"What kind of oath?"

"Don't be silly now," he said, rolling and squeezing the Coca-Cola bottle cap between his fingers. "We already talked about this."

"Let's not rush," I whispered. "Let's do an Istikhara prayer to seek Allah's guidance. And then we'll decide."

"I already did my prayer," he said with a cold smile. He was looking at me as if daring me to speak.

"Let me do mine," I said.

March 21

My mother tried to wake me a few times, but I pretended to be in a coma.

An hour later, I brought her a cup of coffee. I sat beside her as she sipped and watched me from the corner of her eye.

"Do you like your coffee?" I asked her. "Lots of foam."

"I don't care for foam."

"You always say a cup of coffee with no foam is for the drains."

She shrugged. "Foam is foam, and coffee is coffee."

I laughed. "The house of Aziz has a new philosopher."

"Laugh as much as you like. It is written in the Quran: 'As for the scum, it is cast away as jetsam, but that which profits people remains on the earth.' I thought you knew your Quran."

"Foam is not scum."

"Same thing. Water and scum. Coffee and foam. Look at you, you're wasting your time and missing school. Do you want to keep washing dishes all your life?"

"I also make coffee. People come from all over Jerusalem to drink my coffee."

"So you want to keep making coffee all your life?"

"No."

"Then focus on what is real—your life, your future."

I turned to face her. "I'll figure things out."

"No, you won't. Your head is in the clouds."

Holding her phone in her hand, she showed me the screen. "Look what your aunt has sent me."

"Pictures? I don't care for her pictures."

"She sent me links."

"For what?"

"Canadian high schools that accept exchange students from all over the world. There are many scholarships for international students."

"And?"

She handed me her phone. "Take a look. This school is close to her address. You could live with her, in her apartment downtown. Look what she sent me—"

Without looking, I pushed the phone back at her. "Are you sending me away?" I stood up and paced across the living room. "You can't be serious."

She folded her legs on the sofa. "I'm doing this for your future. For you to have a normal life. You're my only son. Do you think it's easy for me to do this? You're only fifteen!"

"Almost sixteen."

"And soon, inshallah, you'll make us proud and get into a good university. But if you keep on going your way, you'll be another Mustafa."

My knees bumped against the coffee table, nearly spilling her coffee on the carpet. "You're talking about my friend! Don't belittle him. He left school because he had to leave school. End of story."

"He left because he's not smart enough," she said.

"He's smart. Very smart. He needed to help his father."

"Excuses, excuses."

"I'm working to help my father."

She shook her head. "That's what I'm saying. I don't want you to help your father. He doesn't need help."

"He does. He complains all the time."

She shook her head again. "Your father would complain even if you threw a million shekels in his lap."

"Don't worry so much," I told her. "You always worry and make me nervous."

"I *am* worried," she said. "I want you to get into the best schools. Two of your cousins are studying medicine abroad. They are not smarter than you. You're throwing your life away."

"I'm not throwing anything away."

"If you keep hanging out with Mustafa and Yousef, you will be throwing your life away. I don't want you to hang out with them."

Throwing my cup into the sink, I glanced at her as she sat, steadily drinking her coffee, looking through the back door at the neighbours' roofs and all the yellow and white things under the bright sun. Her quiet eyes irritated me, and I kicked the refrigerator.

She underestimated me. She did not know that I had made a pact with God. That the flat stones of the sanctuary and the lights and the inscriptions on the blue walls of the Dome of the Rock were my witnesses. She did not know that everything—absolutely everything—was driving me toward this point.

"You know what? I will not be another Mustafa. My dreams are bigger. My dream is to be another Hassan. That is my future."

25

March 21
Night

The clock hit eleven, and we closed the café to celebrate Olga's birthday. When Olga walked in wearing a pink skirt, the boys whistled, and the girls clapped and released balloons. Marwan twirled with Olga, holding a stack of cups as though it was a burning torch. Dafna laid a blue tarp on the floor. I was setting out plates and forks when she said, "It's a party! You're supposed to smile."

When I told her I was still sad about my grandfather, she dropped everything and we went to smoke in the back. Crouching down against the short wall that separated us from the street, she folded her arms and pursed her lips, waiting. I gave her the only cigarette in my pack. I was not going to smoke. The act of smoking was boring me. Everything was boring me: standing, sitting, sleeping, eating, drinking, watching people smoke and stand and sit and eat and drink.

"We'll share it," she said.

I did not respond, and she went on, "Were you close to him, your grandfather?"

I nodded.

"What did he teach you?"

"To be kind and gentle," I said.

"Mine taught me to be kind and strong," she said, flexing her arms.

Combining strength and kindness is hard work, I thought. I tried to remember if I had ever met a strong person who was not an imbecile.

She rubbed her knees and gave me the rest of the cigarette. "What do you do besides washing dishes and making good coffee?"

"I read. I run. Then I read some more."

"Where do you run?"

"In the Old City," I said. "And outside the walls."

"I run in the forest near our apartment building," she said. "I need an open space."

She thought I ran for fun. She didn't need to know I only ran when I was being chased.

"I don't need an open space. A crowded alleyway will do."

"You're funny," she said, tapping me on the thigh. "I want to teach you all the Hebrew words and see if you stay funny."

She slid her arm through mine, and we went back inside.

Marwan saw us and pulled me into a corner. "She likes you," he said, slapping me on the head. "Do something about it."

"She likes everybody," I said.

"You need to have the heart of a lion," he said, gnashing his teeth, and then he went to mix drinks behind the counter. I followed him to see where he had hidden the bottles. Bending over a small cooler, he said, "What do you fancy, Lionheart?"

"Coke," I said, and he took his time banging out the ice cubes and pouring the drink.

Itzik joined us and started showing Marwan photos of his new car—a Corvette. He had gotten it from a good friend who had finished his army service and was going on a tour across India.

"'You have to take it,' my friend told me, so I did!" Itzik said.

"Good for you, brother," Marwan said. "One day, I'll get one of those." He mixed liquids in a metal cup, dipped in his little finger, and sucked it. Then Olga leaned over and sucked his little finger. "Yum," she said, and he gnashed his teeth at her.

We sang "Happy Birthday" in English, Hebrew, and Arabic. Olga clapped, then blew out the two candles in the shape of 16, and we whistled.

We gathered on the floor to eat and Dafna sat beside me. "I don't like when girls sit separately," she said. Looking at my empty cup, she asked if I wanted more, and I nodded. She ran to the cooler, and Itzik took her spot. When she returned with my Coke, she had to squeeze between us. I gulped my drink quickly, avoiding the jokes and winks between her and Itzik. His silver chain danced around his neck as they flirted. They went to smoke outside and did not ask me to join them.

Weird music drifted across the café as I gazed at Olga's skirt. It was short, and she shifted her position endlessly. Then she spilled her drink on her legs. Marwan ran his hand along the hem of her short skirt, then onto her wet thigh. Then they left.

I looked around: My workmates talked in speedy Hebrew, and I couldn't understand a thing, or maybe I did but was becoming dumb because a thousand ideas swam in my head. Long story short, nobody wanted to talk to me, and I decided to leave.

On my way to the toilet, I saw Marwan's silhouette out back. He was leaning against the dumpster, looking up at the sky. I went to talk to him, but then I froze at the slippery doorstep. He was not alone. He stood with his legs apart, and his hands held Olga's head. She was on her knees.

I panicked and rushed to the toilet. I stood in front of the mirror and splashed my face. It was red and oily. I straightened my shirt and pounded the sink.

Flicking open the buttons of my shirt, I impersonated Itzik, "Corvette. Corvette. Corvette. Tour India. Tour Europe. Tour Old City. Tour Silwan. Tour my ass. He can go fuck himself, his Corvette, and his army!"

I laughed at my twisted face in the mirror. It took me a few seconds to recognize myself. I was warm and light-headed. Breathing into my hand, I smelled something strange: alcohol? I had only drunk Coke, and I had watched Marwan carefully as he poured the can into the plastic cup. But Dafna had brought me the second cup. I started to shake.

There was a knock on the door. "Hold on," I said.

When I opened the door, it was her. "It's you!" I said, and she giggled.

Her arm and waist created a loophole with the door frame. I buttoned my shirt and took one step in her direction. I waited for her to back up, but she didn't budge, and I stared at her belly button and the chain with a butterfly until my head spun. Then I found myself pushed against the sink. She closed the door and leaned into me. She threw her arm around my neck, and I could smell alcohol and Itzik's tobacco on her breath.

"Close your eyes," she said.

My fingers brushed against her belly chain. My nose ran along the line between her neck and her shoulder. She kissed me on the cheek.

I pulled away. "Do you want to dance?" I said.

A strange thing to say when you're shaking, or maybe not.

She blew hot air onto my neck. I had to get out. I pushed her aside and ran away. I jumped over the short wall behind the dumpster and ran toward King David Street. It was a foggy night, so foggy that the streetlights were Cyclops and the bulbs on the city walls were fireflies. Looking down, I could not locate my shoes, as though I were wading into a mysterious river that separated the two sides of the city. Crossing the road, I hummed a tune to control my nerves. When I reached the other side, the air was heavy and buzzing with bugs and sirens.

March 22

It was early morning and I stayed awake, battling my desires. I was thirsty; I did not drink. I was hungry; I did not eat. Wrapping myself in a thick blanket, burying my head inside, I tried to fall asleep. It did not work. To match the beating of my heart, I drummed on the hollow wall separating my sofa from my parents' room. Then I flipped off the blanket and went to the bathroom.

My mother was awake. Her prayer dress caressed the corridor floor as I stood over the sink. We performed the dawn prayer together, and then I laid my head in her lap. She raised her hands and prayed for me. She asked God to take good care of my grandfather's soul and give my grandmother happier returns.

"Amen," I said.

"Amen," she said, and her voice cracked at the *a* and the *e*.

She ruffled my hair and said it was too long. Her face was tired but beautiful. The green beads of her eyes gave her the grace of a queen and the purity of a secluded lake. Her white prayer dress sent waves of comfort through my chest.

I looked up at the ceiling, searching for cracks to hide all my dark thoughts in. Then I remembered when I was a little boy and she would take me down into the tight cave under the Dome of the Rock and hide clumps of her soft hair inside the stone for God's angels to pull out, untangle, and translate inside the chambers of heaven. She would touch her belly and murmur prayers, asking for another child to be her companion and mine.

"I'm sorry," I told her.

"For what?"
"For everything."

Afternoon

I walked to Jaffa Road amid shouts and car horns until I reached the spot where Hassan had been killed. Squatting in the middle of the sidewalk, I pretended I was tying my shoelaces or searching for a lost coin. People walked past me—some meandered around my shoes; some hit me by accident; some hit me because they wanted to hit me.

I wanted his death to give me clues, the way encrusted swords in museums gave clues to wins and defeats. I was looking for a message other than his still picture on posters and banners. I was looking for a mental note from his last minutes on this earth.

Oh, Turner of the Hearts! Keep my heart firm. Oh, Turner of the Hearts! Keep my heart firm. Oh, Turner of the Hearts! Keep my heart firm.

I sat on the end of a bench where an old couple were eating. They faced one another, and a striped handkerchief lay between their wrinkled hands. Half a challah gleamed under the sun as he took a bite, and she took a bite. They smiled at one another, loosening and unravelling the loaf of bread as though undoing a girl's braided hair. They looked so happy with the small piece of bread, and I wondered if my parents would be that happy when I was in heaven.

I walked through the Mahane Yehuda Market, swivelling my head as people bumped against barrels of spices and fruits and vegetables. Customers' hands held tightly to oranges and avocados, threatening to squeeze them dry should they fail to get the price they wanted. Few young people walked by—early afternoons were for old people, who knew one another and only came here to chat, which happened all the time in the Old City. People talked and pretended to buy when all they wanted was to kill time.

The sight of spoiled food on the ground made me think of jellyfish. Lingering near a spice shop, I was suffocated by the smell. I covered my mouth with the back of my hand; then I emptied my stomach in front of one of the barrels. Passersby yelled at me. Without hearing a word from my mouth, they yelled.

I ran back to Jaffa Road, back to the same bench. It was empty now. I was about to call Mustafa, but then I changed my mind and looked at his social media. His most recent post said, *If we fall, we only fall on the corpses of our enemies.*

He must have heard back from the Carlo people.

I called him. The phone rang and rang. Finally, he answered. "Mustafa, what ... where?—"

"I'll come to your place."

"When?"

"This week."

He hung up, and I walked to work.

Evening

Dafna's face was stone, and her eyes no longer sought mine. It was for the best. She had put a spell on me. She had the nails and eyebrows of a jinn. But she was also an angel. I needed to steer away from the door of the devil and his shapeshifting ways. Besides, she must have been embarrassed she had kissed an Arab.

As I made coffee or washed dishes, her face and her voice interrupted the clarity of my mind. I burned with jealousy when Marwan or Itzik talked to her, laughed with her.

Marwan caught me thinking and pulled me outside to smoke. We stayed silent for a minute or two, puffing smoke into each other's faces.

Finally he said, "Give me the news, Lionheart."

"Don't call me Lionheart!"

"Okay. How did it go, hunter?"

I sighed.

"Your sigh could move mountains," he said, laughing loudly. "Listen, forget about her. She's only giving you blue balls. It hurts. You have to be careful with that kind of thing, especially you, a good Muslim. With all the dark matter inside your balls, you might never have babies."

"Dark matter?" I was about to laugh but held it inside me, not wanting to give him the pleasure of thinking he was funny at my expense.

"I'll take you somewhere tonight," he said. "I'll make you forget love and—"

"Who said anything about love?"

"Relax, sensitive soul! You want to have fun or not?"

"Not your kind of fun."

He shook his head. "My kind of fun is the only kind of fun. So tonight I'll pick you up. Take a shower, wear something nice. I know someone in Tel Aviv who will happily take care of you. Or we could go to Ramallah, if you prefer. Let's go to Ramallah."

I got up. "Praise the prophet, and let's get back to the kitchen."

He pulled me back. "We're going to Ramallah. Let's keep it local. Let me tell you a story. Once, I dated this girl from Ramallah—tall, long hair, magnificent breasts, the works. I used to sneak her through the checkpoints to Jerusalem. I took her once to the beach, and Aziz, I swear to Allah, I sucked on those nipples like a monkey. She was a woman, a real woman." He raised his cigarette above his head. "I wonder what happened to her—"

I threw my cigarette at him. "Stop! You disgust me!"

As I passed through the kitchen, Itzik was calling my name. He wanted me to clean the floor behind the coffee machine. "So much dirt and clutter," he said. "Dafna's not happy."

"I've been busy," I said.

"You don't look very busy," he said, rolling his eyes.

I snatched the broom from the corner and swept the floor. There was trash from Olga's party that nobody had bothered to clean: straws, silver glitter, and bottle caps. I threw everything in a garbage bag and mopped the floor until it shone like a mirror. Then I went outside and crouched down by the café's front door. It was past ten o'clock. Most businesses were closed, and the streetcar was throwing out more light than passengers.

Soon I overheard Dafna's voice. "Where's Aziz?"

I ignored her, but when she called my name again, I waved my arm.

"The floor is still dirty," she said, standing in the doorway. "It has not been cleaned properly."

"No problem," I said. "I'll clean it again."

"It doesn't look clean at all," she said again, but without looking at me. "You should not smoke by the entrance. Just because Uri's not here doesn't mean it's balagan!"

I threw my cigarette away and was about to get back to work when she stopped me. "Give me a cigarette," she said, tucking a strand of hair behind her ear. "Todah," she said, lighting her cigarette with a pink lighter.

"Ain baaya, no problem," I said, lowering my eyes.

She stepped out. "It's fine. Let's smoke by the corner."

"I've got to clean the floor," I said.

"It can wait," she said, crouching down.

We sat on the dirty ground, minding nothing except the hissing lights of our cigarettes and the gliding of the streetcar toward the west. I puffed and stole glances—one glance after another. I drank in every detail: her face, hair, silver earrings, yellow bracelet. Our thighs touched. So did our arms. We remained silent, but my heart pounded. I wondered if she could hear it. She was so close. I was sure she could hear every beat of my heart.

At the turn of the road, a pair of women soldiers leaned against a signpost and chatted loudly. They carried duffle bags and seemed to be on their way to somewhere or back from somewhere. Dafna waved them over. She went inside and brought them Coca-Cola, for free. They drank their Cokes and chatted with her, then tried to talk to me. When I spoke, they noticed my accent. They nodded and walked off.

"They're so cute," she said. "Don't you find them cute? The boots, the shirts, the large buttons, the way they walk, like they're models. Supermodels!"

"Maybe," I said.

She laughed. "Maybe, what?"

"They might look cute if they weren't wearing a uniform."

She slapped my arm. "You want them to be naked!"

That was not what I meant. But then I remembered my dreams of women soldiers. They came with false promises and the necessary shower at dawn.

She narrowed her eyes. She was waiting for me to explain myself. I looked over my shoulder. Itzik was arranging the tables and shutting off the lights.

"They carry weapons," I said.

"Of course they carry weapons," she said. "They have to protect themselves and the people on the streets."

"From what?"

"Are you serious?" she said, brushing dirt off her pants. "War and terrorists!"

My eyes were burning. I must have used too much bleach while cleaning the floor. The streetcar was approaching from the west, its headlights piercing the hazy night. The streetcar stopped at the station in front of us, and the soldiers lifted their duffle bags, adjusted their rifles, and hopped on.

"Will you wear it, the uniform?" I asked her.

"Ma hakesher?" she said. "What's that got to do with anything? My mother wore it, so did my father."

Her face turned grey and featureless. I pictured her at a well-guarded checkpoint, in a bulletproof vest, rifle slung over her shoulders, hair collected under a green beret, face sweating under the scorching sun.

"What about you? Are you going to wear it? Are you going to become a soldier?"

"Ma hakesher?" she repeated angrily.

"Ma hakesher?" I responded without thinking.

She went back inside, and I pursed my lips and stared at the sidewalk.

26

March 23

It was Purim week and people from the west side of the city wore costumes and cheerful makeup. They gathered around musicians in the street and bobbed their heads and watched strings vibrate and pipes sway and took pictures and shared them as though there was nothing else to watch and share in the entire universe. Some walked slowly, some fast and steady, with all the confidence in the world, as though nothing terrible could ever happen to them.

I carried a stack of clean dishes and approached the front window. The café was not busy, and in the contrast between the silence inside and the noise outside, I looked out and daydreamed. All the people in my life came together—Dafna was standing on the sidewalk and musicians played happy tunes. They tossed her a tambourine and she caught it with two fingers. She played a song the musicians knew. Pedestrians stopped what they were doing and watched and clapped. She danced barefoot, shaking her hips, holding her arms up to the seventh heaven. She looked my way, and the trees were green, and the sky was blue. Also on the sidewalk, Hassan held a newspaper and squinted at the headlines. Soldiers wearing boots with pointy teeth kicked him in the ankle. He did not turn. He had his own teeth on both ankles. Ustaz Salim wore round glasses, like Einstein. He took off his glasses, wiped them, and put them on again. He was speaking Russian to Olga, and they talked over each other and frowned and laughed. Nuha hugged her cat, Lolo, their faces glued to the window. With her paws, Lolo started knocking on the glass. She seemed upset, mewing and hissing. I waved at her to stop, and the dishes fell on the floor and shattered into dust.

Marwan came quickly and cleaned everything up. "Take a break," he said. "But not here. Go for a walk and come back."

The moment I stepped out of the café, my phone rang. It was Mustafa.

"Where are you?" I asked. "When are we going to meet?"

"Friday," he said.

March 25

I finished the Friday prayer and waited for Mustafa across from the bakery. He knew everybody. I also knew people, but while I preferred to keep to myself, he smiled and waved and talked and talked, again and again. Sometimes it was hard to wait for him to finish visiting, so I would leave him to it and we would meet up at the turn in the road. This time, I had to keep waiting.

Five or six lines were forming inside and outside the

bakery, and people cut in front of one another, hands waving cash. Abu-Yousef's head bent down toward the cash register and popped up like the head of a fat lizard. "Arabs and order do not mix!" he said.

It was a hot day, and women spread blankets and mattresses in the sun on balconies and roofs to burn off the sweat and piss and mildew. People with no roofs jammed bedsheets and mattresses into their doorways and window bars. A pair of cranky men hunched over a backgammon table, yelling combinations as the dice rolled. The newlywed neighbour from last month strutted past me, wearing red pyjamas and brown slippers. Water must not have touched his skin since his wedding night. He stank like a goat.

Mustafa walked out of the bakery with a large spinach pie and a disk of La Vache Qui Rit cheese. He offered me a piece, and I shrugged. He patted my stomach. "Do you have a bug?"

On the roof, we dangled our legs in the wind and people-watched.

"Did you do your Istikhara prayer?" he asked me.

"I didn't."

"Why?" he said, throwing away the rest of the pie.

"I wanted us to talk first," I said.

He looked at me but was not actually looking at me. A cloud of words hovered behind his eyes like mosquitoes in the middle of July.

"We need to hide," he finally said.

Shifting on the thin slab of concrete, I tried to stay calm. "Why do we need to hide? Did you get the call? Did they finally call you?"

"Let's not talk about the call now. First things first."

"No," I said loudly. "If we hide, we raise suspicion. First, tell me, did the Carlo people call you?"

He squeezed my wrist. "Stop talking about the call. You'll get us caught if you keep babbling like that. Captain Moussa was in my neighbourhood this morning. He talked to my father, told him I needed to behave or else. The balls on that motherfucker!"

"He didn't come here," I said.

"You got your head in the sand. He was here. He got Yousef."

"Again? What did he have on him? Did Yousef know about the plan? Tell me the truth!"

"Your voice. Lower your voice!"

I grabbed a pebble and flung it down. "What should we do? Tell me now."

He swallowed the cheese triangles, tossed the container behind him, and lay on his stomach. "We are at war! Soon, we'll be ripping out stones and pavement to build trenches and barricades." He stretched his arms toward the new settlement. He mimicked a handgun, a machine gun, then an RPG. "This roof is a perfect place for an RPG launcher," he said.

"Stop that," I said. "So you're not going to get us caught talking like this?"

"Like what?"

"Like your RPG shit!"

He sat up and threw his arm over my shoulder. "Aziz, you need to open your mind and use your imagination. Have you heard the saying: 'Dreams of yesterday are facts of today, and dreams of today are facts of tomorrow'?"

"Dreams are dreams and facts are facts," I said.

"Look at Gaza. You remember what the fighters did in Gaza in 2014? They shot rockets at Tel Aviv. Rockets, Aziz! Who would have dreamed of that?"

We looked down at the shops as they reopened, unstacking what had been stacked, unwrapping what had been wrapped. Friday is a full week packed into one day—busy before the Muslim prayer; silent during the prayer; busy until sundown. Then the Jewish prayers and, afterward, the silence of Shabbat.

"You understand me?" he said, and I nodded. "Stop nodding when you don't understand."

"Leave me alone," I said, and he laughed loudly.

He grabbed my empty wooden crate and put it in his lap. He positioned the crate to look like a Quran stand, imitating Abu-Hassan. "Let me tell you my plan. It was in front of us the entire time, and we missed it!"

"What are you talking about?"

"The café."

"What about it?"

"We'll attack the café." He nudged me. "Your café. Marwan's café. Whatever you call it."

"Where I work?"

"Yes." He leaned closer. "And it has to be done very soon."

"What are we going to do?"

"Smash the doors and windows, burn it to the ground, boom, boom, boom, whatever."

"And the people inside?"

"What about them?"

"What's going to happen to them?"

"You're becoming soft now?"

"You don't spit in the well you drink from."

He snickered. "Of course you do. If it's poisoned, you spit and spit and spit."

"Your brother works there. I work there."

"I'll make sure he's somewhere else. And you? You know where you will be. Right?" He nudged me again.

I tucked my head between my knees.

"I need to use your cistern," he said.

"Why?"

"I'll tell you later."

"Why don't you use your place?" I said.

"Yours is safer."

"It's not."

"Nobody comes to your cistern. Nobody uses it. I know it. Remember when we used to piss inside it, competing for who could make the loudest noise?"

"You're joking at a time like this?" I yelled at him. "Can you be serious for one second?"

"As you like," he said, nodding. "But I do want to use your cistern."

"It's not safe," I said. "Think of another place. Anywhere. I don't care."

"You don't care? What do you mean?"

"I mean what I said." I looked down at nothing in particular.

I took a deep breath. He did the same.

"Are you having doubts?" Veins throbbed across his shaved head. "Answer me," he demanded. "I just asked you, are you having doubts?"

I felt like I was falling, like I had felt after my last bad dream of a faceless man. I folded my arms and looked up at a rusty antenna. The pigeons were gone. They must have been hiding, worried about too much sun.

"I'm not sure," I said, still looking up at the antenna.

"About what? Our cause? Our fight? Our dignity? Our freedom? Our slaughtered friend? You're not sure about what exactly? About not being a coward, a traitor?"

"You're calling me a traitor now?"

"I'm asking you if you're having second thoughts."

I sat up. "I told you I'm not sure."

"About what exactly?" he said again loudly.

"Not sure if I want to die!"

He looked away, and I looked away. We stayed like that for minutes, or hours. Time diverges and gets lost when people look away.

My mother's voice came from below. "I made tea," she said.

She stood in front of a full clothesline, wringing one last piece to the last drop, and then throwing it on the sagging line. We climbed down to the terrace, and she greeted Mustafa.

"Long time no see! My son visits you all the time, but you never think about visiting us?"

"I don't want to bother you," he said, looking down at the wet ground.

"Don't say that. You're a second son to me. God bless your mother's soul."

She went inside and returned with the teakettle and three glasses. We sat in the sun.

"I remember this kettle," Mustafa said with a boyish laugh. "It's at least ten years old."

She nodded and stared at her fingers. "I bought two. One I kept, and one I gave to your mother."

We drank our tea, and she lifted the tray and pointed at the solar heater. "Can you help us? You're a handy boy, unlike Aziz. We don't have hot water, and when it comes, it's nothing but lukewarm drops."

I folded my arms for fear I might hurt myself, the solar heater, the pipes, my own mother. She was not supposed to be here.

"Forget the solar heater," I told her, embarrassed. "I'll buy you a new water heater. I'll pay for the electricity. I already told you."

"Why waste money?" Mustafa said. He glanced down at the broken glass cover and the shards on the ground. He crawled on the ground, checking the pipes, the joints, and the rusty valves. "You need a new cover to contain the heat, but the piping seems fine." He stood up and said, "I know a good plumber. I'll give his number to Aziz."

She clapped like a schoolgirl. "You are a godsend! Thank you! Aziz takes cold showers every morning. He's always sick."

I pulled Mustafa's arm. "Let's go."

My mother went on, "When I hear the shower in the early morning, I feel bad. But I tell myself, 'He's going to a cold country. He might as well toughen up for the Canadian weather.'"

I was dumbfounded. "Don't listen to her," I told him. "She's just joking."

Mustafa ran to the edge of the terrace and climbed down to the lower courtyard.

"Wait!" I shouted. But he was gone.

Night

When my father got home, I was getting ready for bed. After locking the door, he sat on the opposite sofa. He looked tired.

"She's not here," I said. "Check with the neighbours."

"I'm not looking for your mother. How are you doing?"

"You came all the way from work to ask me this?"

He was sweating, and I started to feel bad. I brought him a towel, and he wiped the sweat off his face and the back of his neck.

"Is this about my aunt?" I asked him. "Because if it is, I'm not going. You can go, fly away, enjoy yourselves, migrate like birds across the oceans, but don't sell the house. You must promise you'll never sell. I'm staying. I'll keep the house. I'll protect it."

He locked the back door and turned on the television. "Watch the news with me," he said.

I was not ready for another lecture about politics, but I kept my mouth shut.

He switched to the Israeli channel. There was live coverage from the city centre. The news ticker said *Terrorist attack.*

Another ticker said *One terrorist killed in a car-ramming attack.*

The area on the screen looked familiar. Police cars had blocked the side roads and ambulances were on the scene. The reporter said only one car was involved in the attack.

My father pointed at the screen. "Your friend Mustafa. He was killed inside that car."

I saw no cars, only floating colours. "How do you know?"

"I passed through Bab Hutta," he mumbled. "I saw his father standing in the alleyway. The police were surrounding his house. I couldn't talk to him. The neighbours told me."

"How did they know? How did they know that quickly?"

He shook his head and muted the television. I scanned the living room as though seeing it for the first time, then I got up. Walking toward the kitchen, I staggered like a sheep tangled in a wire. I started opening cupboards and drawers, hurling every fork and spoon and ladle on the floor.

My father grabbed me around the waist. "Settle down!"

I pulled out a knife.

He seized my arm and yelled, "In the name of Allah, settle down!" He kept holding me.

"Let go!" I shrieked.

"Calm down," my father whispered. "Calm down."

He pulled me back to the living room as the news ticker rolled from left to right and from right to left. In all languages, the lie repeated itself over and over.

"It's not him," I said, knocking my head against the back door. "He's up there on the roof. Let me show you. Open the door. Please open the door. Let's go and check on him. He's waiting for me. Can't you hear his voice? He's laughing at you. He's teasing you like he always does. Listen to him. Listen!"

27

March 27

The soldiers pounded on the roof. They kicked the doors, barged in, and rolled me out of bed. They tied my hands and pushed me against the wall. They rummaged through the kitchen, spreading silverware and dry sage and mint on the ground. Their dog walked over the dry leaves and sniffed the rugs.

Captain Moussa was the size of Uncle Fahmi but with glasses and a gun at his waist. He showed my father a piece of paper and signalled to the soldiers to drag me out to the terrace. As they did, I tripped over the doorstep. My mother groaned. Outside, the soldiers scanned the satellite dish, cables, solar heater, and steel bars projecting from the floor waiting for the possibility of an added room or an accidental death.

Captain Moussa shook the branches of the lemon tree and shone his flashlight down below. "What's down there?" he asked my father.

"A table and a cistern."

"Show me the cistern," he said.

They dragged me down the stairs, opened the cistern, and let the dog sniff the old water. A soldier pointed his flashlight inside. The dog nodded like a human, sat to the side, and whimpered.

"There is nothing in the cistern," my father said. "We don't use it."

Captain Moussa ignored him and pointed his flashlight inside the hole filled with a soup of dead pigeons, piss, and lemon leaves.

My father moved closer to where the flashlights beamed. The soldiers pushed him back and away.

"Don't touch me," he said. "Don't you dare touch me."

My hands were tied behind my back, but my eyes roved, probing the light and the whimpering dog by the mouth of the cistern. Mustafa could not have had enough time to hide anything in the cistern. Or could he? Could he?

Two soldiers remained by the cistern, while others rushed me back up the stairs and into the messed-up kitchen.

Captain Moussa asked, "Where is the storage room?"

"We don't have a storage room," my father told him.

"Then where do you store your things?"

"Inside the house," I mumbled, and he glared at me.

"Keep your mouth shut, boy," the captain said in fluent Arabic. "You had the chance to talk to me before. Remember?"

He ordered a new search. Standing by the kitchen counter, he admired a set of knives my father had purchased recently. One of them struck his fancy. His fingers walked over the handle, and he laid the sharp edge against his palm.

"Do you know why we're here?" he said. "Mustafa was your friend, right?"

I coughed, and my mother ran to get water. The captain snatched the glass from her hand. "See how your mother is worried about you? Is this how you reward her?"

She cursed at him, and he snorted. Turning his back and waving his other hand, he said, "He's coming with us."

My mother ran to the closet and returned with a pair of jeans and my heaviest sweatshirt. Sitting on the floor in front of me, she pulled my pyjamas down my skinny legs in front of everyone: the captain, the dog, the soldiers, my father.

"I'll do it!" I said, trying to keep my balance. "Leave it to me. I'll do it."

I stumbled and fell on the rucked-up carpet. My mother dressed me quickly, as though she knew my body better than I did.

They blindfolded me, marched me out, and threw me by the side of the road. My back landed on someone's leg, and I shifted to the nearest wall. My ears pricked up at the breath of neighbours and their shoes rubbing against pebbles. I was not the only one who had been arrested. I was not alone.

Later

The blindfold was tight, and I twitched as they dragged me up the road. One soldier did not like my twitching and kicked me in the leg. I groaned. He pinned me to the ground and the rest of them piled on my chest. When they stood me up, my jaw was stiff and I tasted salt and metal around the corners of my mouth.

At the police station, they uncovered my eyes and walked me through a labyrinth of corridors. It was a slow walk, each step an echo that stretched to the Dead Sea and back. They threw me in a cell with a dirty mattress and a pit latrine with dry dung. They locked the metal door and left me alone. Sweat ran down my face and behind my ears, and I needed to use the latrine, but the hole in the ground scared me more than my burning bladder.

Shortly after, I was taken to a clean room with a desk, a monitor, a high chair behind the desk, and two small chairs on the other side of the desk. I was left for some time, until Captain Moussa walked in. He had changed into a new shirt. He sat behind the desk and leaned back until the chair squeaked. He opened a black briefcase, pulled out a laptop and a file, and hummed a song that had an Arabic tune.

"Do you know this song?" he asked me.

I shook my head. He hummed it again, squinting at me as though it would help prime my ear to pick up the frequency of his song.

"Forget it," he said, arms up in frustration.

He handed me a wet napkin. "Clean your face."

I moved the napkin across my face as he pulled out a sandwich from a bag and started to eat. "Fantastic," he said, biting through the crunchy bread and shifting his eyes between the monitor and the sandwich filling. "Not as good as Abu Shukri's, of course. You're so lucky to live in the Old City. If I lived there—oh God, if I lived there—I would eat falafel five times a day."

Setting aside the rest of his sandwich, he got up and sat in the chair opposite me. Pulling my chair closer, he said, "This is better."

Electricity moved through me.

"Relax," he said, offering me a cigarette. "Smoke?"

"No."

"Very good, Aziz. Smoking is a very bad habit. You know, I have a kid your age. He smokes, not in front of me, but I know all about it. I swear to Allah, he's making my life difficult. I want to take him to the theatre, the library, a football game, but he says no. Whatever I suggest, he says, 'No, no, no.' He prefers to stay home, hopping from screen to screen. It annoys me, but it's his life, not mine. Do you do anything with your father?"

"Sometimes."

"Good. What else do you do? Like last Friday, what did you do?"

"Friday? I went to Al-Aqsa. And then I went home."

"Nice! Who did you see there?"

"People."

"People, huh? Very funny, Aziz," he said, rolling his tongue inside his mouth. "That's fine. I want you to relax and talk to me like you're talking to your father."

He opened a bag of chips. He shoved his fingers inside, and the bag wrapped around his hand like a glove. The chips crunched under his teeth, and I winced.

He pushed the bag in my face. "Want some?"

"No, thank you," I said, and he raised his eyebrows at my manners. That's what he wanted me to do—first to thank him, then to be his snitch. I blinked a few times. I needed to wake up.

"Look," he said, slouching over. "If you answer my questions, if you tell me the truth, I'll let you go home. I promise. You'll be in your mother's arms in no time, with a kiss on the cheek."

I was not going to give him the pleasure of my nod this time.

He chucked the empty chip bag at a basket in the corner. He missed, walked over, picked up the bag, and dumped it into the basket. He came back and sat in front of me.

"Okay, I don't have all day. Tell me, who did you see on Friday?"

"Marwan, a friend of mine."

"What did you talk about?"

"Normal things."

"Normal things?" He kicked me in the shin twice, and I swallowed a scream.

"About work."

"Where was Mustafa? Was he with you? Did you talk about work with Mustafa? I thought you were friends. I thought he was your only friend."

He was. I looked down at my laceless shoes. My eyes got lost in the holes.

"I have many friends," I said.

"Like who? Mahmoud and Yousef? Do you like them? I like Mahmoud. He's a funny guy. We know each other very well. Of course, we have our disagreements, but he's a good guy."

He walked back to his desk, pulled out a cigarette, and gave it to me. "You have a long day ahead of you," he said.

I craved that cigarette. When I stuck it in my mouth,

my upper lip tingled. I avoided looking into the captain's eyes as he lit the cigarette for me. Smoke filled the room, and my eyes blinked. He turned the monitor around and pointed to the screen. "Let's talk about Mustafa now. Okay?"

He pushed a button and crossed his arms. "I'm going to show you something, and I want you to focus. Good?"

I stared at his big hands.

"Look here, stupid! Here!" he said, slapping my head and twisting it to face the screen.

There was a big intersection, cars and buses driving in all directions. A digital clock at the top of the screen counted the minutes and seconds. Time moved slowly as the number of people huddling at the bus stop increased. The bus approached as pedestrians carrying light and heavy things moved toward the curb. Then a small white car cruised alongside the bus, cut it off, and swerved in front of it. The car coasted toward the sidewalk. Some people ran away, and some were struck down, their limbs turning and twisting. Two soldiers glided into view and started shooting. The video was silent, but the BANG BANG BANG sounded in my head. The scene ended with an armed civilian opening the car door and shooting until the driver's body was slumped on the asphalt.

Captain Moussa's voice cut through the noise in my head. "He got what he deserved, no?"

On the screen, half the body was showing. It was wearing the same jeans and the same black shirt as Mustafa from our last day together.

"Did he tell you about his plan? He was your friend. Did he tell you?"

I shrugged and looked down.

Directing my head toward the screen again, he said, "Tell me the truth, what did he tell you?"

The bus stop looked familiar. It was not too far from the café. Had he lost his way? Had he changed his plan?

"He said he was going to the Malcha Mall," I told the captain.

"Malcha Mall? What did he want to do in the mall?"

"See a movie."

"What?"

"He was going to the movies," I repeated, my lie bouncing in my lap.

"Your friend drove a hundred klicks to kill Jews," he said, pointing his finger at my head. "He timed it around sundown. Your piece-of-shit friend wanted to kill people who were going to eat and pray." He pointed at the screen. "We finished him before he could harm more people. And you come here to tell me he went to see a movie!"

He made a phone call, and two guards with big muscles came in and dragged me back to the cell. They told me to stand still and covered my head with a bag that smelled like animal shit. The stench flowed through my nostrils, past my clenched teeth, and into my throat. I couldn't breathe.

Later

Captain Moussa came into the cell with a guard and pulled the bag off my head. I gasped for air.

"What do you want from me?" I panted.

"Good question. See? Now you're asking good questions."

He wiped my face with a damp cloth and gave me a bottle of water.

Leaning close, he said, "Your friend's corpse is on a slab in Abu Kabir now. He is not with us anymore. Gone! Thank God nobody got killed. Several wounded, in the hospital, but they will go on with their lives. You have a future ahead of you. I don't want you to lie for Mustafa. Lying is wrong, right?"

I sniffled, nodding.

"I want you to tell me something that could save many lives. I know Mustafa had a gun. We wouldn't want it to get into the wrong hands, right?"

He kicked me in the back of my legs. Only now did I feel the pain of standing for so long.

"Where did he hide the gun?"

"I don't know."

"You do know."

"I don't."

He showed me a set of pictures. Two of them had me carrying something in my hand; behind me, someone held a flag and another carried a bottle, about to throw it.

"Not me," I said instantly.

"Your friends told on you." He pointed to the boys in the picture. "They were here for only one night, but they told me everything and I let them go. They were smart. Are you smart, Aziz? Do you understand the consequences for this kind of thing, Aziz?"

"I swear I did not—"

He slapped me on the neck. "Don't swear!"

He drank from his bottle of water and then shuffled another set of pictures.

"You see these? You can't say that you don't know these places." He pointed at my house and Mustafa's. "I could tip them over like this"—he flicked his finger—"and they would vanish, abracadabra. You see, Aziz, like this. That would be your punishment."

There were other pictures of my house and Mustafa's, razed to the ground, with arrows pointing at each blank space. "I can make it real," he said. "Like this—" he flicked my ear this time. The pain streamed through my neck and down to my knees.

"Where did Mustafa hide his gun? Tell me."

He hit me on the knees. I wanted to collapse, but the guard held me still.

"Do you mean the toy gun?" I said.

"Toy gun?"

"Mustafa used to have a toy gun," I said, looking at my fingers as they made the gun sign. "It looked real. You might find it if you look under his bed or in his drawers."

Captain Moussa put the bag back over my head.

Later

I was moved to a different cell with speakers mounted on high shelves. They were silent at first, but then drums rolled with the sounds of forest bugs and frogs and monkeys. Then orange lights came on, and freezing air. I couldn't sleep. I had strange dreams. I was a thick-skinned orange. My long, sharp nails scraped and burrowed into my flesh. My wounds festered and bubbled like bone soup. Ants came out of every hole and crack. Wherever I looked, I found them. I gasped for air, teeth chattering.

I could not tell how many days and nights I had been here, but it must have been plenty. I smelled bad. I smelled of my own piss, my own sweat, and their spit. Staring at the door, I waited for someone to stop the freezing air and the orange light. I stared at the door as though I were practising magic on the knob and hinges. When the guard brought me tuna and corn and soggy bread, I did not eat them. Then one night, he came and saw the food uneaten. He said I would become famished soon, and then he would give me no food.

At night, the guards brought new prisoners to the jail. Sometimes screams came from the corridor, though I could not hear footsteps or doors opening and closing. I would stay quiet and slap the slices of bread on my ears. I thought I was going crazy. So I kept talking to myself. Because when you talk to yourself, you are in control. Yousef had told me this once. I wondered what had happened to him, and if he was my neighbour here. Now it would be good to have him around. I would not see his eyes winking or his mouth twisting. Now I would not mind his jokes. On the contrary, I would laugh until it hurt. I would laugh because Mustafa would have laughed. I crept closer to the wall and shouted, "Yousef, are you there? Yousef, can you hear me?"

The guards came and said they would beat me until the whole compound could hear my cries. So I sat in the corner by the latrine pit and confided to imaginary friends. We told stories and confessed our sins and fed each other soggy bread with holy stamps, similar to those carved on jewellery and old caves—the name of Allah and the tears of the Virgin Mary. My imaginary friends were all dead; they had been dead for so long. And because they had been dead for so long, they were always nice, always smiling.

One Morning

Captain Moussa squatted by my trembling knees.

"I'm going to let you go," he said, holding up my phone and pointing to the screen. "Here's my number. We'll be in touch. If you don't call, I will. I'll climb up your stairs and grab you by the neck. I want us to be friends. You understand?"

The stench of his last meal filled the air between us, and I held my breath and stared at the hair in his nostrils and the greasy spots on his glasses.

"Whatever you say," I said. "Whatever you say."

28

April 1

It was about seven in the morning when the guards let me out, pushing me into the parking lot where my father and my uncle were waiting. A ray of sunlight fell on my forearm as we went down our alley. Children half my height kicked a deflated ball and screamed as it bounced, soaring high, hitting the tips of shuttered windows. When it came down, their faces beamed. I glanced at the alley's walls, and my face was nowhere to be found. No posters. No banners.

Standing in the doorway, looking over my shoulder, I saw nobody was coming to lift me off the ground and parade me like a hero.

I am the martyr's friend!, I was about to shout. *I am the martyr's friend.*

I froze, guilty for being alive.

The house was full. It stank of tobacco and body odour from visitors who had come to see the blue crescent under my left eye. My father and uncle talked about the lawyer they had hired. He was able to get me out without extra fines or house arrest. My uncle had paid the full amount.

My mother had cooked rice and lamb and seven kinds of vegetables. I couldn't eat. Every mouthful tasted like jail. Every ten or fifteen minutes, my mother took me in her arms, leaving tears on my neck. She would not let anyone get near me. I was hers, hers only, as though she wanted me to trek back into her womb, when water and blood were the same thing, and she knew everything.

April 2

The clock hit three in the morning, and I was awake. Then it was four. I flipped and turned, my shadow swaying slowly like a caravan of camels braving endless dunes. My eyes were shut, but my ears were awake. I could hear the cracking of knuckles, the creaking of beds, the wet feet, the dry feet, arms stretched, arms folded, arms folded at the back of the head, and arms folded over the belly.

I walked to the kitchen sink and poured water into a bowl. I pushed my mouth into the bowl like an animal. I shuffled to the bathroom and sat on the toilet. White wax stretched across the sink and the bathtub. Electricity must have been lost the night before. I peeled the wax off, sniffed it, and flicked it to the floor. I washed my head, face, and arms.

When I came out, my father was standing in the corridor.

"Take a shower if you want," he said.

"I'm cold."

"I fixed the water heater," he said. "Take a shower and rest."

His eyes were narrowed but without menace. They wanted to tell me something.

"I can't rest," I told him.

I left for Al-Aqsa. The mosque felt like a bright tunnel, and I shuffled my feet into the deep end toward a row of copies of the Quran laid against marble walls. My head felt heavy, and I sat down, opened the Quran, and started reading. But then the rubbing and rustling of pages made me think of the papers they had forced me to sign before letting me go. Something about not causing trouble. I had hesitated. "The lawyer said nothing about signing papers," I told Captain Moussa, and he only said, "Sign."

I dozed off on the warm and fuzzy carpet. Shortly after, a voice nudged me awake. "Son, don't leave the Quran on the floor."

I was not going to wake up because of a stranger, but the man's voice was kind and gentle. "Keep the Quran close to your chest," he said.

It was Mustafa's father. He bent down and rested his hand on my stiff arm. "I did not know it was you," he said. "Forgive me, son. Sorrow blinds the eyes."

"Please forgive me, uncle," I said, getting up. I hugged him and then kissed his hand.

There was a moment of no talking, and then he said, "All God's work."

He cleared his throat. "They took me to the police station, then they took Marwan. For three days, they interrogated us. We hired a lawyer. He told us there was no reason to worry."

He said nothing about why not to worry or what not to worry about—bringing back Mustafa's body or keeping their new roof or both?

The details must have been heavy on his tongue. I had seen evidence, the video footage. I was going to ask him if he had seen it. If Captain Moussa had forced him to look into the screen and see his son getting shot, then slumping out of the car's driver's seat. My head was pounding. It could all still be a lie. Why would I believe Captain Moussa and not believe Mustafa's father?

He looked frail. I asked him about his health.

"'Only in remembrance of Allah do hearts find rest,'" he said. His eyes were closed as he told me to take care of myself.

I left him but kept turning to look back until the mihrab was too far and he was too small to see. I had a feeling I was missing something without knowing what exactly, like when you study for an exam, and the exam comes, and you squeeze your brains with every period and comma. With every line, you feel there are lost words. Those words only come later, after you have left the exam room.

Going home, I passed by the Quran School. I laid my hand on the door's metal handle. It was closed, and I stood at the threshold like a pool of muddy water. I remembered our gatherings outside the low wooden door. I could hear Mustafa's laughter, and I could feel his hand slapping my head when I had said something borrowed from a book. He would phrase my words as his own, and they would rhyme. They would always rhyme. I remembered Abu-Hassan's pride, looking at all of us gathered around him, exchanging nods and smiles and whispers.

Captain Moussa had not asked me about him—not a single question. He didn't need information about him, or maybe he didn't need him, or maybe they worked together.

The last thought was crazy, but it lingered heavily in my head. It made me angry, and I ran through the alleyways as though I was being chased. I ran and I bumped into shopkeepers and peasant women and peddlers and mothers and their little boys and girls and queues and tour guides and glossy maps. The tourists were back. They were not afraid anymore. They streamed through the Old City, following all the stages of pain that Christ had endured. Mustafa's dream had been to teach them how to walk without maps, to dump everything and get lost, to let the landmarks find them, let the alleyways and the mess in the alleyways find them.

At the bakery, Abu-Yousef was on his own, rubbing his knees and glancing up at the neighbour's window, trying to find a good angle on her bedroom mirror. I blocked his view.

"Aziz, is that you?" he said.

I gave him a quick nod, walked in, and opened the refrigerator. I did not know what to buy. I did not even know why I had come to the bakery. When the cold gust blew across my face, I grabbed a carton of milk and shut the door.

"They let you out so fast," he said, walking over to the register. "Five days?"

"What do you mean?"

"My son is still inside."

"Is he?"

"Yes, he is a tiger."

Pounding on the counter with my carton of milk, I shouted, "Your son is a tiger! Not one tiger—a tribe of tigers, a jungle. Your son is a jungle."

Evening

Aunt Sarah called. When I said, "Salam alaikum, Aunt Sarah," she burst into tears. I could not see her tears, but there were sniffles travelling across land and water.

"What did they do to you?" she asked me.

"Nothing."

"It can't be nothing."

"Jail is for men."

"You are a boy!" she screamed into my ear.

I put her on speaker and told her that the jasmine tree she had planted years before was alive, that the almonds near my grandparents' house were very green.

"Is it still winter in Canada?" I asked her.

"Yes, still winter."

"Is it true that when snow melts, Canadians fall into rivers and freeze to death?"

She let out a breath of laughter. "Who told you that?"

"It was on the news the other day."

"Don't believe everything on the news," she said. "Spring is a shy season, but it comes. As your grandfather used to say, 'No season shies away from its time.'"

April 3

On social media, there was a page called "Mustafa the Martyr."

I wanted to post my own stories on that page, but I also wanted nothing to do with it. And because of that, I felt weak and ashamed.

In one photo, he was making shotokan moves at a karate lesson. He seemed focused, stepping forward, flexing, preparing to turn. He loved karate—punches, kicks, blocks, open-hand strikes. I had been in the same class, though never shared the same feelings. I was ten; he was eleven. Behind him in the photo was a line of ten boys and one dot in the middle. That was me—the dot in the middle.

In another photo, he wore a military uniform and held a gun. Under the photo, it said: *Our hero-martyr Mustafa Salman, who carried out the heroic car-ramming attack in Jerusalem.*

"Lies!" I yelled.

April 4

At school, my classmates asked if I knew the martyr.

"Yes, the martyr was my friend," I said. They nodded, and some patted me on the shoulder.

I went to Mustafa's house and stood by the door for five long minutes, expecting him to whistle from above or yell, "Come up, you fool! Why are you standing down there?"

I turned the knob. The door was open. I climbed upstairs and paced across the unfinished roof. I kicked damaged bricks, loose wires, and construction tools.

Where is the gun?

Why didn't you use it? Did it jam on you?

Shovelling through a pile of gravel, I dug deep, shifting most of it onto a new pile, then sifting through it for sharp, pointy objects. Lifting bag after bag of cement, I found Mustafa's slingshot. It was fastened with duct tape to the bottom bag. I tore off the tape, accidentally ripping a hole in the bag, which released grey powder over my arms and shoes.

A number of cavities spread across the newly constructed ceiling. Some as big as a rat hole, some as tiny as dice. Would he have hidden a gun inside the new concrete, down one of those rat holes originally made for wiring?

Clamping my fingers around the smooth olive wood, I remembered how proud the slingshot had made him. Holding it in my hand, I scanned a pair of wooden planks leaning against the would-be bathroom. I lifted a stone and placed it in the leather pouch. I shot at the plank to the right, and then at the one to the left. I shot at a lizard trying to find a home in the holes and cavities. I imagined a hundred lizards that might know where a gun was hidden. I shot at all of them.

I stomped the ground with every shot. "Talk to me!" I said. "Tell me your secret!"

A ladder was lying down beside the cement bags. I dragged it and was about to climb it to search through the ceiling cavities when I heard something downstairs. I dropped the ladder and tiptoed alongside the pile of gravel; then, hiding the slingshot under my shirt, I jumped over the stone wall shared with the neighbours.

I hopped onto the next roof and the next and the next.

Night

I was lying on the sofa when Marwan called and said we should meet at work.

"I thought they would have fired me," I told him.

"You were on vacation. Just tell them you were on vacation."

The word *vacation* stayed with me all night. Five-day vacation, all-inclusive: memory excursions, yoga positions with drums, lookouts, exotic air and light. Abu-Yousef might be right. I had been released too early, too easily. No wonder my face was not glued onto the walls. I deserved no glory. I deserved no kindness.

I sat up and searched for the number Captain Moussa had saved in my phone—a toll-free number with instructions written underneath—when to dial and what to say after. Simple words, big font. He must be waiting for my call, and he might not wait long. If I failed to call, he might call me, or come up the stairs, and then things would get more complicated—I would spend the rest of my life in prison and my family would lose the house.

Just like his son, Abu-Yousef was a big mouth. What if he told people I was a collaborator? What if he convinced everybody that I had told on Yousef and others? Who would people believe: the elder of the neighbourhood, a shopkeeper from a household of shopkeepers, with a family tree as tall as the YMCA tower, or a boy from a nameless peasant family?

My name would be written on the walls, but below it, instead of *hero* or *martyr*, it would say *traitor*. Like Nuha, I could be kicked out of the neighbourhood, out of the city, out of life—shot in the back like they did with informers during the First Intifada.

I swiped the screen before I could accidentally dial the number. Pacing across the living room, I tried to recall the moment Captain Moussa had thought he could make me a snitch. When I took the cigarette? When I cried? When I paid attention to his monitor? When I signed the papers? When exactly? Did I make a deal? Did the lawyer make a deal on my behalf? When did the deal start, and when would it end?

New photos had popped up on the "Mustafa the Martyr" page. Again, he was holding a gun, the same gun. I hugged his slingshot.

Enough with your jokes, Mustafa. You think I'm a coward? You can stop now. I confess: I am a coward! May the cowards never sleep!

29

April 5

The sink at work was dry except for scattered drops of water, and the wide plughole was gleaming. I asked Marwan if they had replaced the old sink. He shook his head and went back to slicing onions. When the faucet let out a sudden drop, I jumped backward, almost hitting one of the kitchen boys.

Marwan rubbed his nose with the hand that held the knife. He looked in my direction, then quickly turned and started searching for something. "Get me the other knife!" he shouted at his assistant, who was panting behind him, trying to catch up. The assistant took his time, searching for the knife while dripping sweat over the cold roast beef and the cherry tomatoes.

"Donkey!" Marwan yelled at him. "You'll live and die a donkey!"

I went to look for Dafna. She was not in the dining area, but Olga said they needed help. Pulling up my sleeves, I cringed every time I heard Hebrew words. I left plenty of room in every cup for the hot liquid not to spill over, and as music played in the background, I let the faucets and steamers run their own music to mask everything.

At the first break, I asked Marwan if his family had heard anything from the police.

"We're in the dark," he said, propelling potato peels under a table. He wouldn't look me in the eye.

"Bastards," I said, and he pulled me aside and whispered in my ear, "Don't talk about this stuff here. They don't know. I don't want them to know."

I left him alone. His family had been harassed and interrogated. Who was I to cause him more pain?

I wanted the night to end. But Marwan had lied for me, so I had to play nice and get along. I had no energy for small talk, but I spread nods and smiles. Yet Olga and Itzik looked at me like they were meeting me for the first time, like they were meeting a difficult customer.

When it was eleven o'clock, I left through the back door. Dafna saw me and waved, her eyes full of words.

"How was your vacation?" she asked.

"Very good," I said in English.

"Did you forget your Hebrew?" she said softly.

"It's heavy on my tongue," I said.

She pursed her lips. She was being nice, and I was being a brute. I wanted to slip my hand into hers like I had done by the juice shop in the Old City. I craved the feel of her fingers and the look on her face as I said, "Until next time..."

Will there ever be a next time?

"Tell me, where did you go?" she said. She played with her yellow-and-brown bracelet, and I wanted to sneak in between the beads and take a nap, a long nap.

"To the north," I said. "We kayaked down the Dan River and fed the crocodiles."

She laughed loudly. Her laughter could melt dolomite. "Crocodiles! In the Dan?"

What would she do if I confessed that crocodiles had stopped living here a long time ago? What would she say if I told her about my time in jail? Would she be disappointed? Would she stop thinking of me as cool and calm and funny? Would she swear at my sad blood and tell me to find another café to make bubbles with the faucets and steamers?

"I want to quit," I said.

"How come? Do you want to work fewer hours?"

"I'm not feeling well."

"Take two days off," she said. "But come back."

April 6

My mother was not wearing black for the first time since my grandfather's passing.

"You look beautiful," I told her.

"Sadness is in the heart," she said.

She slipped fresh jasmine into a vase. The white petals leaned over the maqluba's caked rice, making the kitchen table look enticing, though the smells of jasmine and rice did not get along very well.

The three of us sat down. My father started to eat straight from the serving tray while my mother scooped rice and meat onto my plate and hers. A pile was forming on my plate, and I told her to stop. She said something about getting me back to normal. "You need more meat on your bones," she said.

"He needs more muscles," my father said.

I was not in the mood to talk about muscles.

"How's the maqluba?" she asked him with a hesitant smile.

He chewed quietly, his eyes dancing between the rice and his phone. Then, without warning, he howled and threw his spoon on the floor. He stuck out his tongue and stared at a small bone or a shard of glass between his fingers that he had pulled out of his mouth.

"It could have killed me," he said. "And this isn't the first time! Every time you get close to the stove something awful happens. You burn the food, or your fingers. Yesterday, the mujadara, the day before, the tajine, the day before that, you opened a can of tuna and left a dozen lemon seeds."

"My father died," she said quietly. Her hands shook, and she bent over to look at his plate. "It's only a small bone."

He threw it at her and made the cuckoo sign, twirling his finger beside his ear.

I got scared. She got scared. The rats behind the kitchen walls were also scared. My eyes lingered on his dancing hand, and I stopped eating. I was looking at a demon.

I got up, snatched his plate, held it high above his head, and then dropped it. The mix of rice and meat splashed all over his shirt.

"Don't talk to her that way," I said. "Show your wife some respect, or find another house. You're happy when you're with other people. Why don't you leave, live somewhere else? It'll be good for you, good for us. Good for everybody!"

I folded my arms and waited for him to get out.

His eyes were burning red, and he grabbed the vase off the table, poured the jasmine water on the scattered rice, and chased after me with the vase. I ran into my parents' room and locked the door behind me. He pushed the door, and I pushed back.

"I will kick you out of this house! You are not my son," he said. "You are a curse."

I heard my mother panting behind him. "Leave him alone. This is between you and me."

Their footsteps went back to the kitchen. I opened the door slightly and peeked out.

"Nuha told me everything," my mother said.

"She's lying," he said. "You doubt your husband and believe a woman like Nuha?"

"I didn't want to believe her. I told her she was imagining things."

"You should trust me."

"No!" she screamed. "You deserve no trust. I'm tired. I'm leaving you."

She walked into her room. When I tried to say something, she told me to leave her alone. She was crying and packing her clothes. The metal hangers clinked and clacked as she shoved things into a suitcase. When my father came in, she refused to talk. Standing in the doorway, he pleaded with her not to go. He looked at me with needy eyes. I folded my arms. I did not want her to leave, but his desperation gave me a strange satisfaction.

"Nothing happened," he said, chasing after her between the bedroom and the bathroom, between the bathroom and the kitchen.

"Keep telling yourself that," she said with a sneer.

"We should talk. We should not fight. It's not good for the family."

Her voice thundered. "You broke the family! You broke everything. I should have done this years ago—when you forbade me from working, when you became married to your phone, when you ignored your son and used his money to fool around with our neighbour. Shame on you, Omar! Shame. Your only son had to get a job to pay the bills because you were fucking around in Ramallah!"

"I made a mistake," he mumbled.

She zipped her suitcase shut. "You made many mistakes."

"Let's save the family," he said. "Let's save our marriage, even if we have to leave the city. This city is full of crooks. I swear to Allah I cannot stand it anymore." He followed her to the door. "If you leave, I'll kill myself."

"Maybe you should," she said, storming out with her suitcase.

April 7

The sun was barely out when I came home. I had stayed the night at my uncle's house. The smell of yesterday's meal lingered in the living room. I opened all the doors and windows. I sat at the kitchen table and called my mother. She did not answer. I called her several times. Nothing, not even a chance to leave her a voice mail.

I called my aunt in Canada. She was not excited to hear my voice. Even when I joked, she remained quiet.

"I have no good words to say," she told me. "Your father is a bully and a judgmental prick."

"He's been trying to fix things. He cried after my mother left," I said. "It's very hard for men to cry."

"Men can cry," she said. "They *should* cry."

"She has to come back."

"Your father is not nice to her. Why does she have to?"

I didn't want to say, "For me," and sound like a child. So I said, "I don't have time for this."

"What do you mean?" she said.

"I don't have time for this!" I was crying.

"What's wrong, habibi?"

"I have to go to school. I'm late."

"I'll see what I can do," she said.

30

April 8

After school I dropped my backpack at home and walked to work. I listened to nasheed that I had saved from my time at the Circle of Sincere Hearts. I had only kept it because Mustafa liked it. As I crossed the street, elbowing my way to Jaffa Road, my phone rang.

I answered. No sound on the other side, not a single breath.

I looked at the screen. No caller ID.

Metres away from the café, I received another call. This time, the line was open for a longer time.

I said, "Hello, salam, shalom."

Nothing.

I started to panic.

I huddled in a corner and began browsing my social media pages. There was one missed call, but with no ID. My heart was pounding. Going through old missed calls, I felt paralyzed.

Who could it be? I had deleted the Carlo people's

phone number long ago. Could it be them? Or Captain Moussa?

I browsed the news. Nothing new. Even the "Mustafa the Martyr" page was inactive. For the last twenty-four hours, it had been inactive. Something must have happened. My phone must be monitored, bugged to its tiniest screw.

But I knew nothing. I was nothing.

Afternoon

When I got to work Olga was inviting Marwan to the beach in Tel Aviv. He told her that he was busy. She tapped him on the arm and went back inside without looking at me.

I stood beside him. "Does she know?"

"What?"

"About me," I said. "My vacation."

"Nobody knows."

"Are you sure?"

"Relax!" He raised his arm. "Get to work and stop wasting my time."

"Wasting your time? We always smoke. What's changed?"

He did not answer.

"So they don't know about Mustafa? Are you happy that nobody knows?"

"Yes," he said. "It's better that way."

I took a deep breath. "Maybe you should tell them."

He signalled toward the door. "Maybe you should mind your own business."

"He's your brother," I said loudly. "I can't believe you didn't tell them about your brother."

He pushed me against the dumpster. "I said, mind your own business!"

"Let's talk somewhere else."

"I don't want to talk. And if you want to keep this job, keep your mouth shut."

"Why are you talking to me this way?" I said, feeling hurt.

"What way?"

"Like you don't know me."

"*Do* I know you?"

"You only know them. You only know how to please them."

Marwan seized me by the wrist and pulled me to the corner. "Listen, I'll tell you something, and it will be the last thing I say about this: Right from the start, when I asked you if my brother was in trouble, what did you say? 'It's all good, Marwan! No problem, Marwan.' We could have stopped it, asshole! Why didn't you say something?"

His question fell on my head like a hammer. I could only say, "But I didn't know—"

"Shut up and listen. The night Mustafa died, he took my car. He said he was looking for work. I knew he was lying. I asked him if he needed money, and he said, 'I need no more money. Be good, brother.' I didn't get mad, even though he was preaching to me. The night before, when he threw a glass of water at me because I was drunk, I did not react. He was my little brother. He wanted me to wake up. I might never wake up, but he will always be my little brother."

I rested my hand on his forearm as he continued.

"My father has taught me that there are things better left hidden. Life will always come at us with things we fail to understand or explain. That's why, from now on, I will wait for my brother's body to be released. I will wait, and then I will bury him. And after I bury him, I'll ask Allah for His mercy and forgiveness."

April 14

My father woke me up with a cup of coffee. He asked about my exams and I told him not to worry.

"You can stop working at the café," he said. "We have enough money."

"Inshallah," I said. I knew he didn't have money. His car was worn-out and battered, and the two packs of cigarettes he smoked daily demanded their own salary.

"Inshallah, yes, or inshallah, no?" he asked me.

"I can do both," I said. "Work and study."

"How did you get so stubborn?"

"I inherited your genes," I told him, trying to make him laugh.

"You mean your mother's," he said.

I tidied up the house and cleaned out the refrigerator, got rid of the mouldy labneh and rotten mortadella. I had zaatar and an old tomato for my lunch. I grabbed the oil jar and dribbled some on a slice of stale bread. I thought of my grandfather's fine face and his strong hands during the olive harvest. While hunting for the fallen olives under rocks, between the thorns, my fingers would bleed, getting stuck in the wrong places. He would nod and say, "The harder it is, the more it's worth."

Slicing the old tomato, I cut the tip of my finger. Blood streamed out and trickled over the counter, the floor, and the stove. I cleaned up, and then, throwing the stained cloth in the sink, I remembered my mother's warning: "This knife needs stable hands."

Standing in the doorway, I called her. She answered. "Come home," I said.

"Inshallah," she said.

"When?"

"I don't know."

"How come?"

"I don't know," she said. "Why don't you come over? Your grandmother misses you."

Afternoon

People appeared and then disappeared through Damascus Gate. I drank Red Bull, which was warm and tasted like urine. I was about to throw the can away, but then I saw soldiers standing by the garbage bin. They watched me, and I watched them. They had guns and cameras, but I had the advantage of knowing the inside of my own head.

But that did not mean they could not frighten me. Because the unknown calls kept coming. Mornings during school and evenings at work. It was either Captain Moussa, looking for the missing gun, or the Carlo people, looking for money. Mustafa must have owed them. And now they were chasing me. Maybe. Maybe not. I was going crazy, and nobody was going to help me.

I was placing the Red Bull between my feet when I saw

Ustaz Salim. He was climbing up the steep stone stairs on his way to Sultan Suleiman Street. He tried to take large strides with his new cane. His hair had gone white and his shoulders bowed.

I ran to him. "Ustaz Salim, do you remember me?"

"Who are you?"

"Aziz from the Rashidiya School. From your physics class. I sat—"

"I remember you. Didn't you sit by the window?"

I nodded.

"You're a curious one. It's good to be curious. Very good."

"How are you today?"

He smiled. "Today I am fine. Yesterday I was fine. Tomorrow, I don't know." His right hand trembled as it clasped the cane.

"Do you need help?" I said.

He shrugged. "Ten more steps and I will be just fine." A crammed pushcart full of used furniture bumped down the stairs. "They should ban those carts from the Old City," he said. "Dangerous things. The boys who drive them are also dangerous, not paying attention to anyone except themselves." He paused, looking at the scattered clouds in the sky. "Nice day today."

"Where are you headed?" I asked.

"Taking the bus to the Hebrew University. They have a nice green area up the hill. I took you there before. Remember when I took your class to Givat Ram? Or maybe it was another class."

"Yes, I do," I said, remembering how we had disappointed him by not completing all the experiments he had organized for us with professors from the university. We had run away to sit on the open lawns and watch university girls stretching on the wet grass. Only Hassan and two other students from the whole class had remained in the lab that sunny day. Afterward, he decided to take only those three with him to the university and ignore the rest.

"You should study there," he murmured, his face drooping.

"Where?"

He murmured again, "Givat Ram."

I was having difficulty hearing him. "What did you say?"

The tip of his cane made scraping sounds as it scratched the edge of the stairs. "Why aren't you listening? The Hebrew University, I said. You don't listen. You only make noise."

He went up the stairs without looking over his shoulder. For someone who had been shot in the back, he didn't look so bad. He was still rude and unkind and ungrateful, but he was funny in his own way.

I went back to sit on the stairs of Damascus Gate. Captain Moussa knew where I lived. He could reach me anytime he wanted. He knew how I spent my days and how many sandwiches I ate. But I was not going to play his game. It was *his* game. Not mine. I would play my own game. I would be the message as well as the messenger.

I stopped into a phone shop and bought a new SIM card. Then I went into a public toilet and flushed my old SIM card with Captain Moussa's phone number. I stepped outside and smoked a cigarette. It burned in seconds, but it tasted good. It tasted very good.

I went to the bakery and stood in the doorway. The settlers were not buying bread today. *Very soon they will come*, I thought. *Very soon they will come. They will buy bread like they always do.*

An hour passed, and only the Haredim were rolling through the alley that afternoon. They whizzed by like projectiles. They wore fur until May. How could they take the heat wearing those coats?

Soon I lost my sense of time. I was intentionally not looking at my phone.

My hands were running over my front pockets when Abu-Yousef asked if I wanted to buy something or only fuck around. He was holding one long bagel. I felt sorry for the bagel. He was biting into it, enjoying it as though it was begging to be swallowed. He was over sixty, but his legs were strong like the trunk of an oak tree and his teeth solid and shining. He would live a long life. But not forever. Nobody lives forever. I gave him one of those looks I had learned from his son and told him I was there to fuck around. He whimpered like a dog and went back inside his bakery.

I held my backpack to my chest and looked up and down the road. It was getting dark, and I could not tell if the evening was approaching or another rainstorm was on its way. It had rained plenty this year. Never before had I noticed this much rain in Jerusalem. More rain means better olives and sweeter tomatoes, they say, though the price of tomatoes was through the roof. Nothing made sense anymore.

When my mother called, I was still standing by the bakery.

"Are you back?" I asked her.

"No," she said. "I just wanted to know if you were okay."

"I'm fine ... Bye."

"Wait," she said. "Are you eating well?"

"Yes, but I have a headache."

"Go home," she said.

I threw my backpack in the doorway, sat at the kitchen table, and rocked in the chair until it was about to break. The smell of fried liver drifted in from the neighbour's house. The smell of onions also drifted, but the smell of the lamb's organ was stronger. It made me nauseous. All sorts of meat were making me nauseous these days. All of them. Fear grew like nettles on the walls of my stomach.

The front door was half-open. I closed it and made sure the small window in the back door was closed. I crossed over to the kitchen, sat on the chair, and threw my arms on the table.

The clattering of dishes came from my neighbour's house, with the mother yelling at her children to sit and eat like the rest of God's creatures. She yelled many times until there was no sound. From the side of my eye, I looked down at the backpack where it lay on the rug. I pulled it over to my side and let it hug my leg. I petted the backpack like a good boy would pet his dog. I opened the zipper, slipped the knife out, and threw it in the sink.

31

April 22

It was Friday, but I just stood in the alleyway and watched people leave the mosque with their prayer rugs and their children and their beads hanging from their sweaty fingers. My uncle came home carrying a load of grocery bags. I helped him up the stairs, and he told me to come inside.

"Not hungry," I said.

"Everything okay?"

"Fine," I said, growling like a wolf, a hungry but wary wolf.

Wiping his forehead with a used napkin, he said, "Today is your birthday, isn't it?"

"Tomorrow," I said. He always remembered it, one day before or after, but he remembered it.

"It's nice to be sixteen, don't you think?"

I nodded.

"Next week," he said, "I'll take you to the Ministry of the Interior and we'll submit the application for your ID card."

"Don't worry. My father will do it for me."

"No discussion," he said. "I have time. I'll take you, and then we'll go eat something nice. You pick the restaurant!"

"Tamam," I said.

"Tamam," he said, squeezing my arm. "You are a man now."

Then, pointing his finger up the road, he said, "Last night some young men were arguing and one of them killed the other. People are fighting just to pass the time. I'm going to mediate between the families. Tell your father I'll be waiting for him so we can go together." His eyes pierced me. "You should come with us. It will be good for you."

"Why would it be good for me?"

"Mixing with the men," he said. "Better than staying home."

Then I asked him about the suitcase full of books in their guest room.

"Why do you ask?"

"I'm building my own library, and I need it," I said.

He got excited. "I'll give you a sturdy bookshelf," he said. "One of my friends is a carpenter."

As I was hauling the suitcase through his doorway, he said, "You know, these books belonged to your father. They're all yours now."

I DROPPED THE SUITCASE INSIDE the front door. My father was sitting at the far end of the living room, his face unshaven and a cigarette dangling from the corner of his mouth. He looked miserable.

"Is your mother back?" he said.

"No."

"Whose suitcase is that then?"

"Yours," I said.

He did not move a muscle. "Mine? Where did you find it?"

"My uncle's guest room. There are books inside."

"I see," he said. "I thought he threw them away." He turned on the television.

"They're your books," I said. "Do you want me to arrange them for you?"

Without looking at me, he stood up, flipped through the channels, then turned the TV off and dropped to the couch like a sack of flour.

"I was thinking, maybe we could have a bookshelf here," I said.

"Where?"

I pointed at the television.

"And where would we put the television?"

"Throw it away."

A light smile appeared on his face. He got up, dragged the suitcase over, and dropped it on the floor. He opened it and patted the dusty books. Raising his hands toward his face, he blew the dust with force. As he sat on his knees, grabbing his books one at a time, feather bookmarks fell out and landed beside his feet.

I helped him sort the good books from the old and mouldy ones. They were books from a long time ago, but books that I would read—*Duas for Success in Life and Afterlife, Diseases of the Heart and their Cures, Islam: Religion of the Future, Message to the Muslim Youth*. Souvenirs had collected at the bottom and at the edges of the suitcase: rosaries, greeting cards.

"You read all these books?" I asked him.

He nodded.

My father, of all people, reading Islamic books?

Brushing my hands against covers and titles, I noticed a book that reminded me of Yousef's. Same cover, same title, same miracles. My father's book stamp with his name hung in the top corner. It was a faded blue stamp from the eighties of last century. He noticed my gaze and folded his arms behind his neck, lips clenched on his cigarette.

"I remember this book," he said. "I was about your age when I got it."

"Did you read it?"

"I read it." Silence. Then he said, "I also know what happened to the Mujahideen."

"They won," I said.

"Maybe. But then they killed one another. They said they would free Jerusalem, but then they killed one another and crushed their own people."

"So do you think these stories are lies? They can't all be lies."

"Maybe. Maybe not. My problem with this book is that it shows the Mujahideen as angels. Nobody is an angel."

He scanned the suitcase for a minute and then said, "When I was a kid, classmates introduced me to this young man who had graduated from university abroad. 'You should meet him,' they said. 'He's smart, calm, kind, strong, reads all kinds of books, speaks all kinds of languages.' He was exactly as they said. I was only twelve years old."

"Twelve?"

He smiled. "Yes. At the time, my family lived near your maternal grandparents in Silwan. We were neighbours. That's how I met your mother."

He told me to open the back door for some air.

"This young man told us stories about troubled Muslims who lived in Afghanistan, Kashmir, Somalia, and other places we had no idea existed. He said Muslims who did not support other Muslims were out of line, out of *Ummah*. He told us stories of our oppressed brothers paying the price for defending Muslim land. We were excited to hear about them. It was like resurrecting the companions of Prophet Muhammad. Hamza was back now, but with a Kalashnikov, and Khalid ibn al-Walid was also back, but with an RPG. You understand? This teacher gave us books and took us on trips and picnics. We swam and rode horses and wrestled, and he handed us trophies. He was popular. He had charisma. In the beginning, we were only ten boys, and then we became twenty, fifty, then hundreds."

"Is it true you were friends with Abu-Hassan back then?"

"When Abdullah and I were kids, we played hopscotch and chased after girls and birds. Then we started following our teacher and stopped chasing after girls and birds. As I was finishing high school, the First Intifada started. Some of my friends went to jail, some left the country, some stayed out of trouble. Your grandfather took me to Jordan. I came back to Jerusalem as soon as I finished studying history in university, after the Oslo Accords. My parents remained in Jordan. I thought things would improve, especially after Arafat won the Nobel Peace Prize. I thought I could find a good job here, or in Ramallah. But I had a file. Some security officer, the Captain Moussa of that time, prevented me from teaching. Then things went from bad to worse—explosions, demolitions, arrests. Ten times what you see now, the most hopeless of times."

He lit a cigarette.

"But Abdullah came from a rich family. After high school, his father sent him to London, where he went out with English women. He drank alcohol and took drugs."

"Drugs?" I said, pronouncing the word as slowly as possible. "I don't believe it."

"You think I'm lying to you?" he said calmly. "Ask around. It's true he has millions of online followers, but the internet is not always right."

I remembered the broken fountain with the statue in Abu-Hassan's front yard and remained silent.

My father went on. "He only spent one year in London, but he brought shame to his family. His father flew him back here and put him to work at one of his stores. When his father died a few years later, I went to console Abdullah. We talked, recalled our past together, and promised to meet again. But when I phoned him afterward, he ignored me. I did not hear from him for a long time—until he had cloned himself in the image of our old teacher."

My father kicked the suitcase and went to the sink. He filled a glass with water and gulped it down in one swallow. He sat at the kitchen table, lit a cigarette, and said, "I should have crushed him, snapped his tongue out, and thrown it to stray cats and dogs. It's not right what he did to you and Mustafa. It's not right. People like him can't be trusted."

He told me to sit with him at the table. I hesitated because of his fiery eyes, but then I sat.

Shaking his head, he continued. "I feel sorry for him. I swear to Allah, I feel sorry for him. He lost his son. But I'm also angry at him, not only because I'm your father, but because we were good friends."

Looking up at the ceiling, eyes dancing around the dusty light bulb, he went on. "When we were kids, he thought highly of himself because of his father's reputation, their family roots in the city, and their possessions. He loved to dress up, and he spoke in the most polished sentences. When we went to restaurants, I would dip my fingers into my plate and he would use a fork. He used to make fun of me. But he would use his fingers when he ate with our old teacher, who did it because of tradition. Now, with his lecturing and preaching, he's using the same old tricks, but with the words of God to make himself feel and look extra good, extra special. I've seen his videos on the internet. He claims that he has taught himself, as if he received the revelations. He's a liar. People with no hope, like our people, trust the likes of Abu-Hassan because they resemble glorious men from history books. In reality though, these men are chameleons. They don't speak the truth. The famous proverb says: 'In the land of the blind, the one-eyed man is king.' Abu-Hassan is a one-eyed man, you understand?"

He played with his key chain. "I'm only a taxi driver. I spend my days doing the easiest job in the world, the least demanding of all jobs. I steer the wheel and I hit the gas. When I have a chance to help, I help. When a peasant woman from the West Bank asks me for a lift, I give her a lift. When a construction worker is stranded at night and he waves at me to stop, I stop. Most of the time, I don't charge. I'm happy when I see their eyes flicker as they gaze at the city walls."

He pointed at the mouldy books. "But I will never forget what I studied at university and what I read when I was younger. History taught me not to trust charlatans, especially in this land of ours. We suffered so much at the hands of charlatans and loudmouths."

"So what happened to your old teacher?" I asked him.

"My old teacher was always good with words. He's a politician now. I saw him once on television, sitting with politicians from another party. They debated for two hours and, in the end, I couldn't understand if they were getting anywhere. It's always been like that. Your grandfather once said that after the arson attack on Al-Aqsa in 1969, the drunks and addicts of Jerusalem were the first to run to the mosque to help put out the fire. Then came the politicians."

"I didn't know that," I said.

"Of course you didn't. Because at school they teach you about this and that leader conquering this and that land. They don't teach you about the everyday lives of simple people like us. Real education comes from the streets. It comes from people who don't talk much."

Pink and yellow stripes covered the sky. The call to prayer rang out:

Allahu Akbar, Allahu Akbar
Allahu Akbar, Allahu Akbar
Hayya 'alas-Salah, Hayya 'alas-Salah
Hayya 'alal-Falah, Hayya 'alal-Falah

If the dawn call to prayer is the mother of all calls, the sunset call is the grandmother. It always comes with the nagging feeling of not having done what you were supposed to get done during the day. It comes with a weakness that touches every nerve and muscle.

My father buried his head in his hands.

32

May 1

Tourists came to the café in droves, sweat running down their plump red cheeks. They had paraded earlier in front of the Church of the Holy Sepulchre and along Via Dolorosa and now stood in a long line, taking pictures of the salads. I was filling the containers when a tourist pulled off his straw hat and pointed at the baba ghanoush. "Hello! What's this?"

He had an American accent, though it was hard to tell nowadays. So many people talked like Americans in the movies.

"Baba ghanoush," I said, licking the sweat from the edge of my lip.

"And this?"

"Matbucha."

He looked confused, so I said, "Eggplants, and tomatoes with roasted peppers." Noticing the growing line behind him, I continued, pointing at each salad bin. "Tabbouleh, mixed pickles, hummus, fried eggplant, red cabbage, green cabbage, hot peppers, not-so-hot peppers..."

I thought about the versatility of eggplants: roasted, fried, grilled, boiled, half-cooked with olive oil and vinegar, the way my mother made them.

Why is she still gone?

The salad bar was our newest attraction. Uri had introduced it to compete with nearby restaurants. He trusted Marwan to prepare the salads and trusted me to run it because my hands could scoop and load without thinking. I had gained this skill from communicating with hundreds of people while making coffee every day. And I did not have to be their friend.

The matbucha was about to disappear, the kitchen boys were late, and Marwan was not working today.

Uri jumped up and down and yelled, "Where is the matbucha?!"

I ignored him.

He yelled again, and I ignored him again.

It was a hot day and I imagined a swimming pool in the middle of the dining area, like the ones that grace the high roofs of West Jerusalem hotels. My body was floating and I was looking directly into the sun. There was nothing on my mind except the cool water splashing under my armpits and the mysteries of buoyancy.

I could smell Uri's sweat. He was standing beside me, and then he kicked me in the shin. I felt a sting in my leg as though shrapnel had cut through my skin and was now swimming through my veins. His voice overlapped with Captain Moussa's, and I found myself snubbing him out of spite. I pretended he was not there and kept smiling at the line of happy tourists. I wished them pleasant holidays as they made quick appointments with God and His sites.

"Where is the matbucha?" Uri asked once again.

I dropped the serving spoon on the floor and growled, "In your mother's vagina!"

I ran to the kitchen, dunked my head in the sink, and went outside to lean against the dumpster—the only place with decent shade. Olga came out and shouted at me. Then Itzik came and shouted. They threw the few Arabic words they knew at me. All swear words. Blocking the back door, they whispered and pointed at me: the trapped mouse everyone wanted to kick into the gutter.

Then Dafna came. "What's wrong with you?" she said.

I grabbed an empty can of sardines and threw it behind me. "What's wrong with *him*?" I said, sniffing my fingers. I wrinkled my nose.

"Get back inside and apologize," she said.

"*He* needs to apologize," I said. "He kicked me in the shin a minute ago. He kicked me! He hates me."

"Why?"

"Because I am an Arab."

She patted me on the back. "He's the boss. You know what he's like."

"*You're* the boss," I said, and her eyes sparkled.

She gave me a cigarette. Then she looked up at the clouds and laughed. "Never heard anyone say anything like that to Uri before." She stretched her arms so wide she hit my nose. "I'm sorry, did I hit you?"

"Not the first time," I said.

She flicked her finger at my chest and hit the amulet under my shirt. "What are you hiding?"

"An amulet," I said. "My mother told me to wear it for protection."

She pointed to the hamsa tattoo on her calf. "I have permanent protection here. See? It's stuck on me."

As though fondling a sleepy cat, her fingers cuddled the inked hand. It looked nice, the tattoo. Everything she touched or that touched her looked nice. Tomorrow, I could bring her a gift. Something she had liked when we visited the Old City—a necklace with hanging spruce balls, an olive-wood rosary that releases oil and fragrance, or a bracelet with stones from the Western Wall. Or maybe all of them in a box.

"Do you like cats?" she asked, interrupting my thoughts.

"Real cats?"

"No, robot cats," she said with a snicker.

"Robot cats on drugs."

She laughed loudly. "Robot cats on drugs!"

I laughed with her and found my arm lying over her shoulder.

Suddenly Uri was in front of us, his face red. "Get back to work," he told Dafna.

"And you." He pointed at me. "I don't want to see your face here again."

Night

When I arrived home, my head was spinning. The lights were on and the back door open. My father and Uncle Fahmi sat outside on a mattress. They cracked sunflower seeds and spoke loudly. They did not notice me. *Good.* I slipped through the corridor toward my parents' room.

Then I smelled my mother. I ran down the corridor and flung the bedroom door open.

She was inside, arranging her clothes. We both gasped and I hugged her tightly.

"I missed you," I told her.

"I missed you more," she said.

"Don't do it again!"

I sat at the kitchen table as she tossed mint in four cups. She poured tea from our old kettle and hummed, a dreamy look in her eyes. "Let's sit outside."

The sky was clear and the moon full and solid. I sat down and looked at the moon as my father's keys dangled between his fingers. He must be going somewhere. I wanted him to stay.

He was in the middle of a story: "It was a fortune, you understand, Fahmi? One could live a thousand years and never spend it. Three jars of pure gold. Can you believe it? Those sons of dogs took everything. The cave was on our land, and they gave us nothing, not a single coin. Two years later, they took the land."

He was telling the story of the three jars of Roman gold, a thirty-year-old story, maybe older. He had told it many times before.

"I was the same age as Aziz," he continued, speaking softly, as though he were Ali Baba afraid he would get caught by the forty thieves. "We went at night, after the police and archaeologists had left. We carried shovels and baskets and flashlights and searched the grounds, scraping and poking through the rock, each cave's head leading to the tail of another. We had to stop at dawn, afraid we would get stuck and never find our way out."

His eyes were sparkling as though he had just found that gold.

"You left empty-handed?" my uncle asked. He knew the story but wanted to amuse my father.

"I only found the ears of a broken jar," he said. "I kept them for years and years. I don't know where they are now." He looked at my mother. "Khawla, have you seen the ears of the broken jar?"

"I only see your big ears," she said.

We laughed, and a cheeky smile spread over my mother's face.

My uncle cut into the round tray of knafeh he had brought. "It's too dry," he complained. "Needs more sugar," he said, adding syrup.

"I'll tell your wife," my father said.

"We only live once," he responded, adding another serving to his plate.

The knafeh was about to disappear from the large orange tray while I scanned my dirty hands.

"Eat," my mother said.

"Not in the mood," I said.

"How's work?" my father asked, chewing on the cheesy pastry.

"I got fired," I told him.

"This is good news," he said.

May 15

I went to see Uri. He sat at a corner table and told me to sit across from him. Pulling off a paper clip that held hundred-shekel bills, he shuffled the bills and slapped them into my clammy hand. He gave me two nods, and I thanked him and got up.

Passing by the kitchen, I could hear the rattle of dishes and Marwan's curses at the kitchen boys. He saw me and called out from the kitchen window. We shook hands and then sat out back in the sun. He took one deep breath after the other.

"My father has prepared Mustafa's tomb beside our mother. We might get the call any minute now," he said. "A midnight call to come to the station, take the body, and bury him immediately."

The image of the white headstones flanking the Kidron Valley hit me. The millions of white headstones hit me—all of them. The ones with names, and the nameless, the old ones behind the Tomb of Zechariah near the river of Armageddon, and the new ones near the city wall and on the Mount of Olives.

Not wanting me to see his tears, Marwan turned his face away. He then showed me a piece of paper Mustafa had left inside his pillowcase. It said:

> If you receive news of my martyrdom, do not say goodbye unless you locate my body, unless you find me as you knew me in this life—a face that can be kissed, a hand that can be shaken, a shoulder that can be patted. I do not want my body to be something else in your memory. I want the soil of this land to embrace me, all of me.

Marwan slipped the paper back in his pocket, and we gazed out at the parking lot behind the dumpster, at cars pulling in, pulling out, engines revving, engines dying. He went inside and came back with a bottle of grapefruit juice. I grabbed the cold bottle, lingered for another minute or two, and left.

I drank the juice and loitered near the café, stretching on benches, leaning against spindly trees, looking at the time. When I was tired of standing, I sat; when I tired of sitting, I stood. Crowds waited at bus stops and streetcar stops and lottery kiosks, and I stayed as far as possible from them. I counted my money, then slipped it back into my pocket. The money smelled bad; the sidewalk smelled bad; the air smelled bad. But I was going to wait.

The clouds were collecting flies from far away and mixing them with sand and water. The khamsin storm was about to hit the streets. You never knew how much muddy water the khamsin could carry with her. You only knew when the mud hit you.

Three soldiers came and asked for my ID. I was relaxed. I even grinned.

"Here," I said, handing them my brand-new ID.

They looked at it. They looked at me. Was I the same person?

They asked me why I was sitting on the ground. "For fun," I said.

They told me to stand up and wait until they checked my information on their computer. One hour later, it started to rain. The khamsin was here. It had come from the desert and made a mess. It moved things; it poured mud.

Two hours later, I was still standing, wet all over, legs fixed to the ground, like a lightning rod. Passersby hurried past me, holding phones like guns, umbrellas like rifles.

Then I saw her.

Dafna.

She was crossing the street, less than twenty metres away, behind the soldiers and their wide chests. I nodded to her. The soldiers were watching me; I was not supposed to wave. I nodded. I wanted her to notice me. She did not. I nodded again and waited.

33

June 1

The khamsin storms with their muddy rains passed, and no grave could hold Mustafa; no heart could hold Dafna's laughter. Their memories sat on my shoulders like the two angels, both working for God. As the alleyways and roofs got ready for Ramadan with decorations, I busied myself reading the whole day and the whole night. I avoided people and watched video after video of silly things and sometimes very important things that seemed silly, like climbing goats who did not recognize the laws of physics.

My aunt sent me articles and ebooks on the world of wildlife and its mysteries, about rivers and forests of Palestine that were now dry and dead. She said that once, not too long ago, not only crocodiles had lived in the north, on the banks of the Jordan River, but also lions and bears and ostriches. She referred me to history books, but not the usual history with wars and treaties and the like—stories about humanity and nature. In one book, I read about the spirituality of the Indigenous peoples of

North America, and how it connected them to nature, to animals and rivers and trees. For them and for their ancestors, one life pulsed through the world and ran through every living organism.

My readings would have more impact, my aunt said, if I walked in our nature.

At first, my mother objected. "We have no nature here," she said, to which my aunt responded, "You say that because you never leave your house."

My mother answered, "You tell him to hike the mountains. Did you forget there are settlements on the mountains?"

Eventually, we worked out routes and hikes across Bethlehem, Nablus, Hebron, and Nazareth. I would take the bus, or my father would drop me at a certain spot. I walked and sprinted along winding trails that were sometimes open and smooth but many other times were closed and I had to jump a fence or make a U-turn. I hit beaten and unbeaten paths, among the oaks and willows and sycamores. Sometimes I went down led by gravity. Sometimes by following the sound of hidden waters. When I was tired, I would sit on the roots of ancient oak and olive trees or, if I was lucky, wade through a bubbly spring.

The weather was getting warmer, but the view of our neighbourhood had not changed. The people were the same. Their shouting and cursing were the same. The Dome of the Rock was still gleaming, but nobody was descending the Mount of Olives. Neither the prophets nor the caliphs. Abu-Yousef still sat on his bakery's doorstep, talking to his old friends and throwing stale bread to beggars and junkies. Yousef was still in jail, no sentencing in sight. His father said many confessions had been laid against his son.

Nuha's place had been rented to a family from Galilee—the husband was an engineer; the wife was a lawyer. They had a boy and a girl, and a cat named Zahra.

One day, Nuha called. "I was thinking of you," she said. "I miss my little brother."

My memories of her, and of her kind mother, whizzed through my head like a meteor shower. I was about to cry. I was about to explain how sometimes, on the inside, we think and feel differently from our actions on the outside. I could not articulate it seamlessly, so I reciprocated: "I miss my big sister."

She said she was getting married to a Frenchman. They had met at work.

"Are you going to leave the country?" I asked her.

"We're staying," she said, which was nice to hear.

June 7

My parents had prepared a substantial breakfast: eggs, fried tomatoes with peppers, and meatballs. My father made hummus, and we ate until we couldn't breathe. It was too early for such a meal, and I was late for school. I rushed to the door, but my parents said I could take the day off.

"What prank are you pulling?" I said, folding my arms.

My mother tapped me on the back. "No pranks. Your father needs you."

"What for?"

"You'll see," she said with a nervous smile.

Going down the stairs, I was getting nervous too. "Is there something wrong?" I asked my father.

"We're going to Tel Aviv," he said.

"Tel Aviv? I have an exam."

"The exam can wait," he said. "I'm taking you to the beach."

As we drove along Highway 1, I opened the window and took in the air from the green hills, the pine trees standing behind rolling grass and rocks. Passing the ruins of Lifta, the cars in front of us were slowing down, and I glanced at the row of trees along the road. Through narrow and wide gaps between the trees, I glimpsed empty houses nestled on top of the hill. My father told me to get the binoculars from the glovebox, and I focused on the bushes covering arched windows, on a flock of sheep grazing in the sun and tumbling over heavy shrubs that overtook the roofs, leaving no room for clotheslines or random onlookers. Pricking up my ears, I could hear the rumble of old times: armoured vehicles, gunshots echoing in the valley, shouts of armed men, screams of women and children fleeing through the doors and across the domed roofs. The Nakba vibrated from the rusty window bars, the earth beneath stone remnants, the stretch of trees covering the roadside shoulder.

"You should study biology or ecology," my father said. "It suits you."

"You think so?"

"Why not?"

"I don't know if science suits me," I said. "Sometimes I can't tell reality from dreams."

"It happens," he said with a smile. "But this is where your mother and I can help."

The hills were becoming flat, and I leaned back and watched the speedometer as my father changed lanes and wove through traffic. His hand covered the gear stick without shifting. He was thinking, or daydreaming. What did he daydream about? He could easily have become a history teacher, a headmaster, or professor. He could have lived somewhere else and been somebody else.

On the radio, a patriotic song played, and my father laughed. "Ramallah is preparing for war. We should brace ourselves." He shrugged, his mood shifting rapidly. "When I was your age, I listened to these songs all the time. War songs are the worst. They can kill you from the inside. Because you try to find their meaning, and you fail. These songs are depressing because you can only see the opposite of what they preach. They talk about people sticking together when all you can see is divisiveness, about strength when all you can see is weakness, about dignity when all you can see is humiliation."

A tractor-trailer overtook us, sending gravel onto the windshield. A good distraction. Now my father must be worried the windshield could break again. This time, though, we would only be able to blame careless drivers and bad winds. Looking out the window, I saw plains and pastureland covering the horizon. Soon all this would be beige and brown. Come July, everything would be thorny and hard to touch. Mechanical plows drove nearby, and zigzag scratches spanned a square here and a square there. I wondered how deep the teeth of those plows went into the soil, how deep they went through the soft clay and the soft, wriggling worms. How could this softness take all that pressure? How could the land take all that weight and still bear fruit?

As we took the ramp to Tel Aviv, the Ramallah radio channel died off and incoherent sounds mingled together. Metal-and-glass buildings loomed over our heads, and the smell of the sea seeped into the car as we pulled into a busy street. My father paid at a parking meter, and we walked down the sidewalk. I trailed behind him as he peeked into dim doorways. He glanced up and down the road.

"Are we lost?" I asked him.

He pulled out his phone and checked the directions. We walked through the door of an office building. A security guard with a metal wand checked our belts and then let us in. We stood by the elevator, and my father pushed the button. The elevator gave a heaving groan and then ascended. Soon we were beyond the twentieth floor.

"Are we going to meet God?" I joked.

My father focused on the elevator buttons as they blinked and glowed. "The Canadian visa office," he said, holding up the envelope he had been carrying under his armpit since we left the car. "They will take your photo and fingerprints, and then we'll go to the beach."

Later

Clouds dotted the sky, and the sun was easy on our faces. We dug our feet in the sand and watched fathers throw their babies up in the air and mothers shout at their children not to go too deep in the water. Lovers chased each other, and the retreating waves splashed at the tattoos on their ankles. I thought about protections, permanent and temporary.

Swallows brushed against the clouds, scouting for a nest.

"You'll be free as a bird," my father said.

"I don't want to be free like that. I don't want to run away."

"Who said you'll be running away?"

"This," I said, pointing at the envelope he was holding. It had all my personal information, all forms of identity, or whatever they called identity.

He ruffled my hair. "You're taking a break. This is the least your mother and I can do to protect you."

Wet sand covered my father's feet. It did not bother him, though he would have preferred to sit on a clean rock and appreciate the deep, blue sea from a distance. I also liked the sea from a distance, especially when it frothed and splashed.

Last summer, Mustafa and I had gone to Acre. We visited the old city walls and the cannons, and then watched the locals dive from the top. Mustafa wanted to join them, but I reminded him he did not know how to swim. "Diving is easier than swimming," he said.

Not far from this beach, this seashore, this sun, he lay in the cold. He was waiting to reunite with the soil of this land. God was looking at him from above, from below, from all directions. God saw him, saw us, saw our skin and our scars.

We had come here before, kicked the sand, kicked deflated balls and empty bottles and taken pictures. We had held our arms and legs like trophies, sticking our tongues out at the world.

ACKNOWLEDGEMENTS

I am grateful to everyone at House of Anansi for helping this book see the light of day. To my editor, Shirarose Wilensky, thank you for nurturing the heart of this book and for your sharp eye, kind honesty, and steady guidance. Thanks to Chandra Wohleber for her thoughtful edits.

Special thanks to Maureen Medved, whose support and insight were invaluable during the early stages of this work. Thanks to Ibi Kaslik for her kind words and encouragement when this book was only an idea. For their thoughtful feedback and enthusiasm, many thanks to early readers from the UBC Creative Writing program and the University of Toronto School of Continuing Studies. Thanks to the staff of the Toronto Reference Library for offering a place to write and for their generosity.

Much love to my parents, Salah and Aida, in Jerusalem. Thanks for letting me read when the neighbourhood boys played or ran errands. Thanks to my very dear brothers and sisters. Your passion, strength, and good humour guide my way.

To my partner, Rimah, thank you for cheering me on, reading early drafts, and reminding me why stories matter. To our boy, Adam, you're too young to read this, but one day you will—and when you do, you'll understand how deeply you inspired this book. To our cat, Zahra, you'll always be remembered. Thanks to my sister Rula for always being around.

To old and new friends across the world, thank you for shaping who I am today. I am excited to share this book with you; I know you've been waiting for it.

I would like to thank the Canada Council for the Arts for their support.

And, finally, thank you to every reader who chooses to spend time with this story.

© David Chang

ASHRAF ZAGHAL is a Palestinian Canadian author who was born and raised in Jerusalem. He has published four poetry collections, and his work has been translated into English, French, and Hebrew. He is the editor of an online magazine focused on progressive literature and translation. He holds an MFA in Creative Writing from the University of British Columbia.